Lewis Davis

The Life of Rev. David Edwards

Lewis Davis

The Life of Rev. David Edwards

ISBN/EAN: 9783337333317

Printed in Europe, USA, Canada, Australia, Japan

Cover: Foto ©Raphael Reischuk / pixelio.de

More available books at **www.hansebooks.com**

Rev. David Edwards, D.D.,

LATE A BISHOP

OF THE

UNITED BRETHREN IN CHRIST.

BY THE
REV. LEWIS DAVIS, D. D.

WITH AN INTRODUCTION BY
REV. JAMES W. HOTT, D. D.

SECOND EDITION.

DAYTON, OHIO:
UNITED BRETHREN PUBLISHING HOUSE.
1883.

PREFACE.

IN presenting the following memoir to the Church and the reading public generally, a few words of explanation may not be out of place. The writer was not led to undertake the work through a desire to bring himself before the public as an author; but when a request came from the highest judicatory of the Church, together with the earnest solicitation of many of the friends of Bishop Edwards, the author could not well refuse to undertake the work.

In the General Conference of 1877 a paper was presented and adopted in which the following words occur: "We esteem the life of Bishop D. Edwards as worthy to be forever embalmed in the memory and history of the United Brethren in Christ, as one of its most eloquent preachers, wisest counselors, and most faithful defenders of its holy and honored principles; a mighty man of valor in the cause of Jesus, and a Christian of the purest and noblest order—alike great and good." Mingled feelings of joy and sorrow seemed to fill the hearts of all the members of the General Conference,—joy that he had passed so triumphantly from labor to reward, but sorrow in view of the great vacancy made in the Board of Bishops and in the Church at large.

The feeling had already become deep and abiding, not only in the General Conference, but throughout the Church,

V

that some permanent record should be made of his life and labors. In order to meet this want the following resolution was passed: "That L. Davis be requested to prepare such manuscript for publication, and that such incidents of the life and labors of the late Bishop Edwards as may give interest to the work be forwarded to him, from which to make selections."

Scioto Conference, where the bishop held a membership for more than forty years, also requested me to write his biography. The fact, too, of my long acquaintance with the bishop, and our intimate friendship, was urged by many as a reason why I should undertake the work. I hesitated for a time, but finally yielded to a request which seemed so general and hearty. Little, however, was done before the meeting of the General Conference of 1881. At this session, on account of other pressing duties, I asked release from the work, or assistance in its prosecution. I was not released, but again requested to prosecute the work at once. The Book Committee of the Printing Establishment was directed to furnish such help as might be needed. The committee appointed Prof. A. W. Drury to assist as I might direct. This appointment was very fortunate. The professor devoted over two months during the past summer in collecting and arranging materials for the work, which have been of great service to the author. But for this invaluable help the work would not now be ready for the press. Others, too numerous to mention, by furnishing valuable suggestions and incidents, have contributed no little in helping the work forward.

The author has had free access to the bishop's diary and many of his private letters, written to dear and intimate friends. Files of the *Religious Telescope* and the proceedings of General and annual conferences have also been freely consulted. The object has been to let Bishop Edwards speak for himself. In this way the reader can see the man as he was. We want to know as much as possible of his modes of thinking, the struggles of his heart, his practical way of overcoming sin and Satan, his life-long battle with the ever-varying forms of unbelief and human weakness, and, above all, the secret of that power by which he so gloriously wrought for the Master. It is hoped that his rich endowments and varied attainments have not been overstated. The aim has been to be true to the facts.

What the reader may think of this unpretending memoir I know not. But this I know, that in telling the story of his life—its struggles and triumphs—my own heart has been made stronger for life's battles. I have not done all that I wished—but what I could. And now nothing remains but for me to send forth this volume, with a prayer that the blessing of God may attend it, and that it may have the charitable judgment of the Church.

LEWIS DAVIS.

Dayton, Ohio, February, 1883.

CONTENTS.

CHAPTER VIII.

CHAPTER IX.

CHAPTER X.

CHAPTER XI.

CHAPTER XII.

INTRODUCTION.

THE good man has a twofold immortality. The one belongs to him in the country within the veil, where the soul enters upon a higher and broader life; the other, by the influence of personal character and deeds, mingles with the thought and being of men, and flows down the stream of human life to the end of all things.

It is the mission of biography to contribute largely to the force and faithfulness of this after-life which men live on earth. As the historian gives to succeeding ages the lives and influence of nations, so the biographer places upon newly-forming features of society the influence of a personal life which has completed its earthly pilgrimage.

Bishop Edwards has been in the unseen holy seven years. He has measurably solved the awful mystery of human existence. At present his life is untrammeled by the limitations of time and space, as they belong to us. His life no more bears the tax of wearying toil. Life and death have rolled up the curtains which conceal from us eternal things.

The biographer might have written a panegyric upon the life of Bishop Edwards, which would have revealed his own skill as well as portrayed the enticing features of a remarkable human life. He might have chosen the character he

xi

has handled as a text from which to proclaim certain important moral truths. He might have aimed to furnish rather his own interpretation of the character, meaning, and influence of the life of Bishop Edwards. These possibilities, however, have not been the aim of the author of this volume. He has sought to present the deceased bishop of the past generation to the present generation just as he was. The pen has traced his life in its development of character through sorrows and joys, through struggles and labors, through sufferings and triumphs, threading the history of the Church to its final consummation.

The value of this personal element in the literature of a church can not be too highly appreciated. The Bible gives us the biographies of Joseph and of Ruth and of others of illustrious fame, in stories of marvelous beauty. The Odyssey of Homer gives us the biography of Ulysses. Suetonius tells the story of the lives of the Cæsars. Diogenes Laertius records the biographies of the ancient philosophers, while Plutarch has furnished the ages with the biographies of the greatest among the Greeks and Romans. Ancient, medieval, and modern literature bring us vast treasures of imperishable wealth in the biographies of the good and the great. How fitting, then, that our own Church should more diligently and sacredly garner and guard the influence and memory of its honored dead. This is the first instance in which the biography of any of the deceased bishops of the United Brethren in Christ has been placed in book-form.

Forty years Bishop Edwards labored in the gospel ministry. Twenty-seven years he bore the honors and met the responsibilities of the office of a bishop in a progressive and growing church, which did not hesitate to grapple with the profoundest moral questions of the age. Four years he occupied the editorial chair, conducting the *Religious Tele-*

scope, the official organ of the church of his choice. He died in the bishop's office, in Baltimore, Maryland, June 6, 1876. A deep, oppressive sorrow fell like a pall upon a wide circle of Christian hearts when it was announced that Bishop Edwards was dead.

To hundreds, and even thousands, he whose life is traced in the succeeding pages seems hardly to have passed away. His persuasive voice has scarcely been hushed. The gracious benedictions pronounced at his last conferences still hover over the hosts of God. The strong grasp of his mighty hand still presses the living palm. Bishop Edwards lives alike on account of his strong personal character and because of his deeds.

Born of Welsh parentage, in North Wales, and early emigrating to America, Bishop Edwards' young, strong nature found a genial sphere of development in the broad scope and free air of the New World. He was by nature a mighty man in physical, mental, and moral endowments. He was what the world calls a "self-made man." He was the product of deep, conscious, entire self-surrender to God, and the constant cherishing of high moral ideas and sublime Christian truth. He developed from within. Christ was his supreme teacher. His life was a flame of light, kindled by an invisible sun within. The grace of humility adorned him like robes of spotless purity. When asked where he received his education he replied, "I am not educated." In this he was mistaken. His spirit and thought touched those of great and cultured men. He was capable of profound thought, and was a preacher of wonderful power. He preached largely by inspiration, however thorough his previous preparation. The writer can never cease to remember how he struggled in prayer for divine help before his great pulpit efforts. Then he trusted in God and left results with him. He was sometimes homely, and even rough, in his direct address and illustrations in the pulpit. This homeliness was a weapon which he knew how to wield with powerful effect. In his better and grander pulpit ministrations he far transcended all this, and became vivid, ornate, and unconsciously dramatic. He was pre-eminently a man of prayer, and relied largely upon God for immediate direction. He lived ages, counting time by heart-throbs. He possessed deep heart-consecration to Christ and the Church. Toil was his daily food. To make the best of his opportunities and talents was a ceaseless aim. His convictions upon all matters of religion, moral reform, prudence, and church-work were intense. His soul and life swung unerringly to the side of conscience. His life performed the music composed in higher spheres. This intensity of nature sometimes made his conduct an offense to those who only partially understood him. Even these, however, honored and esteemed him as a man of God.

Bishop Edwards did not grow weak or old, but retained the vitality and strength of life to the last. He had energy enough for forty years more in the ministry. He died at the zenith of usefulness and power. He kept abreast of the progress of the Church, yet scrutinized every new development. His life covered the period in our Church when its enterprises, institutions, and peculiar features of ecclesiastical government really took form. He left the influence of his thought and life in the Church, rather than on it. These facts make this biography the more valuable to the years to come; for,

> "In the wreck of noble lives,
> Something immortal still survives."

The critical Carlyle says, "A well-written life is almost as rare as a well-spent one." In this book these two strangers meet. It is pre-eminently fitting that the long-time friend and fellow-laborer of Bishop Edwards, Dr. L. Davis, should have written this biography. His long personal acquaintance with his subject, his unflinching fidelity to facts, his wide acquaintance with the history of the Church in these years, his simple, ornate style, his ripe scholarship and long Christian life of usefulness, all fit him for this task. Few persons can fully appreciate the labor needed to produce such a volume. As the evening shadows of life are stretching across his pathway, he has turned about and amid other duties sat down and inscribed an "unrhymed heroic poem." The book shows how patient the toil bestowed upon it. In an incidental manner, very much of interesting and profitable history of the Church is given which is nowhere else accessible. This will be found an exceedingly valuable feature of this biography. The pen of the author has been held by a steady hand. He has chiseled a statue of a great and good man. This has been so done as scarcely to leave the marks of the tools upon the image. This late work of a life already so full of labor not only pays a just tribute to a noble character, but confers also a lasting blessing and heritage upon the Church and coming generations. Bishop Edwards is made to rise up and speak with the same voice familiar in days long gone by. Hundreds of old men will here trace the life of one dear to them, and find new consolation in the gospel of Christ. Hundreds of young men will rise up from reading these pages and go out inspired and girded for stronger and nobler lives. To the writer it is no ordinary joy to commend this book to the many readers who have anxiously awaited its appearance. "The memory of the just is blessed."

J. W. HOTT.

Dayton, Ohio, February 1, 1883.

LIFE OF BISHOP EDWARDS.

CHAPTER I.

Parents—Early Years—Home in Wales—Incidents—Emigration to America—Settlement—Incidents—Conversion.

AVID EDWARDS was born May 5, 1816, in Denbigshire, North Wales, one mile from Llangedwin and five miles from Llanfyllin, in Montgomeryshire. Much of this country is rugged and mountainous, presenting a scenery varied and picturesque. Its extended mountain ranges and wide-spread valleys, intersected by deep ravines, are indeed very remarkable. In fact, this part of Wales has always been noted for its romantic charms. This may account, in part, for some of the characteristics of the Welsh. For example, they are very fond of poetry and music. And it is said that their language is especially adapted to poetical effusions. They are also brave, intelligent, generous, and impulsive. But they are more noted for integrity of character than anything else. It is pleasant to know that the subject

2

of our narrative descended from a race so noble
as this, and that he was in fact a native of no
mean country. Many who read these pages will
readily call to mind how often he referred, in
after - years, to his Welsh origin. He would
say, as an apology for some of his bold utterances, which seemed to give offense, " Brethren,
you must remember that I am a Welshman;"
as much as to say, this will help you to understand me. But those who knew him best did
not need this reminder; for it was very apparent that some of the peculiarities of his country-
men clung to him to the last.

Edward Edwards, his father, was twice married,
but had no children by his first wife. His mother's maiden name was Elizabeth Davis. She too
was twice married, her first husband's name being
John Jones. By this marriage she had one son,
named Thomas, who at this writing still lives, a
respected citizen of Delaware, Ohio. Six children
were born of this second marriage,—Elizabeth,
John, Ann, Mary, David, and Sarah, their ages
corresponding to the order here given. John was
an itinerant minister of long standing and great
usefulness in the Methodist Episcopal Church.
But all these members of the Edwards family
have gone to their reward, except Mary.

The parents of young Edwards had lived in

the early part of their married life in Montgomeryshire, three miles from Llansantffraid. Their
home consisted of a small rented property, belonging to the father of Mrs. Edwards. It was
called Penygroise. Upon one corner of this
little estate was built a small Dissenters' church,
in which a few Congregationalists worshiped.
The Edwards family were members of this society; and here they continued to worship while
they remained in Wales. Thus humble and devout, they continued to come to hear the word of
God preached, to attend the Sabbath-school and
the week - night prayer - meeting, even after a
move of one mile and a half had taken them to
the location in Denbigshire, before mentioned.
As promptly as the occasion came, the parents
with their children found their way to the house
of God. Mr. Edwards often said, "My father
and mother were deeply pious. They had the
fear of God before their eyes." The grateful
remembrance of this fact was to him an inspiration and joy all through life.

At the time he was born the family lived in a
plain, neat cottage of four rooms, which, with
four acres of land, was known by the name of
Bronrathro. But even this humble home belonged
to the estate of an English landlord. The family
possessions did not extend beyond the household

furniture, and at one time a horse. Edward Edwards was a mason by trade, and was often intrusted with the supervision of improvements, and even the construction of new buildings. In every relation in life he was noted for his rigid uprightness and strict integrity. One Sabbath a rich land-holder, upon whom he was chiefly dependent, came to consult him concerning a piece of work. Mr. Edwards replied: "Sir, my conscience does not allow me to work or to plan work on the Sabbath-day. Come any other day and I will gladly do for you anything in my power." The rich man, though not a Christian, was not offended at this answer, but was more than ever desirous of trusting his work to one so devoted to principle. Once on the Sabbath, as an exceptional privilege, the children desired to take a walk down the lane. The permission of the father was obtained on the condition that they would not stop to play and would return soon. This rigor will hardly be appreciated by an age that always leans to the side of indulgence and sees nothing good in self-denial. But such was the parental training of young Edwards. In referring to this in after-years he said, "My parents were rigid, but kind, in the government of their children." The positive qualities of the Edwards family were especially due to the mother. She was a woman of clear and settled convictions, of mild but efficient government. This, of course, gave her an ascendant influence over the children as they grew up to manhood and womanhood. These are rich and noble endowments. Were they transmitted? At any rate they re-appear in David the boy and in Edwards the bishop. Besides, the place of his birth and its immediate surroundings must have been eminently fitted to awaken and develop his unusual gifts of nature. The rural scenery of this his first home on earth was indeed most lovely. True, he left it when quite young; but we have his own statement for it, that some of its charms, like visions of beauty, remained with him all through life. And no wonder, for everything here seemed to please and attract. A short half-mile in front of the dwelling ran the beautiful stream Tanat, cool and fresh from the mountains. Beyond were the rising slopes, rough hills, and mountain ranges. Here, close by the way, are splendid gardens, beautiful walks, and rich gifts of nature, newly touched and directed by the hand of Art. Yonder is a noble palace, renovated and improved from what seems to be an ancient castle. This is the summer-resort of an English gentleman. The children of that cottage of four rooms at the foot of the green hill-side might be born poor to all that can be crowded into purses, but no stress of fortune or selfishness of the great could defraud them of the wealth that gives pleasure to the eye and the inspiration of life and joy to the mind. This was Mr. Edwards' boyhood home; and even thus early his highly-gifted mind could appreciate beauty in nature and art. These early impressions and rich endowments he brought to America; and when sanctified by the Spirit of God they made him the mighty preacher that he was. This is the key to the whole complexion of his character and life. Mr. Edwards was characteristically a Welshman. This fact makes it necessary to dwell a little longer upon this phase of his lineage. He himself, as we have said, often referred to this. The Welsh constitute an important remnant of the once widely-spread Celts, who now have so generally fallen before the more powerful Teutons. They are the descendants of the old Britons, who early embraced Christianity, and waged a vigorous and for a long time a hopeful struggle against the arrogant pretensions of the Papacy. The old Culdee Church is a monument to the child-like susceptibility and truth-loving character of the Celts. To our times the Welsh have maintained their character for guilelessness and susceptibility to the truths of the Christian religion. Hence it is that their fire and realism have passed into proverbs. It is well known that when the Welsh mind is touched by the power of the gospel it becomes an unintermitting flame. Does not this fact explain why it was that Mr. Edwards was so mighty in the pulpit and in the council-chamber? His keen susceptibility, fine imagination, and wonderful descriptive powers may be attributed to his Welsh origin.

But the parents of this family caught the spirit of emigration. While Mr. Edwards was at his daily work he often thought with longing desire of America. One Saturday night he spoke of these desires to his wife, and was surprised to find that the same longings had also filled her heart, and that she had for weeks been praying and planning for an opening to enable them to come to the land of plenty and equality. They sought this change especially for the sake of their children. Providence having opened the way, this pious family left their home, in the mountains of North Wales, the 10th of April, 1821, and the second day of the following month set sail from Liverpool in the ship " Thomas Gibbenson," and for eight weeks were out upon the sea. During the voyage a roll of sheet-lead weighing four thousand pounds, becoming loosened from

its fastenings by the rolling of the ship, pitched
to the side of the vessel, crushing the lower
berths in which two of the children were sleep-
ing; but a projecting timber shielded their lives.
Thus under the protection of a kind Providence
the family reached Baltimore, Maryland, where
they remained for two years. Thomas Jones, the
half brother of the other children, soon went on
to Delaware, Ohio.

At Baltimore the father soon found work, and
both parents became members of that branch of
the Presbyterian family called Seceders. These
people were intelligent and devout. Hence it
proved to be a very pleasant church-home for
these Welsh immigrants. So here, for the time
being, the entire family were regular attendants
upon the means of grace. This privilege they
highly appreciated, especially in a new country,
and in the midst of strangers. But here let us
pause for a moment and reflect. In this same
city sleep the ashes of Otterbein. Here he lived,
struggled, and died. His great soul had just
passed from labor to reward. But lo! God is
preparing a Welshman upon whom the mantle
of this great German is soon to fall. Young
Edwards is already in America, and we shall see
in the simple story of his life and labors how
well and nobly he wrought for the Master's cause
in connection with "Otterbein's people."

In 1823 the family moved to Delaware, Ohio, where the father of Edwards still followed his trade. The parents at once united with the Presbyterian Church. As no house of worship had yet been built in Delaware, all religious services, including a flourishing Sabbath-school, were held in the court-house.

Here the family received the full benefit of spiritual and general culture through these services. The impulse and means of mental as well as moral culture were thus supplied. Besides, more than the usual care was given to the advancement of the children at home. Here they were taught reading and writing, the lessons of morality and religion, and, not least, good manners. The parents had discharged their duty well. They had consecrated their children to God in the ordinance of baptism in the little church at Penygroise. In infancy they had taught them to pray. They had daily at the family altar sought the blessing of God upon them. In their tenderest years they had led them to the Sabbath-school. The testimony of Mr. Edwards is, "My parents taught me to pray from my earliest recollection. They also taught me the necessity of a change of heart through faith in Christ. At about seven years of age I was impressed that I would be called to the ministry. From this time I sought

the Lord in secret, and led a moral life. In the
Sabbath-school, as well as under the preaching of
God's word, I would often weep and pray earnestly for the pardon of my sins." How beautiful
is this testimony compared with the neglect that
so often shames the relation of parent and child.

It was well that these parents had so fully discharged their duty, for the husband and father
was soon to be taken away. In 1825 Edward
Edwards died in great peace, leaving the responsibility of the family with the mother and
Thomas, the oldest son, who from his occupation
as a tailor was able to meet the principal expenses
of a frugal living. John and David for the
three succeeding years assisted their elder brother
in the shop, occupied themselves about home,
and took such work from others as they could
perform. During this time young Edwards received only twelve months of regular schooling—
all that he ever received in this way. In his riper
years, however, by the aid of living men and
living books, he pushed forward to a respectable
standing among scholars and thinkers of his
time. But more of this in another place.

At the age of twelve he, with his brother John,
entered the woolen-factory at Delaware as an apprentice, and began to learn the trade of carding
and cloth-dressing.

All of the hands slept in the factory. The first night when he knelt down at his bedside to pray, as was his custom, some of his companions tossed their boots at him. The next night when he knelt down they said in a whisper, loud enough to be distinctly heard, "H-u-s-h, Dave's a p-r-a-y-i-n." But he gave them no heed, and treated them just the same as before. It was not long until they were ready to show him the utmost respect, and in time some of them followed his example. After his connection with the factory it appears that his attendance at Sabbath-school was interrupted. Some ladies came to the factory and solicited five of the boys to attend the Sabbath-school. Three accepted the invitation; the other two refused to attend. One of the two referred to afterward filled a drunkard's grave, and the other still lives, a drunken saloon-keeper. Of the three who went to Sabbath-school one became a Presbyterian deacon, another a Methodist preacher of large usefulness, and the third a United Brethren bishop. This is the substance of a story often told, by the subject of this narrative, to illustrate the importance of Sabbath-school work.

Young Edwards was full of healthful energy, which often vented itself in boyish pranks. He used not many words in the social circle, but always spoke with promptness and to purpose. There is evidence enough even at this early period of his life, that his mind was often exercised upon the great problems that have always pressed upon noble natures. But his thoughts and plans were generally kept to himself. His mind was capable of conversation with itself. Nevertheless his companionable character, while working as a factory hand, is attested by the warm attachment and confidence manifested in after-years by those with whom he had been associated in labor. He continued at Delaware until he was seventeen years of age, receiving but a meager compensation for his work, and that in cloth. But now, having acquired a fair knowledge of his trade, he prepared to leave home, and so changed his place of labor. It is not certain that he knew, at once, just where to go, or at what particular place he might find employment. He was heard to say, in after-years, "I felt like doing something more and better for myself." We know too that he lifted his heart to God in prayer for his protection and guidance. Nor did he pray and trust in vain. It must have been a great trial to the mother to see her boy leave home, "but it seemed for the best." When the time came to leave, his mother said, "Are you sure, David, that you have money enough to go on?" He said, "I have enough." The amount was thirty-seven cents, all told. Here was a chance for the exercise of that faith which so much distinguished him in after-life. His mother now cautioned him against bad company and bad habits; and so, with a mother's blessing, he departed. A kind Providence led him to Rock Mills, about seven miles above Lancaster, Ohio, on the Hocking River. In these mills he found employment, and at once went to hard work. Here the pay was better than at Delaware, but he was away from mother and loved ones. This was not home. "At times," said he, "I felt sad and lonely." Besides, the very things against which his mother cautioned, namely, bad company, and the danger of forming bad habits, seemed now to confront him. In fact his associations at this place put his principles to a severe test. But God was with him.

After he had been at Rock Mills about one year he attended a protracted meeting held by the United Brethren in a neighboring dwelling-house, occupied by a family by the name of Graul. At first he avoided all personal connection with the meeting, but was at length deeply convicted, and resolved, as he expressed it, "to commence seeking for life." He joined the church as a seeker, but it was not until after three months, May 28, 1834, at a meeting held at Jacob Bolenbaugh's, just a short distance from where the protracted meeting was held, that he received a satisfactory evidence of the forgiveness of his sins. The depth of his experience and the energy of his religious life began to suggest to the minds of others, whether God might not have a special work for the converted factory-boy.

CHAPTER II.

T is no easy task to take ourselves back nearly a half century, to the time when Mr. Edwards entered upon his ministerial career; and yet, to understand his life and labors, it is necessary to take some notice of the times in which he wrought, the living forces that were most prominent in society, and the immediate circumstances with which he had to contend. In 1835, when he first looked out upon public life, the population of the United States was only sixteen millions. The frontier line, marking the limit of settlement, ran through Michigan, northern Illinois, and Missouri. Wisconsin and Iowa had not as yet been organized as territories. Ohio had looked upon but a single generation. The churches had scarcely adjusted themselves to the great problems that were to be wrought out through the commingling of the nations in the new world. The country was new, and but

31

sparsely settled, especially in all that vast territory lying west of the Alleghany Mountains.
The churches, too, were generally weak, and but
poorly organized for work. This was especially
true of the United Brethren in Christ. The Church
numbered but eight conferences, and probably
less than twenty thousand members. At this
time, however, no regular records were kept;
hence this uncertainty respecting the number
of its communicants at the time referred to.
United Brethren meeting-houses, in Ohio, could
be counted on one's fingers. The *Religious Telescope* was less than a year old. But little attention had been given to the external and indirect
conditions of success. No general missionary
society, no educational institutions had been established. The Church had just commenced to
pass through that slow and losing process of
transition from the German to the English character. But few of its ministers could preach
or conduct religious services in the English language. True, its doctrines and principles were
then, as now, thoroughly orthodox, and its methods of work such as were usual among evangelical Christians; but these were only formative.
Hence the principles and methods of the Church,
however good, needed to be stated, proved, and
illustrated in practical life. This was the one
great work to be done.

Imperative was the call for laborers. Great, too, was the opposition; and of those who came forward at this time no one has stood, from first to last, nearer the life of the Church, and nearer the center of conflict, than Mr. Edwards. To name his early co-laborers, at least any considerable number of them, would carry us beyond our limits. In the Scioto country, and at large in the Church, men of great self-denial, thorough consecration, and excellent powers for the ministry, entered the conferences and wrought successfully for the Master. The omission of particular mention of these faithful associates, in this connection, should not be understood as detracting from the high estimation in which they deserve to be held. Without them Mr. Edwards would never have been what he was.

We have seen that his origin was indeed humble, that his parents were poor but respectable, that his early educational advantages were very limited, and that he had no family or social connections to lift him into public notice. All these facts have been stated, or clearly intimated. He was nevertheless one of God's noblemen, richly endowed by nature, and, by the power of divine grace, nourished up to a great manhood. At first awkward and disappointing, in time he became easy and assuring in manners. He was

in height about five feet and ten inches, but
was never at any period of his life corpulent.
His eyes were dark, deep, and very penetrating.
The largeness of his head and chest were also
marked features of his personal appearance. But
these were only the external signs of the coming
preacher, editor, and bishop. He is now about to
enter upon a brilliant and useful career, and it is
our pleasant task to mark its unfoldings. But
let us be true to the facts, and at once recognize
the hand of God in every such life of strength,
beauty, and excellence. It begins with a divine
call to the ministry. It is the peculiar preroga-
tive of the great Head of the church to desig-
nate men to preach the gospel. All Protestant
denominations substantially agree on this subject. In all ages and under every dispensation
of religion which God has been pleased to give
to mankind, this principle has been recognized.
It guided in the appointment of Aaron and his
sons to the office of the priesthood, and in filling the prophetical and apostolic offices. This
is the faith and practice of the United Brethren
in Christ. She admits no one to this holy office
who does not give evidence that he is " moved by
the Holy Ghost to preach the gospel." It is well
known that Mr. Edwards held this view as being
essential to the validity of the Christian ministry.

He was often heard to say, publicly and privately, that "none are true ministers of Christ but they who are called of God, as was Aaron." Many have heard him relate his own experience on this subject. It was clear and distinct. His usual way of stating it was, "Soon after my conversion, I felt an inward call to preach the gospel." But his extreme timidity was a great obstacle to him. His quarterly-conference license bears date May 23, 1835. So bashful was he at this time, that when his presence was desired in the conference one of the brethren had to go out and constrain him to come in. On entering the room he seemed not to know what to do with himself. When his license was handed to him he folded it and tucked it in his vest-pocket, not wishing to notice it in the presence of others. Call this a trifle, if you please, but it was not so to him. But that which appalled him most was the nature and the responsibility of the work itself. Thus weighed down, he cried mightily to God for help; and in the deepest anguish of soul he exclaimed, "The load is too heavy, I can not bear it! Oh, what shall I do?" The local class to which he belonged at this time numbered about one hundred members. They had just passed through a most extraordinary revival. A goodly number had been converted and brought into the Church;

and of them six were now licensed to preach. The field of labor to which this class belonged was Pickaway Circuit. It embraced twenty-eight appointments, and a single round required four weeks. Rev. M. Ambrose was preacher in charge. One day, meeting young Edwards, he said, "Can you not go at least one round with me on the circuit?" Edwards hesitated. Some of the brethren in the neighborhood urged him to go and make the trial. They said, "If you have been truly called to preach, you have but to open your mouth and the Lord will fill it." So he bought a horse and a small outfit in clothing and went along. The first appointment was at a private house. Mr. Ambrose preached, and young Edwards tried to exhort. He rose and opened his mouth, as he afterward said, "but nothing more unusual than air filled it." This failure, though a too literal view of Bible language, let it be remembered, did not cause him to lose confidence forever in the great truth of the Holy Spirit's help. After his failure, however, he was discouraged, and made up his mind to return home. Darkness, deep darkness, seemed now to settle down upon his soul. But the Lord's hand was in it. It was for the trial of his faith. Of this his brethren reminded him. So, fortunately, he was induced to go on and try again. Mr.

Ambrose requested him to take turns with him-self in conducting family devotions at the places where they stopped. This he consented to do. So one evening, while leading in the devotions, he became confused, and brought his prayer abruptly to a close, with "Amen and so forth." At other times, too, even in the public congrega-tion, he was known to cut short the difficulty in the same way. Little was thought of the inci-dent just given; but the next morning when the horses were saddled he said in his quick, short way, "Now, I reckon, you'll let me go home. When a fellow like me gets so hard up in prayer that he has to stop and say 'and so forth,' I think he had better go home and stay there." "But," said Mr. Ambrose, "everybody knows that you bought a horse and started round with me. Now, what will they say if you leave the circuit and go home?" So, after an energetic exhortation, he again suffered himself to be led along, but only to meet difficulties of a like kind wherever he went. He especially dreaded the somewhat wealthy congregation at Dresbach's meeting-house. Here he pleaded off from going into the pulpit. Next day, dejected in spirits, he started home, mourning over his ill success. About half way home he thought of the Wednesday evening prayer-meeting. One of the six young preachers before mentioned.would have to open the meeting, and as he had been away four weeks he would likely be the one called on; and worse than all, improvement would be expected. The thought was not out of his mind except when asleep. He was tempted to stay at home. Then he thought he would go, but go late. Acting upon this, he entered the room, found a back seat, and quickly sat down. Philip Coons, the oldest of the young preachers, rose and said aloud, "Brother Edwards, come this way." Hat in hand, he went forward and said, "What do you want with me?" "To open the meeting, of course," was the reply. Knowing that it would be of no use to refuse, and fearing that he might displease the Lord, he said, "Sing a hymn till I come back." He then went out into an adjoining orchard to pray. Here the cloud was lifted from his mind. He then returned and led the meeting with manifest tokens of the Spirit's help. After the meeting the brethren commended the improvement he had made, and said he ought to go another round. These words of comfort and hope were timely, and did him much good. The Master himself seemed now to say to his hitherto troubled heart, "Be of good cheer." These lights and shades in the early experience of Mr. Edwards are not here noticed because they are new. They are, in a measure, common to all pious and sensible young men when just entering upon the work of the ministry. In fact they are often the precursors of the greatest excellence and influence.

About this time Rev. E. Van Demark was placed in charge of Pickaway Circuit. His colleague having resigned, he asked for the help of Mr. Edwards. This was granted. So now he began itinerant work in earnest, November 1, 1835. For the six months closing with the first of the following May he received only twenty dollars for his services. He was well received on the circuit. Mr. Van Demark set a high estimate upon his young associate, but could not get to hear him preach until, arriving late at an appointment at which they had agreed to meet, he heard Edwards announce his text; and knowing that the young preacher would likely sit down if he entered the room, he remained at the door and heard him through. At this time he was hard to follow in a sermon. His utterances were rapid and often very indistinct. Words did not seem to flow, but rather to rush along in broken fragments. His ideas, however, were sound and logical. This all intelligent persons could readily discern. Worldly people sometimes made unfavorable remarks on account of the above-named defects; but the pious were never discouraged, even by the poorest of his efforts. It is to be remembered that at this time he was but nineteen years old. During this year, he having failed, according to his own view, in one of his Sabbath-morning efforts, and having an appointment in the Ortman neighborhood at night, discouragement almost overcame him. Thomas McGrady, with whom he was stopping, found him lying upon the ground, on a hill some distance from the house, trying to die. He felt that he could not preach; and he asked the Lord to take him away. His standard of the preacher's qualifications and work was so high that no ordinary success could satisfy him. There have been a few men in the world incapable of mediocrity, and Mr. Edwards was one of the number. The labor of the year was quite successful, resulting in a number of revivals. He was very studious, always carrying with him a New Testament, Kirkham's Grammar, and other books. He studied much on horseback, and so occupied himself with his books at stopping-places that he was regarded by some as very poor company. His senior colleague assisted him in grammar until the student outstripped the teacher. Often was he found upon his knees in the woods, beside a log or a tree, with his Testament spread out before him—for it was by prayer and study that he sought the meaning of the Word. In 1836 he became a member of Scioto Conference, and from that time he made the fortunes of the Church his fortunes. The United Brethren in Christ were then a feeble band, residing mostly in the rural districts of Pennsylvania, Maryland, Virginia, and Ohio. Mr. Edwards knew nothing of these humble people at this time, except from what he had seen of them in a very few localities; for they had no history, and were entirely unknown to fame. He said, "Those of them that I had met seemed humble, spiritual, and devout; and this pleased me. I then read carefully their book of Discipline, and found them evangelical in doctrine and thoroughly opposed to the spirit of the world." "A sincere love of a pure church-fellowship, shown in their opposition to slavery and all secret orders," he said, "especially pleased me." So he said, "These are the Lord's people, and I will go with them." How true he was to these convictions and to the church of his choice we all know. The next year the conference placed Mr. Edwards on Brush Creek Circuit, along with Rev. John Eckert, a foreign German, of good abilities and long experience in the ministry but not very agreeable in his habits and manner of life. Hence it was feared by some that young

Edwards would suffer by being thus associated with one so aged and peculiar in his methods of work. But this fear was not well founded. His rare good sense and piety led him to accept the situation, and so go to work in earnest. At that time Brush Creek Circuit was large, extending through the greater portion of Highland, Adams, and Brown counties. It was at least three hundred and fifty miles around, and embraced twenty-eight regular appointments, which had to be filled by each preacher every four weeks. It is easy to see that the work must have been very laborious. It was also quite successful. Mr. Edwards received for this year's work fifty-five dollars, all told. It was during this year that he preached for the first time before his mother. Many preachers can tell what a trial that involves. His text was I. Peter iv. 18: "And if the righteous scarcely be saved, where shall the ungodly and the sinner appear?" He succeeded, as he thought, quite well. He was, however, anxious to know what his mother thought of the sermon, and gave her opportunities enough to tell; but she said not a word. When at length others drew from her an expression of opinion she said, "There was terror enough in it." These simple and quiet words of his mother made a deep and abiding impression on his mind. He acknowl-

edged many times, in after-years that this answer had much to do in changing the tone of his
preaching. In referring to it he said, "When I
commenced traveling, such was my zeal that I
expected to drive sinners to Christ by scare,—
mainly by urging the terrors of the law and the
awful retribution which awaits the ungodly. Thus
armed, at it I went; but to my great astonish-
ment and confusion I found that I beat the
church and the congregation to death, in many
instances, by the very means which I expected
would revive and save them. We must preach
the terrors of the law, to be sure; but the law
can not save. The gospel alone can do this."
So we see it took some time for him to develop
into the unctious gospel-preacher. There was, in
fact, a gradual unfolding of all his powers. No
premature ripeness stood in the way of a vigorous and sustained maturity. He early habituated
himself to orderly methods in preaching. Nor
did he even in exhortation depart from this rule.
To this we must ascribe much of his power in
the pulpit and on the rostrum. It is needless to
say that all the leading members of the conference watched the progress of young Edwards
with great interest. Notably among these may
be mentioned Benedum, Hastings, Ambrose, Hanby, Coons, Montgomery, and Van Demark. These

have all been called from labor to reward except
the last one mentioned, who at this writing still
lingers among us, waiting for the chariots of
Israel. Father Benedum, of precious memory,
fell asleep in Jesus the same year that Edwards
traveled Brush Creek Circuit. His loss was keenly
felt.

At the conference of 1837, Van Demark and
Edwards were once more associated in work and
placed on Winchester Circuit. They were mutually pleased at this, and so went to work at once.
The circuit extended through portions of Franklin, Licking, Pickaway, and Fairfield counties. It
was about four hundred miles around, and included thirty appointments, which were to be
filled by each preacher every four weeks. They
traveled this large circuit on horseback. The
people were poor, with but few exceptions, and
of course could not do much for them in the way
of support. But, trusting in God, they went
forward, and were generally provided for. At
the beginning of the year they entered into a
covenant to give themselves to prayer and the
study of God's word, so that they might be more
successful in leading sinners to Christ. Their
prayers were answered and their labors greatly
blessed. Mr. Edwards did not spend his time in
cheap talk; nor was he disposed to listen very

long to the gossiping stories of others, as the following incident will show: In making his first round on Winchester Circuit, he stopped with a family somewhat addicted to this vice. The good lady of the house went on to tell him of a quarrel that had taken place between two of the members of the church. He listened awhile, and then said, "Stop, mother, stop; I do not want to hear any more of it. I have all that I can do to attend to the gospel." This may seem a little abrupt, but the case probably justified it. He knew when to be rigid and severe, and also when to be gentle and kind. At one time during this year Mr. Van Demark was under the necessity of going home, and asked a certain minister to fill some of his appointments. Edwards did not think the brother applied to a very energetic preacher; so he turned to his colleague and said, in a firm tone, "You must fill those appointments yourself. That is according to our agreement." Here again we see that faithfulness to principle which always characterized him. His preaching at this time seemed to be attended with great power. He and his colleague held a protracted meeting in the town of Winchester, with marked success. He was earnest, quick, and intelligent in a high degree, but still speaking with too much rapidity and with his mouth but partially open. A dis-

tinguished gentleman—a member of congress—
hearing him preach during the meeting referred
to, said to Mr. Van Demark, his colleague, "If
you can get that boy to open his mouth he will
make a preacher." The United Brethren at this
time had no house of worship in Winchester. On
one Sabbath the United Brethren congregation
came together at the church of a sister denomination, under the mistaken impression that consent had been given for the use of the church.
It happened that said denomination had arranged
for a class-meeting. Unpleasant feelings were
excited at once, and were but too freely expressed.
Edwards walked back and forth, saying nothing,
but groaning in spirit. But finally he was requested to come in and preach. He did so, and
took for his text, "Behold, how good and how
pleasant it is for brethren to dwell together in
unity!" He entered into the spirit of the text with
great clearness and power, but made no allusion
to the altercation that had just taken place. Here
we see his ready power of appreciating and doing
what is required by circumstances. In other
words, his strong common sense, sweetened with
piety, showed itself. He was mighty in prayer.
This was his chief reliance in trouble. At one
time, during a violent disturbance at a camp-
meeting, he cast himself down in a tent that was

being unroofed by a mob, and prayed with all his
might. The excitement immediately ceased and
order was restored. He said, "The Lord did it;
let him . have the glory." He always kept an
excellent horse, and took good care of him. And,
what ought to find no exception in the ministry,
he was a cleanly and pure man in his person and
habits. His salary for this year's service was
eighty dollars.

At the conference of 1838 Mr. Edwards was
appointed to Raccoon Circuit, with Rev. A. Eby
as colleague. The circuit then included a large
portion of Athens, Vinton, and Meigs counties,
in the hilly regions of southern Ohio. It was
large, and difficult to travel. The people were
generally poor and ignorant, and of course could
not do much in the way of support. Lodging
and board were of the simplest kind. Roads and
bridges had hardly been thought of. Places for
preaching were the cabins of these poor people,
and occasionally a school-house. Appointments
were far between and difficult to reach, as the
travel passed over hills but little less than mountains. But no matter, he went forward trusting
in God, feeling, as he said, "that the Master's
vineyard must be cultivated, whatever it may
cost." The hardships through which he and all
the early ministers of the Church were called to

pass can scarcely be realized by the present generation. Like all men of independent thought
and action, Mr. Edwards was occasionally persecuted. He was not the man to hold opinions on
questions of public interest and say nothing about
them. His bold utterances of truth on the slavery
question more than once brought him into danger.
This did not, however, seriously interrupt his
work on the circuit. Fearless, yet prudent and
sagacious, he always managed so as not to be
hindered in his appropriate work. This was a
year of much prosperity to the Church in the
Raccoon country. He found here some excellent
families and well-to-do people, notwithstanding
the general destitution before mentioned. Some
of these united with the Church, thus giving
greater efficiency and permanency to the circuit.
His salary this year was eighty dollars, — the
usual amount paid to a single man. In 1839 the
conference met at Pleasant Run, where Mr. Edwards was elected to elders' orders, after the
usual probation of three years, and ordained by
Bishop Kumler, senior, along with Lewis Ambrose and W. W. Coons. The occasion was
unusually solemn and impressive. At that time
there was no "Course of Reading" laid down
for licentiate preachers, upon which to be examined before ordination. But it was found that
Edwards had been very diligent in study, and

was already acquainted with some of the best books then in use on theological and religious subjects. The present course of study, to be sure, would have been a help to him; but he could and would study, either with or without such help. From this conference he was sent to Burlington Circuit, in the extreme southern portion of Ohio. This was sending him away from the better portion of the Church to serve a few disheartened and scattered societies in a country exceedingly rough and difficult to travel. But he was not the man to hesitate or falter in the presence of a clearly-defined duty. So, true to his consecration-vows, he went and commenced work at once. Here the situation and circumstances were much the same as those of the preceding year. He found the same hilly country,— all over hilly,—and the people here, as before, generally poor and much in need of the gospel. And how well and nobly he bent himself to the work in hand is still a subject of common talk in many portions of southern Ohio. So the light of his life and the good effects of his preaching still remain on Burlington Circuit. The Lord blessed his labors abundantly; but at the close of the year his health was somewhat impaired. He received as salary for the year ninety-five dollars, and presents thirty-two dollars and fifty cents, all told.

4

few miles east of Athens, Ohio, there lived a very interesting and intelligent family by the name of Hibbard. The parents were members of the Presbyterian Church in the East, but at the time here alluded to belonged to the United Brethren. Mr. Hibbard was a lawyer of good abilities, but had abandoned the profession for the study of divinity and occasional preaching. His son Randolph, studious and scholarly in his habits, was also a preacher of more than ordinary promise. Both father and son were members of Scioto Conference. The young ladies of the family were sprightly and accomplished. They were objects of special attraction to the young people of the neighborhood. Harriet, the oldest of the girls, had already become the wife of Rev. John Miller, also a member of Scioto Conference. This was a well-to-do family, but not in affluent circumstances. It is easy to see that this must have been a very pleasant stopping-place for any one who could appreciate refinement and culture. It was all this and much more to Mr. Edwards, as we shall see presently. While traveling Raccoon Circuit he frequently stopped with this family, and thus formed the acquaintance of Miss Lucretia Hibbard, who was at that time teaching school near Athens, Ohio. Her engaging manners and good solid sense pleased him, and so, after awhile, he proposed marriage, and his proposal was accepted. The nuptials were solemnized on December 10, 1839, Rev. W. K. McKabe officiating. This union proved fortunate in every respect. Mrs. Edwards, as the wife of an itinerant, has ever been a devoted and efficient helper. It was through her judicious management of the financial affairs of the family that he was enabled to devote himself exclusively to one work. She still lives, in fair health, in a pleasant home at Dayton, Ohio.

From overwork and exposure, and perhaps also from a zeal not always directed by prudence, the health of Mr. Edwards had become impaired. His work, especially on Burlington Circuit, had been very severe. By preaching, often in the open air, and in poorly ventilated rooms, he had contracted a disease of the throat, which now threatened to cut short his useful career. He took his case to the Lord, as was his custom in all matters, both temporal and spiritual, and asked direction. After getting all the light he could, it seemed necessary to locate and await the indications of Providence. So with some trembling lest he should depart from the way of duty, at the conference of 1840 he took a location, purposing to return to the active work as soon as possible. He was, however, for this year appointed presiding elder on Jackson Mission, a small field lying in West Virginia, not very remote from his residence in Centerville, Ohio. In 1841 and 1842 he received no appointment, but scarcely passed a Sabbath without preaching. He attended all the annual sessions of conference, and now began to take a large part in the proceedings. Hence his influence was more and more felt.

The sound judgment of Mr. Edwards led him at all times to give the most exact attention to the financial side of his affairs. True, Mrs. Edwards, as before said, was a great help to him in this respect. But he deemed it necessary to keep an eye on all such matters himself, knowing very well how easy it is for a minister to break down in his work by not attending properly to his financial affairs. In his account-book, under date of March 20, 1840, we have an illustration of this phase of his life. "Silver in purse sixty-three dollars, and paper thirty-one dollars." He then adds a figure six, apparently to see how one hundred dollars in assets would look. Mrs. Edwards had added to the common stock what was then regarded a comfortable outfit for house-keeping.

We have seen that Mr. Edwards had learned the trade of carding and cloth-dressing. Now, partially broken down in health, he, naturally enough, turned his attention to this business as a livelihood. There was, "providentially," as he called it, an opening of this kind at Centerville, Ohio. So here he bought, in 1840, a small carding establishment, and went to work. The summer he spent in the mill, meeting with quite good success. For the winter, however, he had no work. Mrs. Edwards suggested that they both teach school. But how could one who had been himself in school so little become a teacher? He could not think of it. But his wife said, "You can,—by getting books, and study. And then you will have a little time for preparation before the schools are to open." He took her advice, and got a good certificate, and both taught. Thus they managed to pay for the little property they had bought. The next year he sold out and moved to Rushville, Fairfield County, Ohio.

Here he carried on the carding and cloth-dressing business with enlarged facilities, but, for a time, in a rented establishment. The following year, in partnership with Mr. George Stults, he bought the mill, and they conducted the business together. · Although busily engaged in these secular affairs, he did not forget his consecration vows. The cause of the Master was still nearest his heart. Every now and then the Lord used him in starting some poor soul in the way of a better life. Among these may be mentioned his partner in business. Nor was he negligent in the improvement of his mind; for during all these years he carried on his studies. In order to do this he kept a desk in the establishment, near the place of his work, upon which was always an open book. In this way he studied geology and other branches. He also took up a new appointment, and formed a class two miles from Rushville. He attended the prayer-meetings with this class, besides being present at the regular church-services at home. It is to be remembered that in the early history of the United Brethren Church, to be a local preacher meant to do no small amount of work. Often the only difference between a local and a traveling preacher was that the former had no regular appointment assigned him, and served without pay. The local preachers of to-day, however, do but little preaching, and in fact but little work of any kind for the Master. Even the average itinerant of the present day does no more preaching, or Christian work generally, than did Mr. Edwards while local. Besides, as a citizen and neighbor, he possessed the highest confidence and esteem of the community. This was shown him in many ways, which, as he often said, did much in making his Rushville home very pleasant. The first child—a daughter —of David and Lucretia Edwards was born here, in 1842. At the close of the second year at Rushville he was fortunate in completely disengaging himself from the business with which he had been occupied, by selling out to his partner. He continued to live at Rushville, however, till the close of the following year.

In 1843 Mr. Edwards was present at conference and prepared to take work. Providence had favored him with restored health and with somewhat improved temporal circumstances. And then he had been so diligent in study, and had so thoroughly maintained the spirit of devotion in his heart, that, all things considered, he was now better prepared for the active work of the ministry than ever before. He seemed especially to have acquired more self-control in preaching. He was appointed to Muskingum Circuit, with Jesse

Wilson as colleague, each of these devoted men being greatly favored by the companionship and influence of the other. The circuit was unusually large, even for those early times. It was said to be five hundred miles around, and was very difficult to travel. At one time during the year he came to the Muskingum River when it was very high, and there being no bridge by which to cross over and so reach his appointment on the other side, he did not know at first what to do. It seemed especially necessary to reach the appointment, because it was intended to be the first of a protracted effort. So, after a careful examination of the situation, he placed his saddle-bags on his shoulder and swam the horse to the opposite bank, and then went on to his appointment and preached in frozen clothes. This adventure being known, the people were more than ever drawn to him, and an excellent revival ensued.

The kind of discipline exercised by Mr. Edwards while on this circuit may be seen by reference to records still preserved. A few cases may not be out of place. "Mrs. M. charged with swearing, but denies the charge. No witnesses. Case laid over till next round." Next round. "Her case resumed, and she expelled." "J. M. charged with fighting and quarreling with his family. Partly denies the charge. Promises to

try to amend, and the class bears with him."
"G. S. charged with whipping his wife and play-
ing the fiddle. Confesses to the latter. The first,
he says, is none of our business. Charges sustained. Expelled." We see here that Mr. Edwards believed that ministers should correct such
abuses, and that the church was never intended
for such trashy and wicked men. An example is
given of a class of one hundred members being
broken up—not during this year, however,—because discipline, though called for by him and
others, was not enforced. Eighty-nine members
were received during this year. His salary was
one hundred and seventy-two dollars and forty-
seven cents.

During the intervals of the General conferences,
the Scioto Conference, for many years, had the
special oversight and control of the publishing
house at Circleville, Ohio. So in the exercise of
this power, Scioto Conference, in 1839, put a
stop to the discussion of the slavery question in
the columns of the *Religious Telescope*. This, Mr.
Edwards, with a few others, denounced as "bad
policy, and unrighteous in the sight of God."
His appeal was most eloquent and touching, especially when he compared this downward movement of the Church to the setting of the sun in
darkness. His nobleness of nature never shone

with more splendor than on this occasion. This misguided policy, however, prevailed until 1844, at which time this "odious gag-rule" was forever removed from the *Religious Telescope*, by a large vote of the conference. Mr. Edwards did much to bring this about. For the next year he was appointed to Circleville Station. This was one of the most important charges in the conference. Important church-interests were being concentrated here. Station-work was yet new in the Church. Of course, he moved his family at once to Circleville. There were one hundred and twenty-five members belonging to the charge, at the time he commenced his labors; and, during the year, forty-two were received. The salary amounted to one hundred and twenty-three dollars and sixty-one cents, and the presents to thirty-eight dollars and seventy-five cents. This was the only year in his entire ministry when he did not lay up something from his salary. Mr. Edwards had just completed his twenty-seventh year when he was appointed to Circleville Station. As to the man, he was still the same that he was ten years before when he became a Christian. He was a man of marked individuality. He was Edwards, —always Edwards. Everything that he said and did was characteristic. Hence what would have been trifles with others were not so with him.

But the accidents of the bashful factory boy were being laid aside. The moral and spiritual elements of his nature were now coming into full play. The devotion, struggle, and one might almost say the agony, of years, were beginning to present some of their ripened fruit. The man who a short time before had shrunk back from all strange contact as from death itself, now began to see in the faces and hearts of his fellow-men what might awaken compassion, but could not move to fear. He had faced and studied the problem of man's nature and condition, and why should he fear the face of man? The Lord was evidently leading him to a higher plane of thought and action; and this made him fearless and mighty in his work. The editor of the *Religious Telescope*, at the time, thus speaks of his pastorate: "Our present very worthy pastor, Rev. D. Edwards, is very well received. Those who attend his ministry appear to be very much delighted with his cogent, pointed, and spiritual sermons. Large and increasing congregations attend his ministry." During the winter of this year Mr. Edwards was awakened one night by the thought of Rev. Jesse Wilson, his colleague of the previous year, who was now in the last stages of consumption. He said to his wife, "Why may not Jesse and his wife come and stay with us?" The answer was favorable; and the next morning, before breakfast, he went down to Mr. Wilson's and told him of his thoughts in the night, and of what he had now to propose. Mr. Wilson replied, "As I was lying awake last night, I wondered if you would not let us come and live with you, and let me die at your house." The two families lived together; and Mr. Edwards often said that Jesse kept the door of heaven open to them to the time of his death, which occurred February first of the same winter.

While at Circleville he made an immense advance in spiritual stature. From this time dates his profession of entire sanctification, and without discussing theories here, he undoubtedly entered upon a new era in his religious life. The flame of his devotion was intenser, purer, steadier, sending its blessings more abroad, and saving less for self, than ever before. He had carefully read and much admired the writings of Wesley and his followers on the subject of sanctification. " Principles of the Interior or Hidden Life," by Prof. Upham, and "Life and Religious Opinions of Madame Guyon," and others of like kind, were his favorite books. Not a few of the members of his charge, as well as others, fully sympathized with him in these tendencies and struggles of his mind and heart. This was especially true of

Jesse Wilson. The influence of this godly man upon the mind of Mr. Edwards was indeed very great. In the struggles and yearnings of their kindred spirits they mutually stimulated each other. Mr. Wilson professed to obtain the blessing of entire sanctification on Christmas-day, 1844, while lying sick at the house of Mr. Edwards. This was regarded as a triumphant vindication of the doctrine taught by these good men; namely, that entire sanctification is by faith in Christ and attainable before death. As the friends of Mr. Wilson gathered around him he said, calmly, "All, all is now peace. Rest, my soul, in Jesus. Glory, glory to God in the highest." The experience of Mr. Edwards can best be read in his own simple and fervid language. "On the second day of January, 1845, having an appointment a few miles in the country, I started about sundown, exceedingly oppressed with a sense of my unworthiness and unholiness. While reflecting upon how poorly qualified I was with such an unholy heart, to preach a pure gospel to others, it was suggested,—'You have been seeking a clean heart for ten years, and you are further from it now than ever before. You had better now give it up, and not make a fool of yourself and expose yourself to persecution. Why not live peaceably as most Christians live?'

I answered, 'God says, Be ye holy, and it is plainly my duty to seek it and obtain it, whether others do or not.'

"The next suggestion was,—for by this time the thoughts presented to mind occupied my entire attention, as much so as if I had heard an audible voice,—'If it is by faith, you may have it now before you preach,' and I began to pray. In an instant these words were presented to my mind as never before; 'Ask and receive.' 'Why, Lord,' said I, 'I have asked a thousand times.' 'True,' said the inward voice, 'You asked, but you have not received or taken the offered blessing.' I at once saw the difficulty. At that instant a revelation was given upon the subject of faith which was worth more to me than all the theology I ever read upon it. I remembered many a time in my former history when the blessing was in reach. I could, as it were, see it, and almost say, it is mine. But this receiving faith was wanting. I saw the blessing held out, and with melting heart and tearful eyes said, 'Lord, I do receive,— I am thine and thou art mine!' It was enough. My heart was filled with love. 'Glory to God.' That was a great turning-point in my religious life. I had from that hour a depth of peace, a constancy of faith, and a clearness of views of divine providence never before enjoyed. Whatever inconsistencies may have marked my life since that time, I am convinced that the above was a real and scriptural experience. And my only regret now is, after nearly sixteen years, that I have not made more proficiency in it, and lived it out more perfectly. But to-day I stand on the same platform, and the merciful Savior who saved me then kindly pardons all past delinquencies, and is still the strength of my heart, and my portion forever. Glory to his holy name." This quotation is lengthy, but it could not well be omitted, nor abridged. It is therefore given entire. It reveals most clearly the triumph of God's grace in the heart of his servant. Many have heard him tell this simple story with throbbing hearts and tearful eyes. And no wonder; for it lets in a flood of light upon the great question of salvation by faith, and faith only.

At the conference of 1845 Mr. Edwards was elected presiding elder, and assigned to Circleville District. As the district was small, or rather fractional, the prospect of support was very poor. On learning of the appointment, Mrs. Edwards cried all night. Mr. Edwards said, "We will trust God." But she said, "We must use some sense." He replied, "To trust God is sensible." So he began his work with firm trust and resolution; but the General Conference, which soon met in Circleville, had for him a different field.

CHAPTER IV.

HE General Conference met at Circleville, Ohio, in May, 1845, at which time Mr. Edwards was elected editor of the *Religious Telescope*, much to his surprise. We may be sure that he never sought the position; nor did he want it when proffered. In fact he was slow to believe that this was any part of his calling. His experience in writing, up to this time, was indeed very limited. He had contributed a few articles to the church-paper, but these had not attracted much notice. He certainly had no general reputation as a writer, at the time he entered this field. He was already a great preacher, and widely known as such. He was at home in the pulpit. This was felt and acknowledged by all who knew him. "Why can he not write as well as speak?" said an influential member of General Conference. "Let us try him," said another. And so it was agreed all around. After his election he said, "Writing goes hard with me; but no matter, the Lord is my helper." This appointment gave universal satisfaction. All seemed to feel that the new editor had something to say. This proved to be true; for the same clearness and energy that had characterized his preaching re-appeared in the use of the pen.

The *Telescope* was in its eleventh volume when Mr. Edwards took charge of it. It had passed through great trials, and many vicissitudes, but had made some advancement. The paper had never met with any direct opposition. Still, its circulation was very limited. The Church had not yet learned the value of this kind of literature. Besides, the want of experience on the part of those who had in charge the special management of the paper occasioned much embarrassment to the enterprise. This was especially true during the editorial career of Rev. William Rhinehart. It was also difficult to secure suitable communications for the paper. A former editor, as a reason for rejecting certain articles sent for publication, said, "They contain nothing but what has been treated in a more able and masterly manner. We have not time to revise, or in fact to remodel, a host of scribbled errors. Other articles contain nothing but invective and criti-

cism; and others there are that contain sentiments contrary to our views of divine things."
The old files of the *Telescope* indicated a decided
preference, on the part of the managers, for
dissertations instead of editorials, for selections
rather than correspondence, and for general and
distant topics instead of those arising from the
immediate affairs of the Church. These defects
had become quite apparent, to many at least, at
the time Mr. Edwards was called to take charge
of the paper. He soon discovered them, and with
his accustomed energy and spirit at once sought
a reformation. The change of the *Telescope* to an
organ of the Church, and for the Church, had
already been made, but was now more fully recognized and emphasized. It most thoroughly sustained the position the Church had taken against
aggressive war, intemperance, slavery, and secret
societies. But what was more and better, the
Telescope, under the leadership of Mr. Edwards,
taught the Church that the position it had taken
against the evils of the times could not be maintained without the aid of the Holy Spirit. This
was urged, in the paper, with great power and
effectiveness.

The work of editing and publishing had previously been performed by the same person. Henceforth there was to be a special publishing agent.

This was a long step forward in the business affairs of the office. It also relieved the new editor of that kind of work which had so greatly embarrassed his predecessors. The ruinous credit-system was to give place to a cash subscription list. This, too, was a move in the right direction. Up to this time the *Telescope* had been a semi-monthly; it was now to be a weekly. All these changes indicated very gratifying progress. The subscription list, however, was only thirty-one hundred. The salary of the editor, including certain contingent expenses, was three hundred and fifty dollars, with house-rent free. This was meager,—too meager, in fact, to be called a salary, —but it did not discourage him. He considered the very little support his brethren in the itiner-ant ranks were receiving, and said, "It will do; let us go to work." A brave and earnest man was now at the helm. This was apparent to all. But the sea was still rough. At least some of the difficulties in conducting the paper yet remained. The work was new to the Church, and newer still to Mr. Edwards. He had everything to learn and but few to help him. Suitable correspondents could not easily be found. A large majority of those who attempted to write for the paper were poorly fitted for anything of the kind. This greatly discouraged him. He said, "They are generally poor, staggering efforts." But this was not the worst feature in the case; a bad spirit was often manifested. "Many of the preachers," said he, "are sensitive, and determined to have the last word. They want everything to be stated exactly as it is." Apparently in reply to these grumbling correspondents, he said, "All this comes from an unsanctified heart. Oh, beware of pride! Let there be in you that lowly mind which was in Jesus Christ. And be ye likewise clothed with humility. Let it not only fill, but cover you all over. Let modesty and self-diffidence appear in all your words and actions. Let all you speak and do show that you are little and base and mean and vile in your own eyes." These burning words expressed the feelings of his own heart. It was not so much a theory as a practice with him. In fact, the Lord had taught him how to abase himself at the time he experienced the great blessing of a full salvation.

In his first editorial Mr. Edwards said, "Custom makes it the duty of those who enter the editorial ranks to give a brief statement of their feelings and views in reference to their future course. In accordance with this custom we appear before you, in the language of Holy Writ, in weakness and in fear and in much trembling." From the first, his strong presence was stamped upon the columns of the *Telescope*. Henceforth the different departments of the paper arose to increasing distinctness. From its earliest history it had been an earnest reform-sheet. This policy was continued by Mr. Edwards. Hence, temperance, national peace, anti-tobacco, anti-secrecy, and antislavery, all received the support of a warm heart and a trenchant pen. Yet effort at specific reform was made much less prominent than the effort to secure the renovation of the individual heart, and thus the purification of all the features of life. Neither agitation nor speculation for their own sake found any welcome. The demand was for " soul, point, and practical utility." " We must," said the editor, " draw the reins a little closer. The *Telescope* must have soul. Each article must have an object in view. Salvation should be marked upon each article, and burn in every line. The Lord baptize anew the editor and each correspondent." His own spirit is clearly manifested in words used during his first year. The Scioto Conference, which was intrusted with large supervision over the *Telescope* in the intervals of the General Conference, met after he had been in the editorial chair four months. Writing from the conference-room, he said, " What the conference may do with the *Telescope* and its imperfect editor is hard to determine yet, but we expect some censure, as some dissatisfaction has been heard. With this we have nothing to do; we have done the best we could under the circumstances. If the brethren say the editor is a poor one and unworthy of such a place, we will have no controversy with them; for it is every word true." He dreaded the disapprobation of his brethren, and sought in every reasonable way to please them. But from his own views of right and duty he would not swerve. At the close of his first year as editor he said, "Duty teaches us that to please all we dare not if we could, and experience teaches that we can not if we would. No editor can maintain a conscience void of offense toward God and man without opposing sin and error. To those who have blamed our course in things as to which we can not conscientiously change we would say, brethren, bear with us, and pray for us. Friendly advice, reproof, dictation, and fault-finding will all be received by us and turned to as good account as we are capable of turning them; and we will endeavor to receive all in meekness, and love our brethren afterward as before. Faith and love will turn everything to our benefit, whether pleasing or displeasing to the natural man."

Many of his editorials are worthy a place in permanent literature. While absolutely destitute of all pretense, they really discuss living issues from their true underlying principles. They do not savor of wearisome labor, but of a spirit that turns all duty into earnest and joyous exertion. He did not excel in the sphere of speculative thought. In fact he did not care to enter this field. And yet some of his sayings let in more light on such subjects than all the labored efforts of the more learned. But his busy life and a practical turn of mind alike led him to view every question in the light of utility. Pure abstract reasoning he called "hair-splitting." His intellect, however, was keen and original in its operations. Hence he could "split a hair" whenever the argument in hand seemed to require it. And this he often did without claiming to be precise.

This portion of Mr. Edwards' life was too much swallowed up in his main work to afford much of incident, yet some incidents have been preserved. He was once laboring over an illegible and confused manuscript on faith, when a brother minister came in. "See here," said he to the brother. "You sit down and write the best article you can on faith and sign that man's name to it." The order, after a little hesitation, was obeyed, and the article as written and signed appeared in the paper. It was his custom to preach somewhere every Sabbath during his editorial career. His services, of course, were in great demand. He had preached at one point in the country quite frequently, and had often been invited to the house of a wealthy member of the church, a farmer, living near by. But for some reason, not very apparent to all, Mr. Edwards did not accept this proffered hospitality. It was generally known, however, that this man was so stingy that he usually sought some occasion for falling out with the circuit preacher, that he might have a better excuse for not paying anything on the salary. He at the same time could palaver over preachers that were not to be paid, thereby keeping up somewhat his reputation for religion. Mr. Edwards saw through this meanness, and resolved to rebuke it. So the next time when the stingy man crowded forward before every one else to invite him to his house, he was met with this answer: "No sir; I won't go home with you. A man that don't pay the preacher, I won't go home with."

At one time his customary seriousness was overcome sufficiently to allow him to publish, according to copy, the following note, which was tacked on to a long and miserably written article: "We wish this Published Punctatim orthagratim as it is here wrote and not tow or three lines as theare sometimes is." The editor may have intended nothing more than a little pleasantry in the publication of this note. We know, at any rate, that he had a keen relish for the ludicrous when not mixed with moral taint. Like John Bunyan, he had a talent for repartee, and occasionally indulged in little sallies of this kind. His chief object, however, seems to have been to punish an ignorant and contumacious critic. This view of the case accords with his well-known disposition to expose all kinds of hollow-hearted pretense.

Neither the first nor the second person appointed publishing agent accepted the office. This made it difficult, for a time, to fill the place acceptably. Hence more work devolved on the editor. This made it necessary for Mr. Edwards to attend various conferences, east and west, on business of the office. He thus attended Virginia Conference, at Hebron, Maryland, in 1847. He had previously offended a majority of this conference by his radical utterances on the slavery question. At the time of this visit the conference was embarrassed by some "peculiar cases" of slave-holding, for which apologists were not wanting. On the conference-floor one member showed his temerity by trying to justify the "domestic institution" from the Bible. This was more than Mr. Edwards could well bear; so he at once charged the member with "heresy." This, of course, produced no little excitement. In this condition of things he was asked to preach. He consented, but with some fear and trembling. He had already been the object of light and cutting remarks from a certain element of the conference. This weighed heavily upon his heart. So, according to his custom, he withdrew to wrestle and plead for the presence and help of the Holy Spirit in his sermon. Nor did he plead in vain. He was just about to go into the pulpit when a company of ministers showered upon him their darts, feathered with levity, but pointed and envenomed by hatred of abolitionism. Being grieved, he turned to them and said, "Brethren, I don't see how you can preach." He said, "At that moment I felt that God had given me the victory." It was indeed a victory in his own spirit, at least, which was clearly manifested in his preaching; for the Lord blessed wonderfully the word as spoken that night by his faithful servant. It is related that while in Virginia, during this trip, he sought to sell his horse, and return home by public conveyance. It was difficult, however, to find one who was desirous of owning the horse of such an abolitionist. Virginia Conference, the next year, by resolution, complained of the editor, though some of the members boldly cast their votes

against such a course. This unpleasantness, however, soon passed away, and Virginia Conference
ever afterward treated him with marked deference and respect.

Mr. Edwards, during his term as editor, was
afflicted for two years with very severe attacks of
neuralgia. His strength was thus being worn
out, and his labor seriously interfered with. During his attacks, which occurred with increasing
frequency and violence, he could do nothing.
The remedies required for relief became quite as
much to be feared as the disease itself. One Sabbath, being detained from church by one of his
attacks, he began to think of what is said in the
New Testament about the cure of diseased persons. He remembered that Jesus "treated all
manner of diseases among the people." Some
of the cases that were helped were much like his.
Then the thought came to him, "Why can not
Jesus cure the people now?" Sure enough; he
began to think almost audibly. "And then," he
said to himself, "it is not more difficult to cure
bodily diseases than pardon sin. Why can he
not cure me?" was the next question. Quickly
came the reply, "I have not asked him." He was
astonished. He fell on his knees and asked the
great Physician to heal him. As he prayed all
sense of his disease departed, and for more than

twenty-five years no sign of it returned. It is
not necessary to affirm or deny that this was a
miracle. The fact alone is stated, and the reader
left to judge for himself. That he found a cure
in the way described is indisputable. We may
be sure, moreover, that divine Providence had a
hand in it. It was God's way in bringing relief
to his servant. Mr. Edwards never connected
the case with any special doctrine or theory of
religion. Whenever he referred to it he simply
said, "The Lord did it." Those who deny special providence and the power of faith, only say
that they themselves are not in a region where a
living God can bless them, or where they have to
do with anything more than natural laws.

The subject of education in the Church was
first made prominent during the period under
review. The General Conference, in 1845, had
signified its favor of educational institutions
under the auspices of the Church. Hence, in the
fall of 1846, measures were first taken by Scioto
Conference, other conferences soon co-operating,
which resulted in the founding of Otterbein University. Other movements of like kind soon
followed in rapid succession. The work was new
to the Church, and needed the support of wise
heads and awakened hearts. While it can not
be said in truth that Mr. Edwards threw himself

into this movement with as much zeal as some others, he nevertheless gave it an earnest and efficient support. His services were especially valuable in showing the importance of maintaining a close connection between education and vital godliness. This was his chief concern when he saw the Church commit itself to this great work. All his editorials and public addresses on this subject clearly show that this was uppermost in his mind. He said, " We must educate, to be sure, but not for its own sake. It is not to be sought as an end, but rather as a means to glorify God and bless mankind." He was right.

The *Telescope* ably supported the cause of missions. The work, however, was carried on mostly by the annual conferences, the general Board that was organized in 1841 doing nothing. The Church felt but little interest in frontier and foreign missions. Nor was there much being done in the home field. Mr. Edwards sought to arouse the Church from this deadly slumber. He asked, " Why this lack of consecration to a cause of so much importance?" Several reasons were assigned in a stirring editorial. " First, a want of information concerning the state of the world, and the little interest the preachers feel on the subject. And then there is not that taste for reading among us that there ought to be. Books and periodicals are not so highly prized as they should be. We never shall be liberal enough to do much as missionaries until books and papers find in us a warmer embrace. Intelligence, liberality, and virtue generally go hand in hand." After stating some other reasons for this lack of interest in the work of missions he said, "Shall this state of-things continue among us? Will we disgrace the name we bear by a carelessness and indifference to the wants of the world in ruins? Will we coolly look on while our sister churches are sending forth missionaries to every corner of our earth, at home and abroad? Will we disregard the command of Christ, 'Go ye into all the world,' when we have both the money and the men? Oh, for a mighty waking up on the subject among preachers and members, until the missionary fire burns in one universal, steady flame of zeal throughout the Church! We must write and pray and preach and give till the whole Church becomes a missionary society. Then and not till then will we imitate our Savior and his early disciples." This short extract is taken from one of his many eloquent appeals to the Church on this subject. He was himself an example of that "steady flame" of missionary zeal which he longed to see characterize the whole Church.

But the great subject on which the mind and

heart of Mr. Edwards were employed more than any other, indeed more than all others, especially during the period over which we are now passing, was holiness of heart and life. This was his central thought on all questions of church-life and spirit. In this field, at least, he was at home. And no wonder, for it was with him a rich experience. He made the *Telescope* ring with this subject as it never did before nor has since. It inspired his best editorials, and governed very largely the selections made. The proclamation of the subject in his first editorial became the key-note for correspondents throughout the entire term. In a word, everything was made to bend to this one all-absorbing theme. No mind was ever more indefatigably employed, no heart ever more fully poured out, in connection with the definition and advocacy of this doctrine, than were the mind and heart of David Edwards. It is doubtful if the particular doctrine of entire sanctification has ever been stated more clearly, more profoundly, and in a way less liable to objection, than as stated by him. One of the proofs is that he carried with him, in this movement, so many of the best minds in the Church, and that, of those who were not convinced, so few ventured to oppose him.

He was very early convinced of the necessity

of seeking that state of grace known as entire sanctification, or holiness of heart. His close connection with Jesse Wilson, and others of like experience, largely influenced him in this direction. He had also closely studied and accepted the experimental and practical views of John Wesley and Professor Upham. The works of these great and good men, with others of like kind, he admired very much. So far as he had any theory on the subject of holiness, these works furnished it. But it was not so much a theory with him as a felt want. He longed to be more and more like the Master. It was, indeed, a hunger and a thirst for righteousness. In this way the Lord led him at the time he believed and entered in. The way this was brought about has already been given in his own words, and hence need not be repeated here. The Scriptures he studied daily and systematically. It was this, in connection with his strong common sense, that kept him from drifting into fanaticism on this subject. Like Mr. Wesley, he seemed to know just where to halt in his views, how to distinguish verbal from real differences in reference to sanctification, and the necessity of finding a common agreement with the undoubted phases of Christian experience. Herein perceive we the rare qualities of his mind and heart, and also the reason why his views have been so generally accepted by the Church. No one could doubt his sincerity, or the substantial fact of his experience. It was from this stand-point that he pressed the question with so much power and effectiveness. It was, indeed, more the practical results in others, than the adoption of any theory or set phrases, that he sought. He would not follow a theory to its last analysis when it seemed to stand in the way of a practical impulse. He had a mind keen enough to appreciate speculative truth; but he would not ascend in a balloon nor go over Niagara Falls to prove himself consistent therewith. He was hence averse to all disputation for its own sake. He said, "We have known much evil, but seldom any good result from controversy. We are aware that we differ from some of our brethren; but we are resolved not to contend *about* sanctification while we are pleading and contending *for* it. The differences we have noticed thus far have been concerning the metaphysical points connected with the doctrine. Our object is higher than to contend for a theory." Again he said, "Even those who were thought to be opposed to this doctrine, when properly understood, do not differ so materially from us who profess to believe in it in full. One brother, who was thought to be very much opposed to perfection, said that if we mean perfection through Christ he had no objection to it, but if we mean a perfection independent of Christ he must oppose it,—with which we heartily agree." The series of editorials on sanctification published in 1849 were especially consecutive in thought, able in argument, and indicative of a profound knowledge of the heart.

Two mistakes are to be avoided. We are not to explain away the doctrine and importance of sanctification by the assumption or proof that some theories concerning it are false; and then we are to be careful against a view that is unduly liable to be misunderstood, or to lead to self-deception or imposture. With the former error Mr. Edwards could at no time be charged. Of the necessity of guarding against the latter he became more and more aware.

While the liability of a view to be perverted is often only an argument that there is something vital in it, that liability is a constant argument against ignorant or reckless advocacy. The doctrine has suffered much from a mechanical propagation, the cheap clap-trap of mushroom experiences, and the heightened peril that always attends whatever is truly pure in quality or exalted in degree. But to make these liabilities or perversions an argument against holiness, would be like declaring against our character as intelligent and immortal beings because of the unspeakable perils which are thereby implied.

In a sketch of the life of a great and good man, some may deem it out of place to speak of his real or supposed defects. But this is not the correct view. At least Mr. Edwards himself did not so regard it. In sketches of this kind, while editor, he more than once speaks of the side of defect, and unfavorably notices those eulogies that are turned off as biographies. He said to a trusted friend, "I fear that people take me to be a much better man than I really am. Sometimes I think that I will write down in a little book all my weaknesses and moral defects,— my secret faults, my inner trials and conflicts with the powers of darkness,—and have them published to the world after my death."

His capacity of giving himself wholly to one thing was indeed marvelous. But this element of strength seemed, at times, to lead him into a one-sided view of things. This was especially true when his keen intellect and ardent temperament led him into fields of thought with which he was but partially acquainted. At one time he read and much admired the Thompsonian system of medicine. But his practical good sense and general intelligence soon led him to give it up as utterly worthless. He also became greatly interested, for a time, in "Millerism," so called. William Miller, the founder of a sect called Millerites, had prophesied that the world would be destroyed in 1843. Mr. Miller was a learned man, and well versed in the Scriptures. Hence his views were presented in a very plausible light. Mr. Edwards, however, soon abandoned this delusion also. These instances will suffice to show that he was at times led away from the more tangible securities of precedent and experience. But this could be said with equal truth of the brightest minds that have ever adorned and instructed the human race.

CHAPTER V.

WRITING, with Mr. Edwards, was not a pleasurable pastime. He gave himself to it, while editor, from a sense of duty; and whatever he did of this kind of work, in after years, was directed by this same strong impulse. It is by this standard that he must be judged as a writer, and not by the artificial rules of those who have made literature a profession. Works of taste and sentiment, as poetry and eloquence, he cared but little about. He certainly could have excelled in this field if he had chosen to enter it. But he did not, for the very good reason that Providence ordered it otherwise. He was destined, as we have seen, for another and a more useful sphere of thought and action. How well and grandly he wrought in his chosen field of Christian activity, thousands can testify. As a preacher, he ranked among the best. His writings, on religious subjects, it must be confessed, possess rare excellence. A few extracts from his numerous editorials

85

will suffice to show with what clearness and power he could wield the pen. In this way Mr. Edwards can be presented to the readers as a writer, and especially as an example of a high type of Christian experience, much better than by anything the author may say. He read and studied much. Works of piety and devotion were his favorites. But no book had so deep and firm a hold on his mind and heart as the Bible. It was indeed with him " THE BOOK," by way of eminence.

In speaking of the supreme authority of the Bible he said, "'Let God be true but every man a liar.' Man by education frequently receives many errors as truth, and holds them sincerely. The Bible itself becomes a mere help to his system of opinions. He reads it not for the purpose of correcting, but to prove his previously formed views. His views are the standard before which everything else must fall, positive Bible assertions not excepted. Such a state of mind is practical infidelity. It is not the simple, teachable, and confiding spirit of that believer who acknowledges in heart and life the supreme authority of God's Word. Viewing the Bible as the word of God, such a man approaches it without any standard of opinion by which to judge of its doctrines. He has learned the weakness and uncertainty of human reason, and his own proneness to error; his own opinions, like his own righteousness, would be sure to lead him away from God. As he has no confidence in his own opinions, as such, so has he no confidence in the opinions of others, further than they are in accordance with the Bible. A plain, positive 'thus saith the Lord' outweighs all the speculations of men. Before this his prejudices, opinions, commentaries, and men-made creeds all fall prostrate. God is his teacher. To him he looks up with the confidence of an unsuspecting infant for all his views of duty, for direction even in the smallest matters. God is his light and his salvation. When he reads the Bible, it is to learn what the Lord has to say to him; when he hears the gospel, it is for the same purpose."

He loved solitude—or, as he called it, being "alone with God." He was not, however, a recluse, or disposed to live without society. He loved society, and was one of its brightest ornaments. In the midst of his family and friends he was cheerful and happy. His intelligence, purity, and ready wit made him a most agreeable companion. But at times he sought the solitude of a wood, a lonely valley, or a private room for meditation and prayer. His spiritual life was thus nourished, and the way of duty made plainer.

He said, " There is no sphere this side of heaven
where the soul of the believer can grow and
expand as it does alone with God, separated from
all earthly things and influences; and yet there
is, perhaps, no duty more frequently neglected by
Christians, especially at the present time, than
such retirement. By this we do not intend to
charge Christians generally with an entire neglect
of what they call secret prayer; but we are far
from believing that those who retire at stated
times every day for prayer are, during their retirement, alone with God in a religious sense. How
often do we take the world with us to our closets,
and, even while on our knees in prayer, suffer our
minds to be occupied with earthly things. Such
praying is little better than mockery. To be
alone with God implies something more than the
retirement of the body from the company, business, and cares of earth; the soul must be drawn
off from the world and self. The Deity is then
manifested to the soul not only as an omnipresent
Being, but as present in a peculiar, indescribable
sense, known only to those who have realized it.
Here the soul seems to pour itself out before the
Lord and unbosom all its griefs and cares, receiving in return the needed supplies of grace and
the assurance of the continued favor and protection of the Father of all our mercies. It is here

that our finite minds are brought into union with the infinite, and receive a portion of the loveliness and benevolence of God. It is sometimes the case that the very countenance glistens with the divine radiance received by the soul in such seasons of deep communion. In order to understand experimentally what is meant by being alone with God, special protracted seasons of prayer are necessary. Such is the constitution of our minds and our relation to the world that it requires time and diligent, protracted effort to disengage our thoughts and affections from earthly things. We are much more easily affected by things of sense than by the unseen realities of the eternal world. Hence we are commanded, after having entered into our closets, to shut the door, and thereby exclude every obtruding thought. O believer, let us examine ourselves with special reference to this point. If we are deficient in this, nothing else can make up our loss. No one can become eminent for piety without much of communion with God in retirement. This point must be insisted on and more generally practiced before we can expect any general revival of true piety among us."

Prayer is both a duty and a privilege. To acknowledge the all-sufficiency of God, and man's utter dependence upon him, is alike the dictate of reason and of revelation. It is also the divinely appointed means by which to obtain both temporal and spiritual blessings. The practice of communion with God in devotional address, worship, and supplication, we call prayer. It is, in a word, the act of a needy and helpless creature seeking relief at the fountain of mercy. Hence we entreat, supplicate, beg, implore, beseech, and petition God for the things we need. All these words and others of like kind Mr. Edwards used freely to express his views and feelings on the subject of prayer. How much time he spent in private devotion is not for us to know. But to pray in secret, we know, was the habit of his life. His public prayers, as thousands can testify, were most appropriate and thrilling. The following extract from an editorial on the subject of "Prevailing Prayer" is a clear statement of his own experience. He said, "This is the great *desideratum* among Christians of the present age. The want of revival influence, the low state of religion, the reasons for the present spiritual dearth, —these and kindred subjects are now the topics of common talk among those who have any zeal for true religion. But is there no remedy for the moral diseases of the church? Yes, there is a never-failing remedy,—importunate, believing, prevailing prayer. God himself has said, 'For all these things will I be inquired of by the house of Israel.' 'Ask and ye shall receive.' Man can prevail with God. This is one of the marks of the condescension of God. He suffers man to lay hold of him, to wrestle with him, even until he overcomes and obtains the desire of his heart. Let ministers weep between the porch and the altar; let every Christian flee to his closet, and there plead, first for himself, until he feels the burden of the Lord, until his stubborn heart is melted and runs out after souls; and then let him present before the throne of God the state of the church, its unbelief, lukewarmness, worldliness, and want of love. But let no one suppose that such a state of mind can be obtained without effort. Unbelief will oppose; self-indulgence and spiritual sloth will hinder; the worldliness of our hearts will stand in the way; the example of others, company, want of time, want of convenient place, and unnumbered other excuses will meet us at every point. But we must break through every hinderance, remembering that 'the kingdom of heaven suffereth violence, and the violent take it by force.' Above all, let faith in God be the moving principle. With it 'nothing shall by any means be impossible to us.'"

That the leaven of the gospel kept from his heart unbelief and bitterness is a very gratifying

fact. In order to show this, the following extracts
are here introduced. They at once let in a flood
of light upon the spirit and life of their author.
Mr. Edwards was not an optimist. In other
words, he did not believe that all events, moral
evil included, are ordered for the best. This
amiable philosophy had no place in his views of
God's government in this world. Hence his de-
nunciations of sin were often terrible. And yet
he could see a "bright side" to things in general,
and especially in the affairs of the church. He
said, "We hear and read much about the corrup-
tion of the church of this age. Infidels, mor-
alists, and Christians all unite in condemning the
church. A spirit of fault-finding and criticism is
spreading among all classes, which, if not checked,
must discourage and paralyze the energies of
those who are laboring for the salvation of Zion.
This arises not so much from a design to injure
the cause of religion as from constantly looking
on the dark side of things. That the church has
many imperfections and grievous errors and sins
is manifest; but there is danger of our looking
so much at these as to cause us to overlook its
virtues. There are bright spots distinctly visible
to those who are not looking for evil instead of
good. It is fully as much our duty to commend
the good as to reprove the evil." In the same

spirit of discrimination and kindly feeling he cautioned against "denunciatory preaching." He said, "By this we mean that kind of preaching that dwells too much on the sins and errors of the people without presenting the proper remedy. It seems that the ministers of the present age are exceedingly prone to this kind of preaching. This has been called the age of reform, and nothing seems popular unless connected with some branch of reform. Almost every public man assumes the responsible title of reformer, and begins at once to denounce the evils from which we are to be reformed. This begets a censorious and denunciatory spirit in the preacher, who now sees nothing but evils in church and state, which are so magnified by contemplation that they call for more vehement and earnest denunciation, until he finally persuades himself that his whole business as a preacher is to proclaim against sin. Brethren, let us examine the subject in the light of the Bible, and if we find ourselves wrong in spirit or practice, let us, for the sake of the church and perishing souls, seek the baptism of love, and follow the foot-steps of Him who came into the world not to destroy men's lives, but to save them."

The favorite theme of Mr. Edwards was holiness of heart and life. If there was any one subject that wholly absorbed him, it was this. Hence his tongue and pen were alike busily employed in its advocacy. He professed to enjoy the blessing himself, and of course could speak from experience. The two following extracts are here introduced as specimens of his skill and power as a writer on this subject. It was his wont to call this state of grace the "beauty of holiness." In one of his happy moods of mind and heart he asked, "What is holiness?" In answer to this question he said, "It is not a mere emotion or passion, neither does it exist in any external act or ceremonies; but it is a moral state and habit—a condition of purity and rectitude. It is not a grace, but the assemblage of all the graces necessary to form the Christian character. It is, in a word, the moral image of God, who is said to be 'glorious in holiness,' and whose nature is love. The heart that is full of love is full of holiness. Yet it abhors sin as the 'abominable thing that God hates.' Such is holiness. It is the harmonious assemblage of all the moral qualities necessary to form a complete character. In it are beautifully blended piety and peace, justice and mercy, and truth and righteousness. An object, to appear beautiful, must exhibit order. All its parts must be properly proportioned and properly placed. In sin there is no order, but everything is by it deranged. Whenever holiness is permitted to enter, it is like a neat housekeeper,—first cleansing the house from all pollution, and then placing everything in its proper place. It places the affections on Christ and heavenly things, regulates the passions, sets reason on the throne, places the world under foot, and brings the whole man into complete subjection to the will of God. This is order. This is true beauty. This is the beauty of holiness. Another feature in the blessed principles of holiness that gives it superior beauty is its fullness. Consider also the fruits of holiness,—the peace, joy, and resignation it brings to its possessor. There is nothing higher even in the abodes of the blessed than holiness. It forms the chief glory of God. Seek, then, my soul, this pearl of great price; let its enrapturing beauties captivate thy affections; let its resplendent glories, as a powerful magnet, draw you to itself, and to God, whose nature and whose name is holy."

It is clear that the doctrine of sanctification is taught in the Bible. That it may be sought and obtained is equally clear. The commands and promises of God to this effect are explicit. Thus far all orthodox Christians agree. It is a question with many, however, as to whether this high state of grace can be attained in the present life. Hence very different answers have been given to this particular form of the question. In an editorial Mr. Edwards raised the question, "Sanctification — When Obtained," and immediately subjoined the following answer: "Among Protestants we know of but four different views on this question. Some say that sanctification is attained at the moment of justification, others that it is a gradual work, others that it is attained at death, and others, still, that it is obtained at any moment subsequent to justification, when it is sought by unwavering faith. We are not prepared to say that the reception, as to time, is absolutely limited to any of the above methods. We have reasons to believe that there are examples of persons receiving it in all of the ways mentioned. To adopt any of the above views as an absolute standard, and to deny this grace to all who do not receive it precisely in the same manner as to time, would be assuming a position not warranted by scripture nor sustained by experience. The Bible nowhere states that it must be received in all cases at the same relative time. The Bible rule is, 'According to your faith be it unto you.' As he that believes with all his heart for justifying grace receives it in that hour, so he that believes with a heart unto righteousness, asking definitely for full sanctification, receives it in the same hour. As our Savior is able to save to the uttermost all that properly approach him, who can say that he might not both justify and sanctify at the same hour or moment the soul whose faith is sufficiently enlightened and strong to grasp and claim both? We know of no divine declaration against the possibility of receiving both at once. On God's part, 'All things are ready.' Yet how comparatively few are prepared to receive the grace of sanctification at the time they seek the pardon of sin! How few have, or can even endure, a full discovery of the evils of their own hearts, their hidden sins, their deep-seated depravity, before receiving the pardon of past sins! While seeking pardon, the mind is almost entirely occupied with its guilt and danger, and the burden of its outward sins; whereas, in seeking sanctification it is wholly occupied with the desire to be cleansed from the filthiness of the flesh and the spirit. While we admit that some do have sufficient light and faith, sufficient consecration and self-denial to ask and receive the blessing of sanctification in connection with justification, we also do cheerfully admit that some do receive it after justification by a gradual process. They are influenced by the best light they have, and are led on step by step, relinquishing and consecrating little by little, in a kind of retail manner, until the Spirit bears witness of their entire salvation. But those who come out in this indefinite manner seldom have a very definite experience, or a very clear light. There are others who receive this grace a short time before death. How often do Christians, when a threatening accident or a dangerous illness presents itself, cry, ' Oh, spare me, that I may recover strength before I go hence and be no more.' The Lord in mercy hears their cry in the extremity of life, and saves them fully. But we would have it definitely understood that although we admit that some do receive the blessing of entire sanctification near the gate of death, it is not the better way; neither does it honor God so much as to ask and receive, and exhibit this grace while in life and health. Neither is it safe for any one who is now convinced of the necessity of it to defer it till death, thus presuming on the mercy of God. Others who have received it on the bed of death may not have had the degree of light that we have. The present is the only safe time."

Those who read these pages need not be told that Mr. Edwards possessed more than ordinary power both as a preacher and a writer. The impression is already deep and abiding that, in these respects at least, he had no superior in the

Church of his choice. But what was the secret of his power? This question can not be answered in a word. The best that the reader can do is to take all the facts connected with his eventful and useful life and then judge for himself. The following extracts, considered as limits to preachers, will help us in making up this judgment. Let us remember that the rules he laid down for others he rigidly imposed upon himself.

Apologies.—What is the principle that moves the preacher to speak of his inexperience, his ignorance, his weariness, or present unfitness to preach? Has self nothing to do with it? Does this not spring from secret, hidden pride,— a desire to have the audience make every possible allowance, so that if he fails he may have it charged to unfavorable present circumstances, and not to any want of talent?

Long Prayer.—We speak not now of secret prayer. No danger of Christians of the present age spending too much time in secret communion with God. We fear that it is by no means the case that those who are the most tedious in their public prayers continue longest in their closets. Reader, is this your case? Are your secret prayers few and short, and your public prayers long and wearisome? If so, have you not reason to believe that you are a hypocrite?

Pastoral Visiting.—Brethren, suffer a word of exhortation. Do you visit your flocks? Do you do it in the spirit of the religion you preach? Does your private conversation make infidels or Christians? Can we turn to the text, "Ye have scattered my flock, and driven them away, and have not visited them," without feeling that we are guilty?

That Same Old Sermon.—The same old sermon preached,

perhaps, several years ago is still dealt out, instead of the fresh, living gospel. What flock can thrive on moldy food? The best of sermons will lose their freshness by age. Every sermon should be new in some of its features. It should be newly studied and arranged; should contain some new truths — we had almost said some new revelation. There is no excuse for not having something new in every sermon. The Bible has a depth that has never yet been fathomed. The Holy Spirit is ever ready to assist and direct the mind into all truth, and to the very truth most applicable to the present congregation. Let us have the living words of God passing through a warm heart and setting everything on fire upon which they fall. The unction, the holy, living unction, is what is needed, giving a new message to every congregation.

CHAPTER VI.

HE General Conference of 1849 met in Germantown, Ohio, May 14, and was opened by Bishop Hanby. Bishops Russel and Glossbrenner were also present. Fourteen annual conferences were entitled to representation. J. Montgomery, D. Edwards, and M. Ambrose represented Scioto Conference. Considering the trying place which he had filled as editor for four years, and the number of strong men in Scioto Conference, his election as delegate was an evidence of the solid character that was accorded to him. At the General Conference he met men of independent and resolute mold, devoted alike to their convictions and the interest of the Church. Notably among these may be mentioned Markwood, Erb, Bright, Kumler, W. Davis, H. Bonebrake, Russel, Rhinehart, Witt, Hanby, Glossbrenner, and Montgomery. Early in the session Mr. Bachtel, of Virginia Conference, presented a resolution alleging on technical

101

grounds the illegality of the Constitution of the Church as inserted in the Discipline. In the vote taken the three Virginia delegates voted in the affirmative, while all the other members, thirty-four in number, voted in the negative. Mr. Edwards, in voting in the negative, indicated the stand which he maintained for life. This early attack upon the Constitution in order to get rid of some of its restrictive provisions thus signally failed. Nor have later attempts of a like kind succeeded better.

On the subject of secret societies, the rule from 1841 to 1849 had been, "Freemasonry in every sense of the word shall be totally prohibited, and in no wise tolerated in our society." Some argued that the prohibition of "Freemasonry" could not be made to include minor orders. But the expression, "in every sense of the word," following the general designation, "Freemasonry," along with the article of the Constitution, adopted at the same time the rule was adopted, must extend the interpretation over the whole family of secret orders. On the proposition to change the former less definite rule to the fuller form,— "Freemasonry in every sense of the word shall be totally prohibited; and there shall be no connection with secret combinations,"—a number of speeches were called out. Mr. Edwards spoke and voted in favor of the proposed change. In this we see how thoroughly devoted he was to a cherished principle of the Church, and how fully he had imbibed the spirit of the fathers. The majority in favor of the resolution was thirty-three against two, which was a most triumphant vindication of a vital principle involved.

A resolution on the subject of slavery elicited some discussion. Mr. Edwards opposed it, though it was strenuously antislavery, because in his view it was not up to the strict requirement of the Discipline, in demanding an immediate emancipation in each and every case of slave-holding. The resolution passed, however, by a vote of twenty-four against seven.

The General conferences of this period were marked by an earnest, aggressive, and preponderating reform spirit. It was manifest that the very life of the Church ran in this channel. Those whose efforts and influence were most marked in the progress and direction of the Church for the following quarter of a century were impelled and molded by it. It supplied, in fact, the very conditions which are necessary for the support of bold and decided characters. Such was Mr. Edwards. He was by nature rigid, and by grace conscientious. These elements of strength, combined with his hearty acceptance of all the reformatory measures of the Church, soon marked him as a great leader.

By this conference Mr. Edwards was re-elected editor of the *Religious Telescope*. But he at once declined to accept the office for a second term. The reason assigned was the want of business capacity on the part of the publishing agent just elected. He remarked that he himself was not fitted for the business department of the *Telescope*, and that the paper could not be properly cared for by two such men. True, the paper had prospered during the preceding term; yet he would be satisfied with nothing short of the greatest possible success. Rev. William Hanby, who had just completed one term as bishop, and who had been Mr. Edwards' predecessor as editor, was now elected his successor in that responsible position.

When the ballots for bishops were counted, it was found that David Edwards was one of those elected, J. J. Glossbrenner and Jacob Erb being his associates. Mr. Glossbrenner had just completed his first term as bishop, and Mr. Erb had filled the office eight years following the General Conference of 1837. Mr. Edwards was thus hurried from one responsible position to another. If he had not been a man that could turn himself wholly and at once to the first duty that presented itself, he would not have become familiarized with it before the next duty was laid upon him. He possessed this capacity, however, in a high degree. In the different steps of his life he presents the unmistakable marks of one called and directed by Providence. So far from planning what was before him, he seemed actually blind to it till each successive change made its own announcement. Seldom does God give to his most eminent servants notice beforehand of the parts they are to perform. But the election of Mr. Edwards to the bishop's office, while a surprise to him, was a choice which the Church was fully prepared to approve.

While promotion to that high office, as is often said, usually develops high-church notions, the effect upon him was not of this character. A brother editor had complimented him on his new dignity; but in his reply he said, "We must object most seriously to the application of the term episcopal, in its popular sense, to our name and office. The episcopal office, as understood in ecclesiastical history and popular usage, is not acknowledged by us. Our bishops are not ordained, only elected, and that only for four years, to preside in the annual and General conferences."

With the following words of review, so characteristic, he closed his work as editor:

"In reviewing briefly our labors for the past four years, we feel deeply humbled in view of the many blunders and mistakes committed, together with the want of spirit and energy, the want of that intellectual and moral power so essential 'to a religious journal, which we feel satisfied must have been noticed by our discerning readers. But we are comforted with the reflection that our aim was right. We now ask God and our readers to pardon wherein we have come short or in any way deviated from the principles of true holiness.

"As to the doctrines we have advocated, our devotion to them remains unchanged. Uncompromising opposition to all sin has been our watch-word from the beginning; and we now only regret that we have not been more energetic and untiring in our efforts. If good has been accomplished, it is of God; and to him be the glory. That more has not been accomplished is from our want of spirituality, our limited experience in the depths and heights of holiness. Oh, how much more God could do with us as instruments if we were more like himself.

"An affectionate farewell to our readers and correspondents. With many of you we are almost familiar, though never having met face to face, and with you we feel a congeniality of spirit. Many of you we hope to greet during the next four years, Providence permitting."

The General Conference assigned him to the Middle District, including White River, St. Joseph, Sandusky, Muskingum, and Scioto conferences. Bishop Erb was given the Eastern, and Bishop Glossbrenner the Western District. The Middle District lay almost wholly in Ohio, Michigan, and Indiana. Agreeably with the provision of the General Conference, Bishop Glossbrenner and Bishop Edwards exchanged rounds in meeting the conferences in 1849, and Bishop Glossbrenner and Bishop Erb made a similar exchange in 1851. Each bishop, however, was to give his labor, while not attending conferences, to his own district.

Having seen Mr. Edwards taken from his editorial chair and elevated to the position of bishop, we are now anxious to see him off on his first tour. We may not always be able to follow him in his journeys, but we must go with him on his first round. The household effects must first be stored away in an unoccupied room; for he will take his family with him, and no more make Circleville his home. Here, in 1847, a second daughter was born; and here, just a few weeks before his time of leaving, an only son, five weeks old, was buried. It is sad to leave; but the preparation for the trip must go forward. But we must not begin to think of the ease and speed of a splendid car as a means of conveyance for the bishop and his family. The great railway system which had been begun less than twenty years before had reached only the oldest of the western states. Hence this method of travel was not so common then as now. So it was decided to undertake the journey with a substantial carriage and a good, stout horse. Mrs. Edwards and the children will go as far as Peoria, Illinois, and there remain with relatives, while the bishop attends the Iowa and Illinois conferences. Iowa Conference was to meet on the twenty-third of August. So the starting must not be delayed beyond the last week in July. But so much of a trip must not be made without some preaching along the way. So he sent forward five appointments, and filled them during the trip. The journey is begun. Bills must be paid here and there for "toll, cakes, horse-feed, tavern-fare, harness-mending, ferriage," and so forth. Thus they made their progress through the country. The roads in many places were very bad. It was frequently convenient to stop with members of the Church. One evening the bishop and his family drew up at the house of a prominent minister of his acquaintance and asked the privilege of stopping over night. The lady hesitated, as her husband was absent and not expected that night. He then said that he was an itinerant minister, traveling with his family, and could not well go farther. He was then coldly told that he might stay. The domestic atmosphere did not become any warmer that evening. The next morning, as they went on their way, they felt it a relief to be out again on the road. During the next day the husband returned and was told that a minister by the name of Edwards, with his family, had stayed over night at his house. "Edwards! Bishop Edwards!" he exclaimed; for he had heard of his passing through the country. He was also told just how coldly the bishop and his family had been entertained. He knew not what to say or do. The next time that he met the bishop he said, "Why did you not tell my wife who you were? If you had just told her that you were Bishop Edwards, you would have been cared for differently." "But," said the bishop, "I do not wish any better treatment for myself than I want for the poorest and humblest itinerant."

Having taken his family to Peoria, he hastened on to meet the conference at Hershey's Schoolhouse, Linn County, Iowa. Here, at the sixth session of Iowa Conference, he had his first experience in presiding. Seventeen of the twenty-five members were present. As want of room was one of the greatest difficulties to be overcome, it had been decided to hold the conference in connection with a camp-meeting. The conference sessions were held in the school-house, while all special religious services were held in the grove. The bishop preached twice in the grove. One sermon was based upon the prayer of the Syrophenician woman, and the other upon the words, "He had in his right hand seven stars." These sermons were a source of great comfort to the brethren. During the conference he frequently said, "Brethren, I am young and inexperienced in conference business, and I want all of you to help me, especially the older ministers." But when occasion seemed to require, he was sufficiently decided and firm. In going to Iowa Conference he traveled about twenty miles with Rev. A. A. Sellers. There were many horse-thieves in the country. Mr. Sellers asked him if he was not afraid they would steal his horse. "No," said he, "they can not steal my horse. I have given him to the Lord, and no thief can take him." His faith thus took hold of a living, present, and protecting God. This was the secret of his strength.

The Illinois Conference, convening August 30, at Lockridge School-house, Ogle County, was next visited. Nineteen of the members were present, and nineteen absent. The non-attendance of so large a number was noticed with regret. The year, however, had been marked with prosperity, and the conference session was peaceful and harmonious. The bishop was made the bearer to those pioneer conferences of very helpful aid from the older portions of the Church. He found the preachers, for the most part, in very destitute circumstances. The little sent from abroad was thankfully received, but it did not go very far in bringing relief. At this conference some poor brother's condition drew on the sympathy of the bishop to such an extent that he made him a small present. But these occasions were frequent, and generally drew from him a portion of his own scanty means. There was at this time an earnest spirit, just beginning to prevail in the Church, especially in favor of home and frontier missions. About this time all of the conferences were formed into home missionary societies.

From this conference Bishop Edwards joined his family at Peoria, and then directed his course eastward. On this trip his horse became so broken down that he had to procure another. This done he started at once to the Wabash Conference, which convened September 13, at Goshen Church, Vigo County, Indiana. The traveling had to be vigorous and systematic in order to meet his engagements promptly. He reached the place, however, in due time. Twenty-five members were present and nineteen absent. This was the fifteenth annual session of the conference. In the beginning of the session there was a lack of spirituality and unity among the members. This grieved the bishop. On Friday evening he preached from the text, "Have salt in yourselves, and have peace one with another." His sermon was very searching, and proved highly salutary. The conference sermon preached on Sabbath was much blessed to the good of the ministry.

From the seat of the Wabash Conference the bishop proceeded to Zion Meeting-house, Harrison County, Indiana. At this place he met the Indiana Conference, September 27, in its twentieth session. Rev. J. G. Pfrimmer came from Pennsylvania and settled in this county in 1808. Through the exertions of this faithful servant of God, the first United Brethren meeting-house west of the Alleghany Mountains was here erected. Father Pfrimmer died in 1825. Many of those who had toiled and suffered in establishing the church at this place had also passed away. The good seed sown remained, however, and had already produced a rich harvest. The bishop, more than once during the conference session, referred to the sacredness of their memory. Twenty-nine members were present and eight absent. At this session the first measures were taken by the conference looking to the founding of Hartsville University. The bishop gave this measure his hearty approval.

After the Indiana Conference adjourned, the bishop proceeded northward, at once, to meet the Miami Conference at Bluffton, Wells County, Indiana, which was the next in order. This was a hard trip, as the distance was considerable, and the road very difficult to travel. He reached Bluffton, however, and opened the conference, October 11, according to appointment. As the ministers had to go on horseback, and as the place was much at one side of the conference district, only thirty-two members were present, while sixty-one were absent. This conference included territory which had been occupied since 1806. This fortieth session of the conference was, indeed, very pleasant and profitable. In the preceding year the net increase of the membership had been one thousand four hundred and sixty-eight. This was extraordinary, and indicated great faithfulness in the labors of that year.

At these conferences the strong reform-spirit against tobacco, slavery, intemperance, and secret orders, manifested itself in earnest speeches and

8

resolutions. This accorded well with the views of the bishop and the sentiment of the Church at large. All the conferences of the Western District had now been visited. The salary of the bishop for 1849, including an appropriation of fifty dollars from the other two districts, was two hundred and one dollars and sixty-four cents above contingent expenses. The salary during the remaining three years increased the average to two hundred and thirty-two dollars and ninety-one cents. The General Conference of 1841 had increased the salary of married bishops, presiding elders, and traveling preachers to two hundred dollars above house-rent and a few other contingencies.

From Bluffton, Bishop Edwards took his family to Fulton County, Ohio, then, however, a part of Lucas County. This selection of a country home in the extreme north-western portion of the state was not without reason. The meagerness of his salary has already been mentioned. Here his mother-in-law lived, and this would make a pleasant and cheap home for Mrs. Edwards and the children during his long absence. And then the father of Mrs. Edwards had given her a small piece of unimproved land near by, to which the bishop could add a little, and this might, after awhile, improve their financial prospects somewhat. This hope, however, proved delusive, for the land was afterward sold without much advance on first cost. He rented the house of his mother-in-law. He had also the benefit of a garden, pasture, and meadow. 'Here he lived in true country style, except that his domestic cares were not very extensive. From these Mrs. Edwards almost entirely relieved him.

Leaving his family here, he went on to Circleville to arrange for the moving of his household goods. This done, it was not long until the family had settled down to ordinary relations in their new home. What will be the effect, upon Bishop Edwards, of this comparative isolation and these pioneer surroundings? To what extent will the Church be deprived of his presence and influence? These questions are fully answered in the fact that he was an itinerant. And then this country home was near Toledo, a great railroad center, and also near the center of his district. He, of course, could not be indifferent to the claims that were upon him at home; yet he never allowed family, society, or business affairs to come between him and his own work. Beyond the simple matter of taking care of his scanty means, he paid but little attention to business. He was not negligent, however, respecting the ordinary affairs of domestic life. He was handy and ready to help when at home. If the bishop was ever especially awkward, it was when he undertook to handle a baby. But even in this, according to the testimony of one who knew best, he made commendable efforts.

It is a gratifying fact that the bishop kept a careful diary through a number of years. In this way some of his best thoughts have been preserved from oblivion. The reading of these daily records enables us to feel anew his warm, throbbing heart, and the influence of his godly life. With the exception of occasional interruptions, this diary runs through a period of fifteen years. Scarcely anything can be better for us than to take a little time from our busy pursuits or sluggish ease and devote it solely to following the now sainted Edwards, as by his cares and struggles he seems to draw so much of heaven to earth and lift so much of earth to heaven. The following will serve as specimens:

January 1, 1850. This day I covenant with God to be more diligent in secret prayer and reading the Bible. Will endeavor to make it a rule to read five chapters every day. Have this day enjoyed a living peace. Faith unbroken. Christ my sanctification near.

Saturday, January 5. Another week is 'gone, and oh, how little progress the soul is making in true spirituality! O Lord, enlarge my poor heart. Received a singular letter from a man in New York, sent by Brother Pratt; savors of come-outism, fanaticism, and censoriousness.

Sunday, January 6. Preached at Knapp's School-house. Good congregation, and good attention. Tolerable liberty. The Lord bless the sermon.

January 7. This day left my dear family in God's care and started on a tour south.

January 12. Quarterly meeting at Gilboa. Preached at eleven o'clock with liberty. Oh, what a weight of glory! The Lord is my light and my salvation. How indescribable is the love, peace, and joy that fill my soul!

Sunday, January 13. Preached at the quarterly meeting on the great salvation. The Lord was present in power. Glory to his name. Boundless love. Oh, such views!

January 14. Love-feast and sacrament. A good time. One brother, a good preacher, claimed the blessing of a clean heart; also a sister in the evening.

January 15. The quarterly meeting continues. The light and glory are overwhelming. Praise the Lord, O my soul.

January 17. Meeting still continues. The Lord is with us in power. Still, it seems that the people trust too much to the preaching of the word.

January 18. Preached at night with great difficulty. Lungs sore, and cough increases. The Lord will bring good out of it. The people will work more themselves.

Sunday, January 20. Still at Gilboa. Good time at love-feast and preaching. Meeting closed at night. Ten additions. A number converted and reclaimed, and some sanctified. Praise the Lord.

January 24. Started for home. Rode thirty-nine miles and put up at Brother Strayer's. Very tired, but all peace within. Frame of mind somewhat jovial.

January 25. Rode twenty-six miles. Arrived safe at home. Found all in usual health. Praise the Lord. He preserveth man and beast and suffers no harm to come nigh our dwelling.

Sunday, January 27. Spent this day at home. Am not able to labor. Soul rather sluggish. How it sympathizes with the poor body.

January 29. Just finished reading the "Philosophy of the Plan of Salvation." Was particularly pleased with the views presented on the miracles of Egypt and the Jewish rites.

January 30. Commenced reading Nevin's "Biblical Antiquities."

February 2. Rose at four. At six and a half started for quarterly meeting at West Unity, fifteen miles distant. Arrived in time to hear the elder preach a skim-milk sermon. Preached from the text, "Let this cup pass." Tolerable liberty, but not with as much power as ought to accompany the gospel.

February 6. Spent this day rather unprofitably. Hardly know where it went. Oh, why is not each day and hour full of God and holiness?

February 11. God be thanked; wife is better. This is also of the Lord. "He healeth all our diseases." Oh, that we could always trust him for perfect care of soul and body.

February 15. The sky is bright outside, but the soul is not as full of life and sunshine as it should be. Oh, for that constant overflowing fullness which I preach as the privilege of others.

February 16. A letter from Brother Pratt; also one from my old friend, Joshua Montgomery. The principal part of the former taken up with Pratt's experience. Hardly know what to make of his state. Can't condemn yet. Don't understand it.

February 18. Spent this day in visiting at D. Butler's and Uncle Abbott's. A kind of a do-nothing day to me; yet all was peace.

February 19. At home, chopping wood, reading Bible and Biblical Antiquities. Confidence in God unshaken. I still will trust God for all things. The outcome must be right.

February 21. Feel much the need of a new anointing of the Holy Ghost to fit me for the work before me. It seems that I run too much in the common channel. Lord, baptize me anew. Amen, and amen.

March 12. All is well. "There is not a cloud that doth arise to hide my Savior from my eyes."

March 13. Wife's health still poor. Have this morning presented her before the Lord anew. Felt encouraged to trust and to believe that all will be right. How and when remains with him.

March 25. Weather cold, but all is pleasant within the spiritual atmosphere. What an unusual state my soul has found.

March 26. Invited to Uncle Abbott's with the family. How difficult to make such visits truly profitable!

April 1. Must have more of the fullness and power of the gospel. Oh, how lean I am.

April 2. Lucretia's health still poor. But all is in the Lord's hands. Had I more faith, might I not ask and get an answer?

April 6. Preached a funeral. Great effect on the congregation; but all through sympathy, I fear.

April 8. Garden plowed. Soul needs plowing up thoroughly. Oh, how is it that I have so little inward and outward power? Why so little of the Holy Ghost? O Lord, show the cause.

April 9. Somewhat gloomy. Seem to be accomplishing nothing. Sinners sleep all around me apparently undisturbed. Am I a Christian at all? Then why doing nothing?

April 10. Feel like crying, "My God, why hast thou forsaken me?"

April 11. Gloomy horror increases. The only such season for eighteen months. Good will, yea must, come from all this.

April 12. Begin to see day-light. See in part the design of my trial. Had been sailing so smoothly so long. Needed just such a lesson on momentary dependence on God. Glory.

April 13. How good the Lord is! He turns even temptation to our spiritual benefit.

April 15. Feel a burning desire to be more usefully employed. Feel as though I ought to preach oftener and better and with more of the power of the Holy Ghost. Horse sick. Wife's health poor. See no way of being out in the work as my soul would dictate.

April 16. All is peace, but a deep sense of my need of a fresh anointing of the Holy Ghost.

April 20. Rode to Bottenburg's. Preached at night. Rather dry. Feel like a backslider. Lord, save me from so great a death.

April 23. How defective is my Christian character. How little fruit unto holiness. The Lord is leaving me to myself to convince me how barren I am without him.

Sunday, April 28. Quarterly meeting at Shafer's. I preached at three o'clock with good liberty. Thank the Lord even for this.

April 29. Love-feast and sacrament. Was impressed to speak of the great salvation. Told my experience, which was blessed to some who seemed on the verge of the land.

May 2. My spiritual state is rather variable. I now have seasons of heaviness. Have I backslidden, or does the Lord intend to lead me up another step? Lord, reveal my true condition. Lead me into all the glorious fullness, whatever the road may be.

May 5. This day I am thirty-four years old. How swiftly

my years are being numbered! How slowly I am progressing in the divine life.

May 10. Spent the forenoon in visiting; not very profitable. Am to preach at four o'clock. O Lord, help. He did help. Was much blessed in preaching the great salvation.

May 22. Visited a young man at the point of death. He says he has peace. But oh! these death-bed conversions,—who can trust them?

May 23. Body is tired. Soul not half enough alive. O Lord, baptize me anew. Amen. Let it come now.

May 24. County-seat located two miles east of my land. Some advantage to me personally. This, too, is of the Lord, and shall return to him.

May 25. Worked hard all day, but do not feel tired. Prayed in the morning for strength. Praise him.

May 31. Left family and horse in God's care, and rode with Brother Bowser to quarterly meeting at Gilead. Lord, anoint me for the work. Oh, for the divine unction.

June 3. Love-feast in a barn. Experiences very shallow. Mere desire to get to heaven to see friends, &c.

June 7. The Lord sent us a little shower. Oh, how refreshing. Thank him for every drop.

June 8. Received a letter from Brother Lawrence on the subject of our difference of views on sanctification. He is tempted at being told that some have been discouraged in seeking through his influence. Lord, teach him.

June 10. Asked the Lord for a sign. Feel that this was wrong. Evidence of weakness of faith. Oh, for an increase of the precious grace. Lord, help.

June 16. The Lord present in preaching. Felt old-fashioned. Yet a lack in results. Oh, for power.

June 19. Preached at Hatfield's. Tolerable liberty. Quite plain and pointed. Some of it will be remembered.

June 21. Dined with Brother Mackey, a wonderful man for dictionary terms, yet a fine kind of a man.

August 7. Getting ready to start to the conference. Lord, prepare the soul.

What do these experiences, taken here and there from the dairy of a part of one year, indicate? A soul fitfully given to God? Rather have we not here what should characterize the experience of every Christian, especially the heart-history of every Christian minister? Many do not know the price that must be paid for an experience fresh and continually renewed. How sad when the first high promptings of the renewed heart are accommodated to a half-way standard. Who can imagine the inner woe of that man, the first gushings of whose spiritual life have become a dried channel? Upon the lips of such men the language of Canaan becomes the weakest and the most repulsive cant. Bishop Edwards could have preached metaphysics from the atmosphere of books, moral practice from that of the world, theology from that of the school or study; but how could he preach the gospel—herald the glad tidings,—except from the influence of the closet and a fresh anointing for the holy work? He must preach the truth from the heart and with the authority of the Court of heaven.

During these months he had preached almost

every Sabbath. He also preached many times through the week. He attended quarterly meetings, protracted meetings, made two trips into Michigan, and kept up a considerable correspondence. It is not the easiest thing for a minister in the country to make and fill school-house appointments in his own neighborhood and at a distance. Again, it is not as easy as many imagine for a man in a general office, and sustaining general relations, and these relations more toward professors of religion than the non-professing classes, to keep up the interest and activity which in others are in some degree produced locally and mechanically. It requires salt, self-direction, and much partaking of the divine nature.

We must now prepare to attend Bishop Edwards as he makes his second round of visiting the conferences. But this time, and for the following two years, he will serve in his own district. The following sad words indicate the spirit with which he started out on this round: "Left my family in the care of my heavenly Father and started for White River Conference. Never before have I left home with so sad a heart. Wife's health quite poor, and one of the children not well. Shall I ever see them all again in this world? For some time I could not banish the thought. Nature felt keenly, and the thought almost found a place, This is hard business. But in a moment it was suggested, The Lord lives and will provide. My faith wavered not, but still the day was spent in sadness. Lord, help. Give me the spirit of resignation. Give me souls, and I shall be content to bear all,—live in poverty and die in penury."

As he proceeded on his way he preached four times. The seventh night he stopped with an old friend, Brother M.,—" the same man that he was years ago; as full of argument and error as ever." White River Conference convened on August 22, 1850, at Andersonville, Indiana, in its fifth annual session. He was so indisposed that he was not able to be in the conference-room the first day. In fact, his health was quite poor throughout 1849 and 1850; and we shall yet find occasions of trial and hinderance from his weak physical condition. His entry for the second day was, " Through divine mercy I am able to attend conference. Went through more work than I expected. The Lord sustained." Third day, "Still better; praise the Lord. Great want of itinerants. O Lord, send forth laborers." Fourth day, Sunday, "Preached the conference sermon. A good time. Very good time in the afternoon at sacrament. The session of conference was characterized by an earnest and enterprising spirit, and closed on Monday forenoon, with a glorious time."

Much hindered and reduced by sickness, he proceeded to Dayton, Indiana, where St. Joseph Conference was to convene on September 5, 1850, in 'its sixth annual session. The bishop had arranged to have the sessions of the different annual conferences opened with an hour's devotional exercises; and at all the conferences of the district this was observed. Much devotion to the work marked the sessions of this conference. The bishop's diary for the fourth day—Sunday—says, "Preached the conference sermon. The Lord was present to help. Praise his holy name." The bishop on returning home found his wife quite sick.

After a very short rest he started for Sandusky Conference, to be held at Bretz Meeting-house, Seneca County, Ohio, on September 20, 1850, which was its eighteenth annual session. In this period Sandusky Conference was marked by an unusually active and progressive spirit. The bishop's journal for the twenty-second—Sunday —says, "Preached the conference sermon. The Lord was present to help. Heard Brother —— at night. Good, straight." The entries of the two following days will give a good idea of the session: "23d. An impressive time on the reading of the report of the Stationing Committee. A remarkable spirit of consecration pervaded the assembly. 24th. Conference closed. A very good session. God was present in power last night while I tried to preach. Glory."

He now started for Scioto Conference, which was to meet at Zion Meeting-house, Perry County, Ohio, on October 3, 1850. The second day he stopped with his brother Thomas, at Delaware. He was feeling "dull,—the natural consequence of a high state of feeling at Sandusky Conference." The bishop reached the neighborhood where Scioto Conference was held, but was not able to go to the conference room during the session. A serious sickness ensued, preventing him also from attending Muskingum Conference. A bishop *pro tempore* was elected by these two conferences, respectively, to preside in his stead. His condition was quite alarming; and his detention from home for a considerable time was an occasion of great anxiety to his family. The Church also began to fear that the bishop's health would fail entirely. But from this fit of sickness he gradually recovered. He returned home as soon as he was able, for rest and recuperation. On the twenty-third of October of this year, the third daughter was born.

During the first months of 1851, he visited various points in Scioto Conference, held protracted meetings, and much of the time preached almost daily. A few notes from his journal will best indicate his spirit and work.

January 11. Came to Winchester. Church is cold. Old sores remain unhealed. Lord, sharpen the Spirit's sword.

January 12. Preached at night. Very plain work.

January 14. Preached. Very close; but God was in it.

January 25. Commenced a protracted meeting at Mount Pleasant. Preached. Had good liberty in enforcing the religion of the Holy Ghost. This is the great lack.

January 29. Tarried with Brother McGrady. A good home for God's poor servants. God put it into the good brother's heart to give poor me a three-dollar bill toward my expenses.

January 30. Spent this day and night with Brother I. Bookwalter. He has lately got hold of faith in simplicity and power.

Oh his return from this work in Scioto Conference he was to preach for Rev. William Mathers, at West Liberty. Having been wrongly directed, he found himself, near evening, seven miles from his appointment and with very bad roads before him. He put his family in a house, borrowed a saddle, and just as the services were beginning arrived at the church. Mr. Mathers said to him that in the circumstances he would have supposed that he would not come. The bishop replied,

"When I found that I could reach the appointment there was no longer a question in my mind as to my duty. If a preacher is not truthful, his preaching will amount to very little."

Bishop Edwards was an occasional contributor to the *Religious Telescope* during this period. In a pointed article on "Skim-milk, Watered," he spoke against the weakening effect of too many words, and the needless regard for what some call system. He also placed the repetition of sermons from which all vital moisture has departed under the head of "vain repetition." He concluded with the following: "Let ministers throw away their old sketches and go to the Bible and seek the illumination of the Holy Ghost; and let them depend as much on one as on the other. From this blessed union of God's word and Spirit a fountain will be opened that will fill the heart."

He concluded an article on unbelief with the following telling observations: "Whoever else you believe or disbelieve, learn to believe God. Irrespective of the opinions of men, without regard to your circumstances, frames, or feelings, believe God; give full credit to the record he has given of his Son, our Savior. He, and only he, that believeth is saved; and that salvation is always in proportion to the measure of faith. 'The righteousness of God is revealed from faith to faith,' This is the lever that raises the gate that lets the waters of salvation flow to the heart. Powerful faith lifts the gate high and overwhelms the soul; but unbelief shuts the gate and leaves the soul unsaved, unblessed."

White River Conference met at White Chapel, Madison County, Indiana, on August 21, 1851. The attendance was large, and the very best feeling prevailed during the entire session. After the usual preliminaries the bishop said, "Now, let us look for fruit. The business of a preacher is to save souls." This was his ever-present thought. All inquiries respecting the labors of the year must hinge on this. It was found that a good degree of success had attended the labors of the preceding year. Many souls had been saved. The reform-spirit was still strong in the conference, and the bishop was quite willing to see it assert itself. Hence, resolutions were passed against all secret orders, the use of tobacco, Sabbath desecration, the Indiana extradition law, and the fugitive-slave law. Vigorous resolutions were also passed in behalf of Hartsville University.

St. Joseph Conference convened on September 5, 1851, at North Manchester, Wabash County, Indiana. The bishop's opening address here was very impressive, especially when he alluded to the passing away of some old difficulties that had

so long affected the conference. "The hand of
God," said he, "is now clearly seen in the organization of the conference, and in the work given
you to do." The bishop showed in this his thorough knowledge of the men before him and the
work they represented. There was but one resolution of general interest passed during the session. This one complained of two prominent
members of Virginia Conference having announced in the *Religious Telescope* that they could not,
and would not, carry out the Discipline of the
Church on slavery and secret societies. Virginia
Conference was urged to correct these abuses.

Sandusky Conference convened on September
18, 1851, at Beaver Creek, Wood County, Ohio.
The conference was large, intelligent, active, and
enterprising. Here sat in council some of the
foremost members of the Church. Notably among
these may be mentioned Biddle, Spayth, Bright,
Lawrence, Briggs, Bowser, Long, Mathers, and
Father John Davis. The bishop always felt at
home in the presence of such men as these. He
was himself keen, quick, and thoroughly posted
in parliamentary law. The labors of the year just
closed were marked with success. There was
reported this year in the lay membership of the
conference a net increase of eleven hundred and
sixty-four. This success was due, at least in part,

to the ceaseless labors of Bishop Edwards, who at this time lived within the bounds of the conference. Here, as elsewhere, much excitement prevailed respecting the attitude of Virginia Conference on the subject of slavery and secret societies. A resolution was passed censuring the conduct of two leading members of said conference for publicly announcing in the *Religious Telescope* that they would not enforce the Discipline of the Church on these subjects. Bishop Edwards was known to be in full sympathy with these efforts to correct the matter complained of, and by this means maintain peace and harmony throughout the Church.

Scioto Conference met on October 2, 1851, at Otterbein Meeting-house, Fayette County, Ohio. As soon as the bishop entered the conference room it was observed that a great change had come over him since his last visit. A year ago he was sick and unable to attend to the business of the conference. But at this session he was in good health and full of cheer. This was indicated alike by his fervent prayer and the strong tone of his opening address. The presence of his old and well-tried friends seemed to inspire him with new courage and vigor. With these faithful and devoted itinerants he had long lived, struggled, and suffered. These brethren had taken him by the hand when he was a feeble, staggering boy, and helped him forward in the work of the Master. The conference was largely attended. Van Demark, Hanby, Montgomery, Fisher, Ambrose, Gillespie, and Kretzinger were among the more aged and widely-known members of this conference at the time referred to. The report showed that the labors of the year just closing had been successful. Many souls had been garnered for the Lord. The spirit of reform was strong and active. Hence resolutions against slavery and secret societies were passed. Education in general, and Otterbein University in particular, were warmly favored. In the adoption of these measures of public interest the life and spirit of Bishop Edwards are clearly seen. His conferences usually reflected his views and sentiments.

The diary for 1852 has unusual interest. Hence the extracts from it will be quite copious.

January 25, 1852. On examining my life, past and present, I find several radical defects, such as sluggish inactivity, aversion to writing, misimprovement of time, etc. Have often resolved upon and even commenced a daily record of my states and employments, but have not hitherto continued till a habit was formed. In God's name and by his strength I this day commence once more.

I was born of the flesh in Wales, May 5, 1816, and of the spirit in Fairfield County, Ohio, May 28, 1834; was baptized anew, and received the evidence of entire consecration to God in Pickaway County, Ohio, January 2, 1845; so that for nearly eighteen years I have had some religion, and for seven years have been trying to live wholly consecrated to God. But what am I yet but a mere cipher, a babe in Christ? I must still plead for mercy. Christ, who died for me, is my only hope. But shall I continue to live so cold, so sluggish, so little by rule? By divine help I will reform. I will rise earlier, will write more, be more methodical in my studies and devotions; will talk and preach more definitely of the great salvation through Christ. Lord, help.

January 29. Commenced reading " Beecher's Lectures to Young Men." The strength, variety, and eloquence of his language so eclipses everything of the kind in me that I hardly know how I can talk or write at all.

Brother P., spoken of below, was a man whose views and life amounted to a hopeless extravagance on the subject of sanctification.

February 4. Received a letter from Brother P. on the new state in which he professes to stand. The train of thought brought up is somewhat painful, and yet I can scarcely tell why. If he is wrong, and is coming out from all that is common for Christians to practice, this would give me sorrow; but if he is right and I wrong, this would be a source of sorrow. But God will guide me aright.

Bishop Edwards next gave an account of making benches and preparing his house for a protracted meeting. The meeting resulted in having twenty-two conversions. He afterward took his wife and two youngest children and started on a long and laborious tour through Muskingum Conference.

March 6. In Muskingum Conference. I tried to preach at night. Some liberty, yet the effort seemed somewhat forced. Oh, when shall I be filled with God!

March 13. Canaan Center. Preached five times at the quarterly meeting. Generally good liberty. Here the elder, in accordance with the desire of the people, debarred persons belonging to secret societies, and those in favor of such societies, from communing. Don't know how this would do elsewhere, but here among Antimasons it does well enough. Yet it seems to me consistent for us to refuse to commune with those whom we would exclude from the Church.

March 20. Went to a quarterly meeting near West Brookfield. Preached four times. Tolerable liberty, but effect not great. Curiosity up; too many preachers present. True piety seems to be at a low ebb here; preachers seem to depend on mechanical effort to save souls. Bro. B. made me a present of a good pair of shoes. God will reward him. Wrote to John Lawrence, expressing my temptation and grief over some things in an editorial, especially on slavery.

March 31. Preached at night. Some intellectual, but no spiritual liberty. This day was spent unprofitably. Find it difficult to converse profitably with the preachers of this conference. They are so full of quibbles. I, too, lack spirituality and faith.

April 2. Spent the forenoon in visiting entire strangers, and conversing on religion. Found it profitable to me, if not to them.

On his return from his Muskingum trip he passed through Westerville.

April 21. Westerville. This day, after serious deliberation, it was agreed upon by Brothers ———— and myself to start, at some future day, a magazine of elevated and uncompromising standing in morals and literature. The object is to advocate true godliness, or unity with God in all things. If this is of God, we crave and expect his blessing. If not of him, we pray it may not succeed. Our plan is to unite ten or fifteen who may be willing to give one hundred dollars each as stock,—the work-not to commence till fifteen hundred subscribers are obtained. The association will meet the first time at Winchester, next fall.

May 22. Received a letter from Brother J. Lawrence, written evidently under excitement occasioned by an article of mine on the slavery question. Will answer it in a religious manner, if God will give me grace.

June 6. Preached a dedication sermon,—my first effort of the kind. Preached again at four. Tolerable liberty both times, but I am not fully alive. Oh, for salvation.

June 8. Preached loudly and zealously, but no inward power. About seven mourners came out; but they hallooed and pounded the benches so that no satisfaction could be taken in talking to them. Think likely enough one or two of them were converted.

June 9. Feel dull and stupid in soul and body. It seems to me that I am a poor preacher and Christian—so little emotion, so little hungering and thirsting for God and souls. I seem not to know how to better my state. I can leave myself in God's hands till he comes to his temple. Oh, that he might come soon. Preached at night. Several conversions, perhaps, but can scarcely tell amidst so much noise and confusion.

June 11. Preached at night. A direct attack upon sinners, but with little apparent effect on them. A real tearing time, after preaching, among the members and converts. I almost fear that such revivals are little better than none. But God can bring some good out of them.

June 27. Am reading "Reformed Pastor," by Baxter. A very soul-stirring, serious work. Oh, how guilty we are as members! Oh, how much I need breaking all up anew!

August 5. This day bid adieu to wife and little ones and left them in God's care, and started on my last round of conferences. The thing that most troubles me is the want of holiness to be useful. When I commenced serving the Lord and the Church in my present capacity, I thought I would be more alive to all the great interests of Zion. Oh, shall the term close without a work for God? The Lord forbid it.

August 8. A dedication. Congregation very large. Occupied nearly an hour and a half in talking—I think a very unpopular discourse here. Knew it would be, but thought it was needed.

White River Conference met at Hartsville, Indiana, August 19, 1852, in its seventh session. Here is the seat of Hartsville University. This institution had been founded but recently, and very much needed the patronage and fostering care of the Church. During the session of this conference the bishop made the following entries in his diary:

August 19. This day comes the trying and responsible business of annual conference. O Lord, help.

August 20. Have been blessed in reading through the Songs of Solomon. How I felt reproved for the coldness of my affections to Christ. The soul that is truly chaste and intent on holiness may read this singular production with profit.

Sunday, August 22. Preached at ten. Some liberty, but

somehow feel dissatisfied with the sermon. I am one of the poorest gospel preachers, especially to occupy so responsible a relation. Oh, that I were more like Christ.

After the close of White River Conference the bishop proceeded to Pipe Creek, Cass County, Indiana. At this place the St. Joseph Conference convened on August 28, 1852. Thirty members were present and ten absent. No action of the conference of general interest. The bishop's diary will let in a little light on the situation.

August 28. Conference commenced fairly. Examinations close. This conference district miserably butchered by a half-hearted itineracy.

September 1. This was a hard day in conference. Tried to preach too. But oh! what a sermon! Well, so be it. God reigns; and even in this his hand is seen. Who needs humbling as much as I do? God is as kind in withholding comforting help as in blessing with light and joy.

September 12. On my way. Tried to preach. Very poor liberty. But God is in this too. It was the best he could do for me.

Sandusky Conference convened at Johnsville, Morrow County, Ohio, on September 16, 1852. Sixty-four members were present and twenty-seven absent. This was, in many respects, a very important session,—none more so, perhaps, in the history of the conference. The spirit of progress showed itself in bold and vigorous measures in behalf of temperance, collegiate and minis-

terial education, and, especially, foreign missions.
Bishop Edwards was highly pleased. The following terse and expressive words are found in his
diary: .

September 21. Conference closed. A very good session.
Several received by licenses and transfer.

It is not too much to say that he always felt a
peculiar pleasure in visiting Scioto Conference.
This he did not disguise. Here he had no un-
friendly critics. His advice was usually accepted
without debate. This deference was awarded
him not solely, nor mainly, because he was bishop
of the conference. True, in this respect he was
held in the highest esteem. But the love and
respect shown him here in his own conference
were chiefly personal. He had some faults, of
course; but who could think or speak of them in
the presence of so many virtues? All seemed to
feel that his guileless spirit and consecrated life
were sufficient guaranties that the business in
hand would be conducted properly. In this spirit
of brotherly love and mutual regard, Bishop Edwards met Scioto Conference, on September 30,
1852, at Canal Winchester, Franklin County,
Ohio. His diary will give us some remarks upon
this session.

August 30. A good conference, on the whole. Preached
twice, with some liberty. At this conference an arrangement

was entered into by a number of brethren to publish a magazine, to be called "*Unity with God*"—the name significant of its design. I was elected as its editor, but could not feel my way clear to accept or decline. It seems to me too much like taking myself out of the hands of the Church. God will give me light against the time when editorial service will be needed. Oh, for divine direction.

Muskingum Conference met on October 14, 1852, at New Rumley, Harrison County, Ohio. Forty members were present, and twenty-eight absent. Here sat in council some of the strong men of the Church, such as S. Weaver, J. Weaver, C. Carter, J. Carter, Slutts, Steward, Brazee, and Bulger. Some of these afterward became widely and favorably known to the Church. J. Weaver, secretary of the conference, and afterward bishop, said, on adjournment, "Thank God for the spirit of unanimity that dwelt among us during our conference session." Bishop Edwards was also highly pleased, as the following extracts from his diary will show:

October 14. A good commencement of conference. Preached at night. God was present.

Sunday, October 17. A grand day. God was present, owning and applying his word. Preached plainly and pointedly.

October 18. Conference closed at ten at night, in a storm of religious fervor. What a conference this has been throughout. Love, consecration, and religious animation.

December 6. In due time arrived at home. Found all right, for which God be praised. .I then for five or six weeks neglected my memorandum, for which I now feel some guilt and some loss. God forgive me. I have this prayer to offer so often in reference to my neglect of this duty that I am ashamed of myself. By divine grace I will begin anew. O Lord, let it be in thy strength.

It was the custom of the bishop, after the close of his conferences, to travel and preach almost incessantly. His zeal and powers of endurance were indeed remarkable. He spent but little time in rest. Preachers and people closely watched all his movements, and whenever they saw that he had a spare Sabbath he was expected and urged to make them a visit. He did not need much urging, however, for preaching was his delight. This was his one work. He spent much of his time laboring in protracted meetings. An extract or two from his diary will show how he struggled to save souls in this way. In the month of - December, 1852, he, with others, conducted a protracted meeting at West Unity, Williams County, Ohio.

December 10. Commenced the meeting in the name of the Lord. First sermon from, "Can these dry bones live ?"
December 11. Have some anxiety for a revival; but why? Is it for self? Am I unwilling to be disappointed, and have it said that I could do nothing? O Lord, search me. Feel very empty. My anxiety too forced, too human. Oh, that

God would annihilate me in my own estimation, and work for his glory in his own way. Oh, my divine "Potter," I am but clay; but thou hast taken me in thine hand. I am on thy wheel. Now, Lord, make me into any shape, and employ me for any use, that will glorify thee. Let this be a new era in my religious history. My feelings this afternoon very peculiar. No message. Powerfully tempted with unbelief. I try to cling to the promises. Such a struggle I have not had for a long time. Well, God says, "Count it all joy." If I continue faithful, this trial is much more precious than gold. Glory. This thought is liberty.

December 14. Conference meeting at sunrise. God was present. Indication good. Visited all day. Preached at night with solemnity and success. Four mourners. A number of others were much affected. Great want of activity and faith in the Church. By whom shall Jacob arise?

Sunday, December 26. Preached at ten, and at night. The meeting closed, though many seemed wounded. Eighteen joined the Church—a good class of persons as a whole, though can not tell how some of the young and uninformed will hold out. They will need good nursing. But this, alas, is the great want in the Church, and a fruitful source of backsliding.

January 12, 1853. Home. Feel somewhat cast down in spirit. Have perhaps been thinking and talking too much of Bro. H.'s hypocrisy, and the evil and trouble he may yet cause the Church. I find that we are in danger of feeling too hard even toward the worst of men. Oh, for wisdom and love.

The conference sessions of 1852 were occasions of much interest. Bishop Edwards visited all of his conferences this year, and presided with great acceptability. His health was much better than it had been the previous year, and the impressions which he made were correspondingly stronger. The foreign missionary movement was favored with his earnest and active support. Many of the leading men of the Church were also working in behalf of this interest. Through the influence of these noble men, guided by the superior judgment of the bishop, Sandusky, Scioto, and Muskingum conferences formed themselves into independent missionary societies. This was the beginning of a great awakening in the Church on the subject of missions. About this time, as we have seen, the question of slavery agitated the Church not a little. Bishop Edwards thought that he could see, especially in some localities, and on the part of a few leading men of the Church, a yielding to the demands of the slave-power. This troubled his mind. Hence, in 1852, some very sharp articles passed between him and Rev. J. Lawrence, editor of the *Religious Telescope*, on this subject. Mr. Lawrence had at least so much yielded to the demands of those who wished some concessions made on the slavery question as to consider mitigated cases of slave-holding. The bishop regarded the ground taken as false and dangerous. He was incapable of treating those tenderly who held a thing as abstractly wrong and yet in actual cases permitted or indulged it; and in attacking a man's position on moral grounds, he knew not how to save easily the moral character of his adversary. He did not profess to be able to distinguish between a man's principles and his character. Himself professedly opposed to abstractions, he settled all moral questions on an abstract basis, and then proceeded regardlessly. This characteristic was strikingly displayed in the controversy in question. The case is here introduced only to exhibit one of the distinctive qualities of Bishop Edwards. Mr. Lawrence easily succeeded in showing his innocent intention, and his antislavery character was not such as to require defense. The bishop, however, was slow to mollify the wounds which he had made. This he could not do as long as he felt that he had spoken the truth. Sympathy could extort no concessions from him when it seemed to antagonize a clearly-defined conviction of right. Hence he would often be thought to be acting from personal feeling, while in fact he would be resisting a slight or injury to principle, which others were too blind, or easy-tempered, to see. One of his best friends—and one who knew him well—said, "When he had once taken a position, he never yielded it—I was going to say, even if he knew it to be wrong." Thus it often seemed; though the fact was that he had a grasp upon the qualities of things unknown to the most of those about him. It is clear that when the abstract barrier is broken down, it is difficult to fortify against the diversified complexions of individual examples. Steadfast principles, along with his extraordinary discernment, promptness, and vigor, made him a trusted leader,—made even his name a tower of strength.

During this his first term, he not only showed himself adequate as a superintendent, but also made himself a powerful element in stimulating the work and directing the interests of the conferences.

CHAPTER VII.

HE General Conference that met at Miltonville, May 9, 1853, was opened with devotional exercises, led by Bishop Edwards. Bishop Erb was not present, and the duty of presiding thus fell entirely upon Bishops Glossbrenner and Edwards. Fourteen annual conferences were represented by forty-two delegates. The session was one of unusual interest and importance. The bishops, when not presiding, took part in the proceedings.

An excellent course of reading for licentiate preachers was defined and enjoined at this session. This was the first of the kind in the United Brethren Church. Bishop Edwards was on the committee that reported this measure, and warmly advocated its adoption. True, the General Conference of 1845 had required systematic reading and study, but did not lay down any complete course. Hence the action of 1853 was a long step forward, and of course did much to increase the power and efficiency of the ministry. This was a favorite measure of Bishop Edwards. While he always insisted on a divinely-called ministry and dependence on the Holy Spirit, he regarded neglect of the ordinary sciences in their secondary relation as shameful and sinful.

The question which elicited much discussion, however, was the nature and extent of human depravity. A few of the members of the General Conference objected to the doctrine of "total" depravity as held by the orthodox church. It was affirmed by those who held this view that before the promise man was totally depraved, but not afterward. That is to say, the death of Christ had so far affected the moral nature and condition of man as to make it improper to use the term "total" as applied to human depravity. There were no differences of opinion respecting the nature or extent of the atonement. The common ground of belief was that Christ did so die for the whole human race as to make salvation attainable by all men. It was also agreed that man in his present condition is, in fact, deeply depraved and sadly in need of Christ's salvation. The only question in dispute related to the extent of man's depravity under Christ's remedial scheme.

While the subject was under discussion, Bishop

Edwards made an earnest speech, which was reported as follows:

" The discussion to me has been pleasant. I am glad to learn that the brethren are not as far apart as has been apprehended. If the brethren mean all they say, why not pass the resolution at once? Mr. Fletcher says that certain doctrines are like the first link in a chain; they draw all the other parts after them. The doctrine of natural, hereditary, total depravity is one of these important links. Tell a man that it is only the outside that is corrupt and he will settle down in his sins. From a child I had myself been trained to church-going and the reading of the Scriptures, but withal did not see the depravity of my own heart. It is of great importance that we all be able to see alike in regard to this vital doctrine. This is a doctrine from which if you remove anything you destroy it all. I go with all my heart for this resolution. The Bible and God's providence concur in its support. Glance back at those ecclesiastical bodies which have denied this doctrine, and you will witness not the light and salt of the world, but all manner of heresy and corruptness. On the other hand, those churches which have held and maintained this doctrine have been saved from all these. Personal experience would teach us here, and confirm the doc-

trine before us. The nearer I approach to the
Lord the more I discover the depravity of my
own heart. If there is no other totally-depraved
person on earth, I know one."

At this General Conference the "Home, Frontier, and Foreign Missionary Society" was formed. The missionary Board established at the
General Conference of 1841 did nothing before
the spring of 1852, and before the meeting of the
present conference only two missionaries had
been appointed by it. Bishop Edwards had given
the missionary movement warm support at Sandusky Conference in 1852, and but little remained for the General Conference of 1853 but to
give it direction and authority. Untold good has
come to the Church and to many perishing souls
through the zeal and methods of missionary
work developed at this time.

At this session of conference it was resolved
that a magazine, denominated " The Unity with
God, and Magazine of Sacred Literature," be
published. For more than a year prior to the
conference, the magazine had been in contemplation; and a voluntary association had been formed
for its publication. The plan was a favorite one
with Bishop Edwards from the beginning. There
was some opposition to the publication of the
magazine in the independent manner proposed;

but its publication under the direction of the Church met with general favor. Bishop Edwards was elected its editor. The following from the prospectus, as drawn up and presented to the General Conference by a committee of which Bishop Edwards was chairman, will give a clear idea of the place the magazine was intended to fill:

· "Among the hundreds of serial publications now issuing from the American press, but few can be regarded as free from religious sectarianism, political partisanism, and a servile cringing to popular favor. Under such circumstances every friend of sound literature and a free Christianity should hail with joy the appearance of any publication, however humble, that will maintain an unreserved and uncompromising allegiance to the cause of truth. The great question should be, What is truth? And having a solution to this problem we should embrace the truth, whatever may be the personal and social sacrifices that it may cost us.

"To give to the public such a periodical as may join the ranks of the few already in the field, battling with error and laboring for the redemption of the entire human race, is the most sincere wish of the publishers of this magazine."

The following may be regarded as characteristics: "First, and above all, the entire regeneration and sanctification of heart and life, exemplified in all the holy and living forms of an experimental and practical Christianity. This we regard as the fixed and unalterable basis of all moral reforms which are founded on truth. It will be one of our particular objects to show that slavery is sinful under all possible and conceivable circumstances. Freemasonry in all its forms and aspects will be freely and fearlessly discussed. It will be shown that all secret, oath-bound societies are anti-social and anti-Christian. It will also be our object to advocate the cause of a proper education. Also, the biographies of distinguished ministers and others, and the movements of the age in reference to the kingdom of Christ, will receive due attention."

The Sabbath-school interest received much attention from the conference. A Sabbath-school paper, called, when published, the *Children's Friend*, was resolved on, Bishop Edwards to be the editor.

The General Conference decided on the removal of the *Telescope* office from Circleville to Dayton, Ohio. Eight new conferences were also arranged for; namely, Rock River, East Des Moines, Oregon, Michigan, Missouri, German, Erie, and Auglaize—first called Maumee. This was a long step forward, and did much in pushing the cause of the Redeemer into new and destitute portions of the West. The Church generally, at this time, demanded aggressive work, and the General Conference thus nobly responded in adopting the measures referred to.

Bishop Edwards was re-elected and assigned to the Southwest District. His colleagues were J. J. Glossbrenner and Lewis Davis. The Southwest District embraced Miami, Indiana, White River, Wabash, Illinois, Missouri, and German conferences.

Shortly after the adjournment of General Conference Bishop Edwards moved with his family to Dayton, Ohio, his appointment as editor of the *Unity Magazine* and *Children's Friend* of course deciding the place of living for the coming four years. He now sold his lands in northern Ohio and turned the money into a lot, with a small house upon it, on east Sixth Street, Dayton.

We can see at a glance that with two additional conferences under his charge, and, in connection with his work as bishop, his new editorial duties, some special arrangement must be made as to the employment of his time. Hence his conference-sessions were grouped within a period of three months in each year, and the remainder of his time was to be devoted to editorial work. During the time while away attending conferences, office-help upon the periodicals was to be furnished by the trustees of the Printing Establishment. Under this arrangement Rev. C. Briggs and Rev. John Lawrence rendered assistance on the *Unity Magazine*, and Mr. Briggs and Mrs. Edwards assisted on the *Children's Friend.* There was nothing very formal in the arrangement, but the logic of the case and the consent of all concerned led to the shaping of matters in this manner. Editorial work filled substantially the place that had been previously occupied in tours of preaching, assisting at quarterly meetings, holding protracted meetings, and other such labor. The change was advantageous to the Church, though not in itself more congenial to the bishop. Yet he preached very frequently, never declining appointments which he could at all fill.

The first number of the *Unity Magazine* was published in November, 1853. It must be conceded that Bishop Edwards possessed special qualifications for the editorship of such a publication. His simple, earnest, Christian spirit, the solid qualities of his mind, his grasp upon sound guiding principles, his close sympathy with the people, his high moral aims, and his vigorous and bold style, gave him no ordinary advantage. At this time, also, there prevailed very much of a church-spirit. What pertained to the Church, or what was put forth in the name of the Church, was quite sure to receive general attention from ministers and people. Yet the Church was scarcely prepared for such a periodical, and after the newness of the enterprise had somewhat worn away it required special efforts to maintain a proper circulation; and two years after the editorial term of Bishop Edwards expired the magazine was discontinued.

No one will find fault at the transcribing of a few paragraphs, from the pen of the editor, upon such selected themes as must ever be of living and absorbing interest.

DESIRE AFTER HOLINESS.

A desire after holiness is implanted in every truly converted soul. This is true not only of those who have been instructed definitely on the subject of holiness, but of every one who is truly regenerated, whatever may have been his views. Even those Christians whose system of belief leads them to doubt its attainability, find themselves possessed of a real living desire for this grace. Whether they make it a definite object of thought or not, the desire for deliverance from all their indwelling corruptions and for complete conformity to the divine image, rises up in the soul like a native, living fountain, seeking vent in streams of tears, sighs, and earnest ejaculations. How many thousand times when alone at work or walking by the way, have they caught themselves exclaiming:

     " Oh, for a closer walk with God."

     " Oh, that my load of sin were gone,
       Oh, that I could at last submit."

Every new temptation, every evil thought, every duty or trial that causes them to reflect on their own weakness or danger, only serves to increase the inward, burning desire for heart-purity.

This thirsting for holiness, with more or less vividness, is perceptible in the first beginnings of religious life, and is inseparable from a healthy religious state in any period. It is the foundation and the evidence of growth in grace. It precedes and accompanies every advance in the divine life. It is not only an inseparable accompaniment, but it is also one of the essential elements of true grace, a part of itself. Wherever grace is, there is a desire for holiness and God. It is as natural for it to call for increase as for the heat of the fire to ascend, or for the stream to seek its level. Wherever grace is found, its natural tendency is to lead the soul to God. And then it will as naturally and certainly lead it upward along the line of the infinite and glorious perfections of the Almighty, expanding and filling its purified faculties interminably.

This desire, in some form, is applicable to all living Christians, whether fully sanctified or not, from the babe in Christ to the fathers and mothers in Israel. In the beginning of the Christian life, before the soul is saved from its old habits and indwelling corruptions, the desire is most ardent for deliverance from these disturbers of its peace. After some progress in this direction, it takes the form of a desire for some needed grace, such as humility, meekness, patience, or charity. Afterward, when the soul has gained many important victories over sin, outward and inward, the same desire for holiness, though now somewhat changed, refined, and elevated, continues to burn within. Its burden now is not merely for deliverance from any form of sin, nor for any particular grace, but its enlarged grasp has laid hold of God himself. Nothing else can now satisfy its longings.

> "Thy gifts, alas, can not suffice,
> Unless thyself be given,"

is its ceaseless language. The intensity of this elevated desire of the advanced Christian is thus earnestly expressed by the psalmist: "As the hart panteth after the water-brooks, so panteth my soul after thee, O God. My soul thirsteth for God, for the living God: when shall I come and appear before God." "My soul thirsteth for thee, my flesh longeth for thee in a dry and thirsty land, where no water is." How earnest this language! The dry, parched, and pleading earth; a panting, famishing heart in a desert land, in full chase to find the cooling stream which alone can save its life. None can understand this language but those who have felt the same burning desire to be lost and swallowed up in the ocean of infinite love. The soul in its desire has now become so enlarged that nothing in earth or heaven can satisfy it. "Whom have I in heaven but thee? and there is none upon earth that I desire besides thee."

A few thoughts of a practical nature are suggested by the above.

I. Holiness is attainable here. Else why are such aspirations after it given to every child of God? Will our God create a desire which he is either unable or unwilling to fill? Is it not written, "Blessed are they which do hunger and thirst after righteousness: *for they shall be filled ?*" Then let every anxious soul give his desire full vent before the mercy-seat. Pour out your heart with the full expectation of receiving, even to the fullest measure, all that Heaven incites you to desire.

II. This subject affords an unerring test of religious char-acter. Those who have no desires for holiness have reason to suspect their present state. Such are undoubtedly in a backslidden state, if indeed they were ever converted. Let such call to mind their former experience; what groanings to be entirely delivered from the body of sin; what longings for more of the mind of Christ. And just in proportion as you yielded to those desires in sincere efforts for complete deliverance did Heaven smile upon you. This ought to have encouraged you to press forward till filled with holy, humble love. But even now, cold and callous as is your soul, if you sincerely repent and return to God, he is faithful and just to forgive and to cleanse from all unrighteousness.

RESPONSIBILITY OF CHRISTIANS.

The responsibility of Christians in this world is most fearful. They are the representatives of Christ. By their spirit and lives will Christianity be judged by the masses of men. They are the light of the world, and the salt of the earth. And if the light in them be darkness, how great is that darkness! How dreadful the consequences to the world if the salt has lost its savor!

There are thousands who know nothing of Christianity only as it is seen in the lives of professors of religion. Being far from God and unacquainted with the Bible, they judge Christianity by the lives of its professed friends. And when Christianity fails to reflect in their lives the full and clear light of the gospel salvation, Christianity suffers in the estimation of those who knew it not. In this way Christ is wounded in the house of his friends, and betrayed into the hands of his enemies. On this very ground many have turned away from God and religion, who might have been saved had they been surrounded by consistent Christian influences.

UNNECESSARY DOTAGE.

Mental imbecility in old age has become so common that it is looked for as an inseparable accompaniment of gray hairs. Many who have scarcely passed the meridian of life, under the influence of this error, suffer their minds to sink into a state of dozy inactivity, and become almost useless. They have been taught to believe that youth is the only time for mental improvement; and if they have unfortunately been deprived of educational advantages in this "seed-time of life," they suppress every mental aspiration with the sluggard's song of "can't learn now; if I had possessed the advantages in youth that young men have now I might have been something." By this popular delusion many a mind has been rocked to sleep, and induced to content itself in ignorance and uselessness.

INFANT BAPTISM.

As to infant baptism, we neither advocate nor oppose it strongly. If religious parents desire to consecrate their children to God in this way, what harm is there in it—especially if they teach them that on consecrating themselves to Christ in riper years they are at liberty to be re-baptized if their views of Bible requirement demand it. We have neither time nor disposition to contend with any one about forms. Let us have the living power, which the best of forms do but faintly shadow forth.

MINISTERIAL EDUCATION.

To lay down any absolute rule defining precisely how much learning a minister must have in order to succeed in his calling, is what no church can or ought to do. Yet every man who gives evidence that God designs him to be a minister should be encouraged, and, if need be, assisted to obtain the best education possible for this important and responsible work. No office needs a more thorough education than that of the ministry; nowhere else can learning be used more profitably. The fact that God has called and employed with much success men of limited literary attainments, should never be used as an argument against a thorough education, so far as Providence opens the way, of all who are called to the work of the ministry. But it must be confessed that much of what is called theological education comes very far short of the training necessary to qualify men to be able ministers of the New Testament. Any school or system whose teaching tends to formality — such as reading instead of preaching, worshiping God by the machinery of fashionable choirs, organs, and fiddles, — that circumscribes and pampers the mind by stereotyped sectarian dogmas, or that virtually exalts literary attainments above religion, is so radically defective as a means of ministerial education that the church of Christ would be better off without than with it. It is these *defects* in theological schools that have brought the subject of ministerial education into such bad repute with many good men. But could we have schools purged from all such defects, where the spirit as well as the letter would be taught, the heart cultivated as well as the intellect, where holiness to the Lord would meet the student at every step in his studies, where self-denial and unreserved dedication to God could be so deeply engraved upon the hearts of the graduates that they would come forth to bless the world with examples of apostolic zeal and self-sacrificing labors, their influence would soon be felt throughout the world. Who will say that such theological schools would not be a blessing? Is there wisdom and piety enough in the churches of this age to institute and sustain schools of this character?

SUCCESS IN THE MINISTRY.

May the ministers of the gospel of Christ confidently expect success in their calling? May they rationally hope to accomplish something worthy of their high vocation on every charge committed to them? These questions may be answered in the affirmative, most unhesitatingly. Otherwise their efforts to save souls and build up the church are only experiments, and they can not labor in faith. The Savior, in his great and universal commission to his apostles and ministers of every age, gives them assurance of success in their labors in the consoling promise, "Lo, I am with you alway, even unto the end of the world." This can mean no less than that he will be with them to bless their labors to the accomplishment of the work committed to them. That other declaration made at the same time, namely, "These signs shall follow them that believe," etc., certainly implies as much. Although its primary application may be to external miracles, yet in a high sense it points to the spiritual power exerted in curing sin-sick souls. It is evident that the apostles and early ministers of the Christian church understood these promises as a guaranty of success, and went forth in the name and strength of the Lord, expecting to make their mark for Christ wherever they could find a place to preach. The Apostle Paul so understood it, and poured out his gratitude on this wise: "Now thanks be unto God, which always causes us to triumph in Christ, and maketh manifest the savor of his knowledge by us *in every place.*" He ran, not as uncertainly; he fought, 'not as one beating the air." He knew what he was about. His success, both in running the Christian race and in the labors of the ministry, was as certain as the promise of the Eternal. And this faith was not disappointed; for souls were converted by thousands, and churches sprung up as if by magic in every country and city where this faithful missionary could gain a hearing.

We see in the writings of Bishop Edwards during this period a more thorough maturity and greater roundness of view. At an earlier period he expressed himself unqualifiedly in favor of general education, and gave his decided influence for schools and colleges under the auspices of the Church. He did not, however, give any encouragement at first to the founding of a theological institute by the Church. But just as soon as this want became more and more felt, and when the Church seemed able and willing to sustain an institution of this kind, he heartily approved of the movement. In fact, he was never opposed to a professional education for the ministry when of the right kind.

But a passing reference ought to be made to those who showed an interest in the purpose of the *Unity Magazine,* and enriched its columns by their contributions. They did their part conscientiously and ably; and whatever changes their views in time may have undergone, their eminence in Christian character and usefulness, in the subsequent history of the Church, indicates that a spirit of definite consecration to God and joyful acceptance of the great salvation produces the surest and the noblest fruit

The first number of the *Children's Friend* made its appearance on May 6, 1854. The subscription soon reached ten thousand copies. But what qualifications had Bishop Edwards for such a paper? Back of the sterner appearances of the man there was ever a simple and tender heart. He also had well-defined ideas and sentiments in reference to what child-training ought to be, and in reference to the privileges and possibilities connected with early piety. These elements may not be susceptible of emphatic statement, and yet along with superior good sense they compose the required qualification for making an impression on children.

In the first number of the *Children's Friend* the editor, addressing the children, said, " This paper is printed on purpose for you. And the editor thinks that you have as good a right to have a paper that you can read and understand and call your own as older folks have." Of course, almost every number must have something on the evils of slavery. Some having objected to this feature of the paper, the editor replied as follows: " The great majority of our readers, so far as they have informed us, seem well pleased with the anti-slavery character of the *Friend*. But a few, who like it in every other respect, wonder why we do not let slavery alone in the children's paper. We

11

answer, because the children will soon be men and women. The presidents, governors, legislators, voters, ministers, and teachers of the next generation must be made out of the children of the present; and it will be for them to say whether slavery shall be tolerated to disturb the peace of the whole country and crush to the earth millions of our race that are yet unborn. We would not edit for the children a hypocritical paper,—one that does not oppose popular sins; we love them too well."

"Uncle Edwards" sought to prepare the children for the realities of life, instead of fanciful and deceptive scenes and encounters. False views of things, unhealthy stimulus, appeals to the lurking enemies within the soul, were entirely disregarded; and yet the simplest motives that prevail with a child's heart, if only innocent, were never disdained.

The conferences attended in 1853 were White-River, Miami, Indiana, Wabash, Illinois, and German. These had all been visited during the preceding term by Bishop Edwards, except the last one mentioned. The German Conference had been organized to meet the wants of the Germans in Ohio, Indiana, and Illinois. Their interests were not sufficiently cared for in connection with the almost exclusively English character of the conferences. The history of the new conference has vindicated the wisdom of those who made this special provision for the Germans. Bishop Edwards at this time could not speak German, but he could approve or direct when matters of business in the conference were brought before him. He always took a deep interest in the German work; and by the Germans he was universally beloved. The Missouri Mission-conference held no session in 1853.

The conferences visited by Bishop Edwards in 1854 were the same as those of the preceding year, with the exception of Illinois. Rev. J. C. Bright, secretary of the missionary society, filled the place of Bishop Edwards at Illinois Conference, as also at Missouri Conference. The occasion of Bishop Edwards' failure to be present at all his conferences was his extremely poor health. During four months he gave up preaching entirely, and was barely able to give even a moderate attention to his editorial duties.

Bishop Edwards was able to attend all his conferences in 1855. The only conference with which he had not before met was the Missouri. Here he found himself surrounded with slavery. Anti-slavery views had penetrated the country to the very smallest extent. In a letter to the *Religious Telescope* he said, "If the churches of the South will not reform,—of which I see no hope,—and take the Bible ground upon this great sin, then the churches in the North that have the truth ought to go South and spread it abroad. It is as much their duty to do this as it is to endeavor to redeem the heathen of distant countries from idolatry, caste, and polygamy."

In 1856 Bishop Edwards attended White River, Indiana, St. Joseph, Sandusky, Scioto, Illinois, Missouri, Michigan, and Maumee conferences. The Missouri Conference met at Rev. S. S. Snyder's, near Lawrence, Kansas. Kansas at this time was the scene of great agitation. The controversy was as to whether it should be a free or a slave state when admitted into the Union. But the scales were already turning in favor of the free-state party. In an account of his trip west this year Bishop Edwards had the following to say of Kansas: "If men will do their work as well as the Creator has done his, Kansas will soon be the glory of all lands. Let it be filled with free schools, free presses, free churches, and, above all, with free men and women fully consecrated to God, and it will soon rank among the foremost of the states of this Union."

A few paragraphs selected from his communications to the *Religious Telescope*, during the period now under review, may not be out of place. They will serve to show how well he was fitted to instruct and guide the church of his choice. Although literature was not his favorite employment, he nevertheless possessed rare power and skill as a writer.

PAY THE PREACHER.

God commands it. He has ordained that they that preach the gospel shall live of the gospel. Thou shalt not muzzle the ox that treadeth out the corn. Reason unites with revelation in declaring that the laborer is worthy of his hire, and that the people who receive his labors are solemnly bound, by every principle of honor and religion, to give him a full equivalent for the time and strength spent in their service. But it is said, "Our preacher does not earn his salary. He devotes much of his time to his own personal affairs." There may be instances in which this is true, and in which the people may be justifiable in withholding; but in most cases it is a mere excuse to justify a sinful delinquency. Men who have talent, spirit, and prudence enough to be useful as preachers, and are not willing to live beyond their income, or in a land of plenty to pinch their families down to the point of meanness to serve those who are getting rich fully as fast as is for their spiritual health, deserve and ought to receive a full and hearty competency from the Church. When the Church fails to support comfortably their families they are driven to the alternative either of quitting the ministry or of devoting a portion of their time to other pursuits. The Apostle Paul himself, in similar circumstances, would have taken a portion of his time from the active duties of the ministry to procure the necessities of life. And if he had been blessed with a family of children to rear and educate, he would have found it necessary to make and sell more tents than he did. The minister sees his brethren educate their children, and provided with means whereby to exercise the virtue of hospitality. He, too, has children he loves. He, also, has a hospitable nature; and besides, he would lead the people in benevolence. But alas for the means! No wonder that a spirit of melancholy is molding his features.

Thus Bishop Edwards addressed the laity. The following extract from an article written at another time shows that he did not intend his remarks to be taken advantage of by the ministry:

But our support! Our support! Well, what of it? If you are really called to the work, and go trusting in God, you will be supported. God has pledged himself on this point. Those who are the most unreservedly devoted to the work of saving souls, who throw their whole souls and bodies into the work, and manifest more concern for souls than for their own bread and butter, are supported. Our people have eyes and hearts, and do open their hands to support those who are whole-hearted and laboring unselfishly for Christ and souls. But it is not to be wondered at if some of those who go hop-skip-and-jump around their circuits, and hasten to their farms and merchandise when the Church is suffering for their labor, should be pinched in their support. Yours for an extended and consecrated itineracy.

PREPARATION FOR THE PULPIT.

Among us as a people too little attention is paid to pulpit preparation. Its importance is not sufficiently appreciated. Indeed, some are even heard to boast that they can preach at any time on five minutes notice; and others condemn all preparation as unnecessary and sinful. It need hardly be stated that those of the classes referred to preach nearly the same sermon from every text and on every occasion. To the honor of the ministry be it said that few now can be found who advocate openly this no-preparation theory. Yet the number who practice upon it, more or less, is not so small. There is a large class of ministers of respectable preaching-talent who have formed habits of mental indolence, which materially cripple their usefulness as preachers. Their chief dependence is upon old sermons,—often borrowed or stolen from more studious ministers,—and upon the impulse of the moment. Fortunately for this class of preachers, many of them possess a good degree of religious fervor, which seems to season what would otherwise be unpalatable. But woe be to their congregation if their "feeling" is absent. A poor sermon well seasoned with good feelings may be heard with patience and profit; but when both thought and feeling are absent the sermon is blank enough. An endless repetition of common-place phrases is neither instructing nor comforting to the soul.

Let no one say that by devoting so much time to mental preparation the Holy Spirit's influences will be discarded. This need not, must not be. A proper preparation for the pulpit will always include the preparation of the heart. The true minister of Jesus Christ will as earnestly seek for spiritual as for mental power. Every sermon ought to be steeped in tears and baptized with the spirit of Jesus in the closet. The minister thus prepared may enter the pulpit saying, in the language of the ancient prophets, "The burden of the word of the Lord." Thomas Shepherd was wont to say, "God will curse that man's labors who goes idly up and down all the week, and then goes into his study Saturday afternoon." God knows that we have not too much time to pray in and weep in, and in which to get our hearts into a fit frame for the duties of the Sabbath. Mr. Jay was in the habit of selecting his text for the next Sabbath as early in the week as possible. By this method he always had something to fill his spare moments. In this way, approaching the subject at different times and from different sides and aspects, it opened to his mind more naturally and easily and with more enlargement and variety.

The General Conference of 1853 made Bishop Edwards one of the vice-presidents of the missionary society, founded at that time. At the first regular meeting of the Board, June 1, 1854, Rev. W. J. Shuey was appointed a missionary to Africa. The Executive Committee was to appoint one or more missionaries to accompany him. Other missions were formed and a number of missionaries sent out. Besides these was the Oregon Mission, together with rude mission-work in the states and territories, which existed prior to the formation of the Board of 1853, and to the care of which it succeeded. Bishop Edwards was also a member of the Executive Committee. The committee during the ensuing year appointed Rev. D. K. Flickinger and Rev. D. C. Kumler as additional missionaries to Africa.

In 1855 the missionary Board met in Cincinnati. A bold expression of opinion, and a determination to prosecute to the greatest success the work of missions, characterized all the proceedings. Two of the missionaries to Africa had returned, after having explored the country for three or four months. It was seen that the African mission required much patience and money in order to make it a success.

Bishop Edwards said in a sermon preached during the session of the Board, "It is not by the number of converts in the missions alone that we are to estimate the result of missionary efforts. The benefit to the societies contributing men and money for the work is amply sufficient to compensate them for all they do. Nothing so expands the hearts of Christians as Christ-like effort to save others. The more enlarged and earnest the plans of any church to save men, the greater will be its prosperity. In proportion as any church withholds its sympathy from the world-wide work of Christian missions, will it wither and lose its vitality.

"The churches need a stronger faith. They should look less at the difficulties, and more at the wants of the heathen and the promises of God. A common degree of faith is not enough. There are superhuman difficulties to surmount. We must rise up and send out men full of faith and of the Holy Ghost. They must have confidence in the truth and in the God of missions. It is God's work; and he is pledged to open up the way and bless the labors of his true servants.

And if miraculous power is needed at any time to give access to the minds of the people, and if it is sought in faith, who will dare say it will not be granted? We must not follow too closely in the steps of others who may have been governed merely by human wisdom. There is yet power in the arm of God; there is yet power in the pure, simple gospel of Christ, if presented as in primitive times, to save even the most degraded heathens of this age. Let then the whole Church engage in this glorious cause with renewed faith, and an unyielding purpose to obey the command of Christ, to preach the gospel to every human being, and 'a little one shall soon become a thousand, and a small one a strong nation.' The Lord will hasten it in his time."

Some thought that the only hope of Africa was through the children. Bishop Edwards said, "We must rely upon the word of God. The darker the picture, the stronger must be our faith." He also said that the report made "dwelt too much upon the gloomy future," and that "unbelief needs no aid." The Board appointed two new missionaries to Africa.

The report of the corresponding secretary, at the subsequent meetings of the Board, showed great progress in mission - work. Rev. J. C. Bright, the corresponding secretary, was the very

LIFE OF BISHOP EDWARDS.

embodiment of the missionary spirit. He was the soul of persuasion whenever the missionary theme was his topic. One of the troubles of the Board, in all these sessions, seemed to be to keep the Executive Committee and the indomitable missionary secretary from doing too much; or rather from putting more missionaries in the field than could be supported.

Not many incidents are preserved from the four years embraced in Bishop Edwards' second term. A few, however, may be given.

Mr. John Dodds had heard him say, incidentally, that if he had money enough he would give his house a second story. So when the bishop went up to his office Mr. Dodds slipped down to his house, laid his plans before Mrs. Edwards, made measurements, and found out when the bishop was going to start away to his conferences. As soon as he was gone Mr. Dodds was on hand with carpenters, lumber, and whatever was necessary in order to give the bishop's house the desired lift. Plastering, painting, and everything belonging to a complete job was done before the bishop's return. The effort was a complete success. When he came home it was very amusing to see him halt, look up at the house, look at the yard, and at adjoining houses, feeling that he was mistaken in the place. This

act of brotherly kindness was highly appreciated
by the bishop and his family.

One Sabbath morning Bishop Edwards filled
an appointment at the First Church, in Dayton.
Brother L., who was to preach somewhat later
the same morning at the Third Church, and
whose week had been full of work, thought he
would drop in for a little while and get a thought
or some inspiration from the bishop. He was
pleased with the naturalness and suggestiveness
of the speaker's thought and treatment; and taking the start which he had received, he went to
his appointment and used the same subject. At
night both preachers were present at the Third
Church. The bishop opened the Bible to give
out his text, and Brother L. judged from the way
the Bible lay open that he was going to repeat
the sermon he had preached at the other church
in the morning. In order to prevent this he
slipped a paper before the bishop, requesting him
not to preach the same sermon, as he had preached it there in the morning himself.

The General Conference of 1853 had placed the
salary of married bishops and traveling preachers at two hundred and fifty dollars, besides certain contingencies. If a bishop received more
than the specified amount, the excess was to go
for other purposes. But as Mr. Edwards was

editor as well as bishop, the receipts from his district were to be turned toward paying the salary that should be fixed by the printing-house Board. After some time had elapsed he found that his expenses were over five hundred dollars per year, and thus much beyond what the publishing Board expected to pay. The bishop said he could not live on less. Mrs. Edwards had been working in the *Telescope* office, had been taking in sewing, and helping in various ways. Some members of the Board said there must be a leak somewhere. But after one of their number had examined the account of expenses kept by Mrs. Edwards he said, "I do not find any particular extravagance, — considerable muslin though." This, of course, was very annoying to the bishop and his family. Most preachers and their families would have a like aversion to producing their account of expenses; but a similar examination would generally turn out to the advantage of the preacher. How many privations, home denials, and attempts to hide the commonest wants would be thus disclosed.

In 1855 Bishop Edwards published an edition of Fletcher's Appeal, with an introduction from his own pen. Many copies were sold. He much admired the writings of Fletcher; and this itself is an evidence of his own clear logic and thoroughly orthodox views.

The four years closing with 1857 had been a season of great prosperity to the Church. At the close of this period the entire membership of the Church was sixty-one thousand three hundred and ninety-nine. This is the first report of numbers that can be relied upon with much confidence respecting the membership of the Church. The bishop's report contained the following: "We rejoice in the belief that the Church at this time is more prosperous, and its operations more efficient in doing good, than at any former period in its history. The past four years, taken as a whole, must be regarded as a season of great prosperity to our Zion. The object for which our fathers, under God, founded the Church,— namely, the extension of the Redeemer's kingdom in the salvation of souls,—is the all-absorbing theme among our ministers and people."

CHAPTER VIII.

Twelfth General Conference—Re-elected Bishop—Diary—
Incidents.

HE twelfth General Conference 'met in Cincinnati, Ohio, May 12, 1857. Some very important questions came before the conference. After quite an exciting discus- sion it was decided that there should be the same liberty of conscience as to the subjects of baptism that there had been from the first as to the mode. Lay delegation was already exciting some attention. The sentiment of the confer- ence was perhaps fully expressed in the remark of Bishop Edwards,—" The desire for lay delega- tion is not great. None of us would oppose it if the brethren want it."

The great subject, however, was the depravity question. The action of the General Conference of 1853 had not proved very satisfactory. But at the present General Conference unexpected and almost unprecedented agreement and harmony were brought about. In the unselfish and glow-

ing devotion of early Christianity, and possibly
here and there in more recent times, there have
been similar examples of the triumph of order over
the spirit of discord. But it must be confessed
that such instances have been rare. The basis of
this agreement was the adoption of the following
question, to be answered by candidates for the
ministry: "Do you believe that man, abstract of
the grace of our Lord Jesus Christ, is fallen from
original righteousness, and is not only entirely
destitute of holiness, but inclined to evil, and
only evil, and that continually?" One member
did not believe the language to be pertinent, as
no man destitute of the grace of God could be
found. Yet the language was true and well considered, regarding, as it did, man as he is in himself. After the vote was taken—fifty-seven affirmative to one negative—the entire conference arose
and sung, "Praise God from whom all blessings flow." A great crisis was passed, and the
happy issue of the long controversy produced
a charitable and hopeful spirit in the Church respecting other points of difference. While
Bishop Edwards was a strong believer in the
doctrine of total depravity, the language agreed
upon fully coincided with his views. The General Conference provided for the formation of
seven new conferences; namely, Parkersburg,

Minnesota, Wisconsin, Lower Wabash, Canada, Kentucky, and Nebraska. The last named was organized in 1859. Bishop Edwards was again elected a member of the missionary Board and a trustee of the printing house. He was also chosen bishop for the third term. His associates were J. J. Glossbrenner and L. Davis, with J. Russel as German bishop. He was again assigned to the Southwestern District, consisting of White River, Wabash, Miami, Auglaize, Indiana, Illinois, Kansas, Kentucky, and Missouri conferences.

The year 1857 marks an important era in the life and labors of Bishop Edwards. His sympathies and qualifications had been brought out in relation to the different interests and demands of the Church. His natural administrative abilities had become disciplined and strengthened. His rich spiritual gifts had become more and more an available pulpit force. His self-command, personal influence over the minds of others, and ability to turn circumstances and occasions to account, eminently fitted him for the position of a Christian bishop. Henceforth he was to give his time and talents, without diversion of any kind, to the responsible office of a superintendent in the Church.

During the entire term, he continued to reside in Dayton. Whenever he was not away from

12

home on his district, he accepted whatever local work presented itself to him. He preached frequently and at many places within the bounds of Miami Conference. The General Conference of 1857 fixed the salary of a married bishop or traveling preacher at three hundred dollars, together with certain additions for contingencies. The object of the General Conference in naming a salary was to secure the best results in the support of the ministry in general, and the greatest contentment and efficiency of the itinerants; and no one can say that the best that could be done at the time was not done.

Bishop Edwards attended all his conferences the first year except Missouri and Kentucky. Missouri Conference was directed to meet with Kansas, and Kentucky with Indiana. The second year he met all his conferences except Kentucky, being detained from this conference on account of sickness. Ex-Bishop Kumler attended the conference in his place. In the fall of this year, by the direction of the Executive Committee of the missionary Board, he organized Nebraska Conference, within the bounds of the Northwest District.

The two following years he presided at all his conferences. By the division of Wabash Conference, in 1858, the district was made to consist of ten conferences. In attending these conferences and meeting the missionary Board, in journeys in the interest of the printing house, in special visits to his own and to other districts, he made one trip to Virginia, two to Pennsylvania, five to Kansas, one to Nebraska, two to Kentucky, and many others to nearer places. Ten years before, such trips would have been impossible. The trip to Iowa, from his home in Ohio, in 1849, was a great undertaking. But railroads and steamboats were bringing the extreme limits of the country much nearer together.

Bishop Edwards wrote scarcely anything during the entire term, except what arose out of pressing occasions and the practical demands of church-work; but his mind was all the more intensely engaged upon the various church-interests, in planning, stimulating, and repelling open and secret foes,—in a word, in endeavoring to care for the Church as one that must give an account. He had great faith in planning new work, and had such thorough and accurate knowledge as to men and measures, and such evident caution, as to inspire confidence and prevent calamity.

But his journal must be relied on for giving the truest and fullest idea of his spirit and activities. Let him paint his own picture—outline, dimensions, coloring, burden of work, life, faults, and all. It is not necessary that frequent comments be made along with the particular selections that are given from the journal. No selection is made unless it is understood to present some characteristic feature or helpful illustration of his life and labors. The nature and value of these entries will generally be obvious. The following selections begin with 1858:

January 1. Spent the day in Decatur, Illinois, in religious visiting. Preached at night from the sacrifice and the altar. Good liberty. Sermon too long, but two were converted. Feel that I am all on the altar, and that God accepts the poor sacrifice.

January 2. Traveled fifty miles to Honey Creek, to a dedication. Walked three miles. Dined and prayed with a Lutheran family. Preached at night. Not very clear. Felt empty afterward. Lord, baptize me anew.

January 3. The Lord gave me unusual liberty in preaching from a new text. Afterward felt too much selfish satisfaction. Lord, forgive me.

How often ministers take to themselves credit for what God has done for them, notwithstanding their promises not to do so; and how few of them afterward ask forgiveness,—at least before they want some more help.

January 7. A beautiful winter day. Feel an unusual longing for the Holy Spirit. Visited several families. Tried to preach at night, with but poor success. Oh, where is our faith? Four mourners.

January 11. Went to Lexington. Quarterly meeting on hand. Tried to preach at night. Oh, what a poor preacher. Tongue thick as a board. It may be the Lord can bring good out of it; but I can not see how.

January 20. Arose with a feeling of gratitude to God for his great goodness to me. Good health, peace of mind, and as delightful a morning as ever I saw. Tried to preach at night. Another of those very dark times; and yet I feel a very great desire to be useful. Oh, why this lack of power! Lord, help.

January 21. Another beautiful day. Lord, let the sun shine into this dark soul. Oh, for power. This may be a selfish thought. Oh, for nothingness, that Christ may reveal his power. I must decrease.

January 24. Preached a dedicatory sermon with much liberty. Guess I offended some pro-slavery persons. Collection materially affected.

January 29. Arrived at home at twelve to-day. All alive and well. Aurelia had been sick, but God mercifully restored her. Heard that three prominent brethren had joined the Masons. Oh, what a shock to confidence. Lord, what is man?

February 4. Try to have victory, but mind somewhat harrassed with little, petty jars. Why is it that my religion fails at home sooner than elsewhere? My family are kind to me; but someway I am stirred by very small things, so as to lose the love I ought to exhibit before the children. Lord, help me.

February 14. At Piqua, Ohio. The morning meeting encouraging. Preached at eleven to about twenty; at night to about thirty. This seemed like doing but little; but we must be humble.

March 16. Dayton. Was tempted by a little, low criticism on my sermons by a brother. Fear his motives; but I will try to profit.

March 17. Have victory over the temptation of yesterday. Have not uttered a word to any one on the subject, nor have I heard the matter alluded to. Will pray for the tempter.

April 18. Rain, rain, rain. In bed. No one went to my appointment in consequence of the rain. Mind at rest. A little affliction is good for the soul.

April 26. Yesterday attended five meetings. Felt victory, but this evening had to punish two of the girls for disobedience and laughing at me. Perhaps was too severe, though did not feel much anger. Lord, teach meekness and wisdom in government. Feel like starting anew in industry and religion. Too cold to study in my room without fire—another drawback. This life is full of drawbacks. Oh, for grace.

May 17. This day visited the grave of my dear father, who died September 15, 1825, aged forty-nine years. Useful reflections crowd upon me as with one foot resting upon his sinking tombstone I make this record. Lord, prepare us all to meet him in glory, where, I trust, he has been for nearly thirty-three years.

May 20. Peace of mind and a season of communion with God in secret prayer. Covenanted to commune more thus in future. Oh, that the covenant may not be broken. Preached at night. Too long, and not very successful.

May 22. This evening Brother Flinchbaugh preached. Good, warm; a little funny, though he was serious. These old German brethren preach the plain truth with feeling hearts. God bless them.

June 5. This is one of the darkest days of my life. Everything seems to go wrong. Missed the train. No freight; no telegraph. Nobody at last to meet me at the depot. Failed to take the bus. Muddy, rain, dark. Made another mistake in seeking lodgings.

June 6. Feel determined to get to my appointment, but misfortunes continue. Hired a buggy. It gave out. Rained all night. Mud and water. Oh! Preached at eleven and four. Good impression, I think. Glad I pressed through difficulties and came.

June 8. Spent this day in visiting in the country. Walked six miles and eat strawberries, etc. Felt condemned and empty for neglecting to pray with the family. Think I will not spend another such day, the Lord helping.

June 10. This day agreed to be one of a company to publish Bernard's Light on Masonry. Lord, if it is thy will give it success.

The publication of the work spoken of here proved to be very successful, many copies being sold and much light spread abroad respecting the dark orders. The bishop lived to see his prayer for its success answered. As a business venture it paid quite well, and still yields a fair profit. He revised the entire work, chiefly in the way of leaving out needless matter. He also wrote an introduction.

July 8. This day took tea with Brother and Sister Sowers. Felt that the conversation and our devotions were profitable. It might be profitable to visit more in the right spirit.

July 12. Our most excellent visit with our northern friends soon to close. Think it has been a benefit to me. I ought to associate much with persons of an affectionate nature. It softens and smooths my rough heart. Oh, for love.

July 18. Tried to preach this afternoon at Crabb's School-house. Poor liberty. Think I undertook too much. Some cause of failure. Oh, when shall I ever become a preacher!

July 25. Able to preach some at ten and a half o'clock. Some liberty. Felt a peculiar desire to get nearer to God and to be baptized anew for my work. Lord, help, that I may go to the conferences in the fullness of the blessing.

August 12. White River Conference commenced at eight o'clock. A pleasant, calm time in the conference prayer-meeting. God was with us through the day. Prospects in money matters poor enough. We will trust God.

August 13. Conference progresses slowly but surely. Tried to preach at night. Too lifeless. Why is it that we can preach sincerely the theory of spiritual power and yet feel so little of it?

August 14. At this conference two members seemed to equivocate on answering the question, "Have you connection with any secret society," and thus threw a suspicion over my mind which it will take time to remove.

Sunday, August 15. A good day. God helped me to preach.

August 18. Came to Goshen, where the Wabash Conference is to be held. Heard a kind of a discourse from an old preacher, with whom I was acquainted twenty-two years ago. Such preaching. Oh, oh! Perhaps I lack charity. God forgive.

August 19. Passed through the day with a peaceful frame of mind. Would in other years have been tempted at some things, but was kept in peace. Bless the Lord for victory.

August 20. God was with us in the conference business to keep our spirits in peace. Bless his name. I yet believe he will grant me more love and meekness.

Sunday, August 21. Preached on the camp-ground from . Judas. A friend afterward sent me a dollar because of the sermon. I hardly know what he saw in it. Brother H. preached at four. Guess he was in the fog some. But he is a good clever man, and will improve.

August 27. Auglaize Conference. This morning feel solemn; not talkative. Drawn out in prayer. Lord, be with us in the conference. A good commencement.

August 28. This conference took very firm ground on secrecy. Erased the name of T. J. D. with some scorching resolutions. Business is progressing rapidly.

August 29. Very cold for this time of year. Mind clear and calm. Oh, that flames of love may kindle in my soul. Am to dedicate a poor church. The Lord help, that I and the people may be dedicated. The Lord helped this forenoon while I was preaching from "Holiness becometh God's house."

August 30. Business goes on finely. Appointments read. Guess all will go off right. Conference closed at twelve at night in a gust of good feeling. All felt first-rate.

September 6. Miami Conference closed about ten this evening. Decidedly the best Miami Conference I have attended. The itinerants right—no reserve. No local men employed. May the Lord make this the best year we have ever had.

September 14. Felt somewhat sad at the thought of leaving home for so long a time, especially on my family's account. Parted with them at six o'clock, and committed them, the house, and myself to God. O Lord, keep us.

September 16. Indiana Conference convened to-day. Our trust is in God for a good, profitable session. Oh, if I were only as holy and zealous for God as I ought to be, I might do something toward stimulating others to love and good works.

All goes on finely. The best statistical reports I ever saw. The stationing committee did its work in one hour. God helps.

Sunday, September 25. Preached at ten and a half o'clock. Tolerable liberty. God grant that it may do good.

October 8. Finished reading Summerfield's life. What a sweet-spirited, saintly man. His life was short, but devoted. He died at twenty-seven, having preached seven years. He had natural gifts; but his great strength lay in his nearness to God, his child-like humility, and tenderness of heart.

October 9. Kansas Conference began yesterday. Had a plain, private conversation with brethren who felt edgewise toward each other. Oh, for love among brethren.

October 14. Arrived at Fannie's. Had a welcome reception. Since a little love does me so much good, I ought to learn to love others; or rather I ought to manifest for their sakes what little affection I have.

Fannie was a girl who had been received into the bishop's family, and who had married and gone west.

October 18. Leavenworth. Am doing nothing for the Lord. What a very poor worm of a man I am! Had a profitable season at dusk, while praying for all the conferences in my district, by name; also, my wife and children and other friends.

October 20. Riding in a full stage. Two or three very profane men. Shall I reprove them? Will wait till I get a good opportunity. How very wicked the people in the West are becoming. Perhaps setting the heart on worldly speculation opens it to all other bad influences.

October 23. In Nebraska. Am to hold a conference, and only one member in it. Am to examine and license several, or reject them.

November 24. Am on board the "Ben Campbell," for Rock Island. Had a remarkable answer to prayer this morning. Who ever trusted God and failed?

December 26. Came home. All well. Too much complaining of the preacher, which caused me to administer too hard a rebuke. God forgive me. I must have more patience. Can there not be mercy and grace for me?

December 31. Went to Arlington, to assist Brother Norris. No meeting. Word sent for night. Preached from "Cities of Refuge." Not much power. Too much trust in man. Felt this as soon as I learned how my coming was received.

Who will undertake to estimate the breadth, extent, various and conscious fullness of the heart-history of even one of these years? Was ever aspiration higher, or struggle so persistent, or so often renewed? We expect to hear him compare himself with men. This is human and common. But Christ is ever the standard by which he judges himself. The purity of Jesus may condemn his defects and short-comings, but it is still the flaming beacon to lead him on, and the sure prophecy of a like purity for himself.

January 1, 1859. Feel the need of spending the coming year more entirely for God than I have the past. Think that I shall be enabled to do more for the cause of holiness. Lord, help me.

January 7. Have started on a preaching tour. Some faith and peace. Preached at night. The Lord helped, and the word seemed to take hold of the people.

January 10. Tried to preach on consecration, but failed

from some cause unknown to me. No power, and but little light.

January 17. Visited twenty-one families. Prospects encouraging. Lord, pour out thy Spirit. Preached at night. Three mourners. Quite a number convicted. Much feeling.

January 20. Felt an unusual solemnity, so that I could hardly preach. Ten mourners. One conversion. Prospect glorious.

March 1. Not much faith of a revival in D. Fear the motive of those who desire it is not such as God can bless. Gained a little help in secret prayer, and a little more while talking to the people on "dry bones."

March 9. Serious temptation about hoops. I hate them. Believe the Lord hates them. But I ought not to sin in my opposing. Fear I did. Oh, for meekness. Preached at night, with more liberty than I expected. Good feeling.

March 10. Left home on a long tour. Preached at Center Point,—long, hard, and loud. Too empty. Too little effected, I fear. Curiosity to hear a strange preacher had something to do with it.

March 13. Beautiful Sabbath morning; but how and what shall I preach? God helped in the morning while encouraging the brethren in the race for eternal life. But at night! Oh! Oh! Choked up. Hoarse. No power.

March 16. Finished the book of Nehemiah. Am reading and marking for use a small book of anecdotes. Read book of Esther through. A very interesting story. Exemplifies the power of prayer and fasting.

March 17. Lower Wabash. Oh, for grace to go through this conference in a right spirit. Reading Job. Am peculiarly struck with his excessive grief. How forcibly he tells his sorrows. Spoke once to-day too harshly. Oh, when shall I get victory over this evil.

March 13. A rather pleasant season to-day; but I still feel the remains of selfishness. Too much concerned for my official reputation. God help.

Sunday, March 20. Felt empty and messageless this morning; but faith claimed the promise, and God came to my help while presenting the missionary interest. Nearly three hundred dollars raised. A powerful prayer-meeting in the afternoon.

March 28. Sent for to preach the funeral of a merchant's wife, who, I fear, died without hope. Oh, what a task. But little good, I fear, is effected by such funerals. At night preached at same place. Rain and dark. Oh! Oh!

July 25. Packing up for another long campaign. Feel some anxiety about a preparation for usefulness. Oh, for the Spirit. Left only twenty dollars with wife, and had but twelve dollars for myself. Left all in God's care. Have very little earthly trust of any kind. But it is better to trust in the Lord than to put confidence in man.

August 4. Preached from Psalms cxviii. 27. Too long. Think I must give up this text. Hard work to preach.

August 12. Kansas Conference commenced. Six members. All present. Preached from II. Corinthians viii. 9. Many tears shed. Suppose the subject applicable.

August 17. Came to the place of the White River Conference. Met the brethren in an unusually pleasant mood. Feel love toward them more than common.

August 18. Tried to preach at night on the promises. God was present, and I and others felt happy. Think good was done. But it was God who did it, and not man.

September 1. In this, the Auglaize Conference, what a want of a true devotional spirit. Many are seemingly substituting theory for religion. Oh, how slowly business progresses. So much talk.

September 6. Answered perhaps too sharply a sister who was complaining of conference. I record it here to mortify the old man.

September 18. Preached a conference sermon in the forenoon, and at night a missionary sermon, on the " Cheerful giver." A little too much lightness in gesture and expression. God forgive.

October 22. This morning feel a thankful and devotional spirit. Am better in health than weeks before. Arrived at the Sandusky Conference as a visitor. Oh, how excited I was to meet so many old and tried friends.

October 23. Tried to preach a missionary sermon. Oh, what a poor preacher. Felt much mortified afterward.

Sunday, October 30. Scioto Conference. Tried to preach at ten from "Open wide thy mouth." Some feeling and loud responses. At three o'clock warm, old-fashioned speaking meeting.

The loud responses referred to were such that the bishop had to wait for quiet to be restored. A chief point in the sermon was in reference to divine interpositions. While the bishop was describing the ascent of Elijah in one of the Lord's beautiful chariots, Brother Joshua Montgomery was especially demonstrative in crying "glory." The bishop turning to him said, "Don't go up yet Joshua; we can't well spare you."

November 30. My own inside state not the sweetest. Can hardly tell the reason. But one thing is clear; I am not enough like Jesus. Oh, for a fullness of love.

December 16. Brother D. preached rather a harsh kind of

a sermon. Oh, how much old-country people need love. It is my great lack.

January 18, 1860. Started for Pennsylvania. Stopped over night at the house of a very dear friend—a visit which will not soon be forgotten. Such exhibitions of affection I am not used to. How strangely this one has affected me. Lord, make it profitable.

February 7. Arrived home at noon. All well. Thank the Lord. Spent the afternoon—hardly know how. Was waked at ten o'clock by Lecta's running in and crying out, "Father, you have another happy daughter." Converted! Thank the Lord for it.

February 11. Preached. Missed my main thought; or rather had no power to amplify or impress it. Oh, what a poor preacher!

March 9. Find that I have but little to say of my spiritual state. Fear I am not as spiritually-minded as I ought to be. Lord, help me and prepare me for thy work. Feel a little more of the spirit of prayer to-day.

March 28. Letters from home, and also from a dear friend. How it excites to get letters of affection. Oh, that I were more worthy of my friends.

May 27. Congregations very good. Not much liberty. A feeling of unworthiness. Fear the people are disposed to trust too much to my efforts. I pity them.

May 28, 1861. Twenty-seven years ago this evening I was born the second time; and yet, what a very poor Christian I am. So often overcome by the least trifles! As a father, husband, preacher, bishop, how very defective I am! It can not be that grace in full measure has not been provided for me. If ever a soul needed mercy I am that soul. Am often deeply humbled in view of my many deficiencies. O God, take my poor heart and purify and strengthen it so that I may be enabled to reflect thy image more perfectly.

May 31. This evening, after weeks of unbroken affection and peace, suffered a mere trifle to disturb my spirit so as to bring on a season of pouting. Oh, when shall I be a man and a complete Christian! Well, one good thing is taught by these seasons,—my own weakness and dependence. But it so destroys my confidence and self-respect that I am sometimes ashamed to look up. What a deep is the human heart! How multitudinous the caverns of the soul! How few ever explore all of them. How few know either their own hearts or those of their most intimate friends! O Lord, search thou me and see if there be any way of wickedness in me. There is victory, there is power with thee. Awake to my help, and that right early.

It is hardly necessary to refer to the many reproaches Bishop Edwards applied to himself. Only the merest novice could understand from them an inferior state of grace. They rather show the keenest sensibility to sin, and the constant purpose to preserve a victory over it by an ever-renewed faith. He not only was resolved not to indulge sin, but he was determined to find it even in its most secret lurking-places, or under its most deceptive garb. It is no wonder, therefore, that he attained an extraordinary knowledge of the heart. Many questions as to faith, the power of grace, and the sanctification of believers are made plain when viewed in the light of his experience.

· Perhaps some of his references to his sermons will be an enigma to some. The expressions, "good liberty," or "poor liberty," were much in use a few years ago. Ministers aimed at results, immediate effects; and they threw themselves forward upon the people, depending upon the Holy Spirit's help to stir up the minds and hearts of the audience. We can easily see that if there. was not something of an unearthly atmosphere, if men's concern was not turned to their souls, and if the preacher's soul was not fitted with a powerful directing tendency for the hour of such close contact and changing emergency, strange and woful consequences would ensue. The help that was necessary was that of the Holy Spirit. Many ministers now ask for this help; but they are careful not to make the success of their sermons depend on such aid. They so stock their minds, and so balance themselves against any contingencies in the audience, that they may at least acquit themselves respectably if they should not be aided by the Holy Spirit. If they do not aim at present and definite results, the risk is reduced to the lowest point; and this, too, it is feared, the people generally prefer.

Bishop Edwards, too, had to preach, most generally, in the face of curiosity, or unreasonable expectation, either of which frequently amounts to disability. How could he, when people came to see how well he could preach, or to analyze

13

him as he preached, make them feel that the problem to be solved was with themselves? For himself he would have preferred the verdict of failure to the fame of victory without trophies for the Master. It is by no means to be understood, however, that the people exercised as severe a judgment on his preaching as he did himself. As a preacher, the people always regarded him as having few equals and no superior in the church of his choice. True, his sermons were not all masterly, but they all received the impress of a superior mind intensely in earnest in the one work of saving souls. In making selections also from his diary, preference has been given to those judgments upon himself which were the most rigorous. The side of his success be passed with little comment. His home life was characterized by great composure. His children have often said, "We never knew an unpleasant word to pass between father and mother."

Bishop Edwards traveled and preached much on his district. He was instrumental in promoting many revivals. A more thorough consecration and increased spirituality were the results of his contact with ministers and members. His texts and subjects assumed a wider range than would have been expected in the case of one going so much from place to place. An exami-

nation of the diary shows that in seventy-one sermons preached in 1859, fifty-one different texts
were used; and that in preaching one hundred
and twenty-seven sermons in 1859, sixty-two different texts were used. Of the other sermons
which he preached during these two years the
texts are not named. The texts used oftenest
were Psalms lxxxi. 10; Hebrews xii. 1; Acts ix.
31; II. Corinthians viii. 9.

The era of church-dedication had fairly begun.
Work of this kind required much of the time
and energies of the bishops. Bishop Edwards
sought to connect with these occasions special
efforts for revivals. Indeed, nothing was regarded
as meeting its purpose if conversions did not
accompany it.

Very little can be given in this chapter of the
nature of incident. Some read biographies only
for their incidents; and others would like to see
those whom they delight to honor as great and
good in nothing but grand and hallowed associations. But unfortunately, or fortunately, our
heroes do not live constantly in extraordinary
circumstances.

The bishops had been constituted by the General Conference a committee to examine the
manuscript of the revised hymn-book. The committee met at Grafton, W. Va., in the winter of

1858. While on his way up the Ohio River he was introduced to a gentleman, a school-teacher by profession. The conversation soon turned upon scientific and literary subjects. The bishop himself, early in life, had tried his hand at the same profession. The gentleman referred to was very fluent and witty in conversation. The bishop seemed thoughtful and cautious, but proved a good listener. One of the topics upon which the teacher expatiated at some length was the mathematical puzzle as to a line continually approaching an object by moves of half the remaining distance, and the impossibility of reaching the object. He said, "Geometricians can demonstrate that there are curves which approach continually to some fixed right line without the possibility of ever meeting it." As the bishop watched the statement of the barriers in the way, the writhing of his face and a peculiar drawing of the air through his teeth, a sure sign that he was about ready for some move, were very noticeable and amusing. For a moment or two he seemed embarrassed, but quickly exclaimed, "I would break right through and get there." By this practical tendency he cut many a Gordian knot.

The bishop's daughters were just reaching what may be called the piano or cabinet-organ period. When they applied to him for an instrument, he replied that they should learn to play right well on the wash-board first.

It was found at the close of the quadrennial term that the Church had improved rapidly in respect to missions, publishing interest, education, and the building of churches. The membership of the Church was reported at over ninety-four thousand—a gain of over thirty-three thousand in four years. In the ten years closing with 1861 the membership had increased from forty thousand to the number above given; or, in other words, doubled itself, with fourteen thousand to spare. This increase was largely due to the unity of sentiment in the Church, and the fact that from the bishops down to the laity the entire membership was characterized by a tireless and aggressive spirit.

CHAPTER IX.

THE thirteenth General Conference met at Westerville, Ohio, May 13, 1861. This was at the beginning of the great civil war, and the members of the conference were filled with the excitement of the war-spirit, or with fearful forebodings of the desolation that would result from civil strife. It was known that slavery was at the bottom of the conflict. The antislavery record and convictions of the United Brethren Church, therefore, made it evident from the beginning that no church would be more agitated or enthusiastic for the Union than the United Brethren Church. And yet the religious needs and duties of men are supreme; and though among the masses these needs and duties may be temporarily obscured or embarrassed by warring elements, they still should command the unyielding and unvarying attention of ministers of the gospel, despite the casualties and calamities of the times.

198

In the General Conference thirty annual conferences were entitled to representation. Quite a noted example occurred, in connection with the opening of this session, of Bishop Edwards' determination to keep the face of his moral consciousness clear, and so preserve his confidence toward God and man. In the conference of 1857, while the depravity question was being considered, he had said some rather hard things in reference to some of the western delegates. He now arose and said, "Four years ago I said some hard things in reference to some of the western delegates. I have been repenting over these things for all this time, and I believe God has forgiven me; and I want the brethren to forgive me." It is but just to say, however, that the bishop had censured himself much more severely in the matter referred to than others had done.

The secret-society question again came up. No modification, however, was proposed further than to prescribe a rule by which offenders against the law of the Church should be tried. The amendment was that those connected with secret societies should be dealt with "as in other cases of immorality." Pending the adoption of the amendment, Bishop Edwards spoke as follows: "We ought not to fear to discuss this question. Advantage has often been taken of our silence. Let us express our convictions frankly and boldly. We do not stand alone on this subject. * * * * The people can not attend to more than one great evil at a time; and when slavery is disposed of, then Christian sentiment in relation to these societies will express itself, and the masses of the people will be moved as they are now in relation to slavery. I have faith in human progress. * * * *. I go for this rule, finally, because it is merciful. Secret societies are like old-fashioned rat-traps,—it is easy to get in, but hard to get out of them. Therefore, decided, frank, scripture measures should be adopted." In the vote to adopt, but five voted in the negative, and one of these afterward transferred his vote to the affirmative.

Sandusky Conference was impeached because of its methods of trying several ministers who had joined the Masons. In the absence of specific direction in the Discipline, the conference had devised a method of its own. The conference required all the members to answer, at the time of the general examination, as to whether they stood connected with any secret society. This was in 1857. All the members answered in the negative. But it was afterward learned that some had answered falsely. In hundreds of similar cases it has been demonstrated, as Bishop Edwards often said, "that Masons, apparently

unimpeachable, will lie without scruple on matters touching their order." It may in part be set
down to the previous character of those who join
the order as indicated by the fact of their joining
such an institution, but in greater part to the
mysterious power that Masonry has to stifle manhood and conscience. The only real objection to
the measure used is the uncertainty of obtaining
the truth from those who have come under this
blight. No one who has any fair comprehension
of the nature and responsibility of the ministerial
office can object to a stricter rule for the ministry
than is used in the civil courts, or in the examination and trial of persons in the ordinary walks
of life.

In 1858 Sandusky Conference again used the
same test; and this led those who had been impli-
cated to acknowledge that they were Masons.
Some made confessions as to the sinfulness of
their course, and promised loyalty to the Church.
One was suspended for one year and one was
expelled. All, however, finally complied with the
requirements of the conference, and continued
in the Church. The course of Sandusky Conference was generally approved, except as some
feared the establishment of a precedent which
might in other cases work injury. Bishop Edwards showed his candor and good sense in the

following remarks: "I can not vote heartily on either side. I am not satisfied that the procedure was strictly in accordance with the rules of the Church. For years we have met this wily foe of secrecy, seeking to make its way into the Church at every crevice. * * * * I am clearly of the opinion that to clandestinely go into the lodge and conceal the fact from the Church is a crime I hardly have language to characterize properly. The rule of Sandusky Conference, however, is a merciful rule, designed to save the brethren." In the vote to sustain the conference · Bishop Edwards voted in the affirmative, there being but three votes in the negative.

At this session seven new conferences were formed,—Fox River, West Des Moines, Indiana German, California, Massachusetts, Western Reserve, and North Michigan. Iowa and North Iowa were permitted to separate. Kentucky and Nebraska mission-conferences ceased for the time to be recognized as conferences.

Bishop Edwards was again elected a member of the missionary Board. He was also elected for his fourth term as bishop. J. J. Glossbrenner, J. Markwood, D. Shuck, and H. Kumler were his colleagues. Thus for the first time the Church had five bishops — a truly strong Board, and one that well represented the Church. Bishop Shuck was assigned to the Pacific coast, and Bishop Kumler presided over the German work. Bishop Glossbrenner was returned to the East District and Bishop Markwood was sent to the Northwest District. Bishop Edwards remained on the Southwest District. His conferences were White River, Miami, Indiana, Illinois, Kansas, Missouri, Scioto, Upper Wabash, and Lower Wabash.

Bishop Edwards was appointed on a committee to prepare a youth's scripture compend. The work appeared in due time, and met with an extensive and continued sale. The little work contains much instruction, and in a very helpful form.

The General Conference closed with the following remarks from Bishop Edwards: "This has been one of the most pleasant General Conferences I have ever attended. Long will I remember the General Conference of 1861. Again the fact has been developed here that on all important questions, on all great moral questions, this Church is a unit. Toward this perfect unity the tendency has been constant for the last ten years. God has had a purpose in raising up this people, but there is danger that the vessel be marred. Let us be watchful. We need to possess a higher spirituality."

Bishop Edwards attended all his conferences

during his entire term, with the exception of the Kansas and Missouri the first year, transit being made impossible for the time by the war. By the same condition Bishop Glossbrenner was shut up for the entire term in Virginia. He attended only one session of conference during the four years; namely, the Virginia, in 1864. A circumstance will indicate how closely he was watched. A sick confederate officer, who had been quartered at the house of Bishop Glossbrenner, and been kindly cared for, was brought before the court and questioned, with a view to obtaining a pretext for arresting and robbing the bishop. Among other things, the sick officer was asked if the bishop prayed in his family. "Yes, every day," was the reply. "Can you discover," said the lawyer, "for which side he prays?" Thus watched and hemmed in within rebel lines, he was scarcely heard of during the first three years of his term.

A considerable part of the duties of Bishop Glossbrenner devolved upon Bishop Edwards. Hence in 1861 he presided at the Muskingum Conference; in 1862 at the Alleghany, Pennsylvania, Erie, Western Reserve, and Muskingum conferences; in 1863 at the same as in 1862, with the addition of North Michigan and Michigan conferences; and in 1864 the Muskingum, Erie

Western Reserve, and North Michigan conferences. He also assisted Bishop Markwood in
presiding at the East Pennsylvania Conference in
1863.

His duties were augmented to no small extent
by the demands that came to him in various
ways from the Eastern District. The result of
this extension of duties was to give him an acquaintance and extend his influence in parts of
the Church which he had not before visited
as superintendent. The extreme parts of the
Northwest District, the Pacific coast, and perhaps
Parkersburg and Virginia conferences, were all
that had not now been visited. Numerous evi-
dences have been preserved of the industry and
labors of Bishop Edwards during this period.
One year, in time of harvest, he was engaged in
holding a successful protracted meeting in Indiana. Another time he preached twenty-five times
in twenty-four days. He was, in fact, an evan-
gelist as well as a bishop.

Let us turn again to his journal. It will be the
last time that we shall have the privilege of the
intimacy which the journal offers, as its last page
closes with 1864.

June 15. Quarterly and dedication meeting commence to-
day. Know not what to preach. Oh, for light and strength.
God, give us some quickening power while preaching from
"'Who art thou, O great Mountain?'"

Sunday, June 16. The text, "The Lord is there," to some extent verified while preaching the dedication sermon. Brother S. preached at four. Good old bread as to doctrine and phrases.

June 23. The Lord was near in the grove in secret prayer, and blessed preacher and people largely while I was talking of the meeting at the transfiguration.

August 12. Feel an unusual need of more faith, communion, and spiritual power. 'Tis certainly for us. The Bible is full of promises of help. In us is no power. Oh, that the Lord would shed forth his Spirit, pour it out upon us. I must have more spirituality. Lord, for the sake of others, bless one so unworthy.

August 14. Started to White River Conference. Felt deeply the need of better preparation for the duties before me. What a poor bishop. A poorer preacher, and a still poorer Christian, I fear. O God, for help.

August 15. A peaceful day. Money matters a little better than feared, but a declension in revival influence and aggressive spirit.

August 16. God was with us in the conference room, and helped at night in preaching.

Sunday, August 18. Brother Markwood preached at ten about the cherubim and coal of fire spoken of by Isaiah. Very good sermon—one hour and forty-five minutes long.

August 22. Miami Conference commenced. Examinations rather superficial. No help from the elders. Oh, that God would help to stir up the preachers. We must have help. J. G. Fee was with us and gave us a good address. He is of the right spirit—the martyr spirit. If we—all Christian ministers—were like him there would be more purity in the world.

August 24. Hard time in the Stationing Committee. Ten

preachers more than needed. Some that were appointed will not go, and some will not accomplish much.

Sunday, August 25. Did not preach much of a sermon to-day. But God was with us, and the meeting was profitable. Indications of a revival this year encouraging. Lord, send it. Amen.

August 26. Conference closed. Generally a harmonious session, but some are hurt about their appointments. Oh, that all had the spirit of consecration.

September 5. Indiana Conference began well; only a little dry and lean in attendance. The war has terribly blighted this region. Brother I. C. preached at night. How much he needs cultivation.

September 7. Nothing unusual to-day. At three preached conference sermon. Some very plain talk. But God was with me, and all passed well.

Sunday, September 8. At ten preached in the grove to a large crowd, with good liberty, from the transfiguration. Preached at night in the Baptist church. Poor and dry.

September 13. This day Father Lane signed over to me notes to the amount of over six thousand dollars for the missionary society,—only a part of what he intends to do. Lord, reward him, and make the donation a blessing to the world.

September 14. Considerable debate to-day. I hurt one brother's feelings by speaking a little short. God, forgive me. A hard time on the Stationing Committee. One selfish brother became offended at a plain, truthful remark.

Sunday, September 15. A long meeting. Preached at eleven to a large congregation in the woods. Gave a lecture at four on Sunday-schools. A good time.

September 16. Preached conference sermon at two. God was with us. Experience meeting at night. The Spirit was freely poured out.

September 17. Learned that I could not get through Missouri on account of the rebellion. Took the cars for home.

September 25. . Started for Muskingum Conference at half past one in the morning. Arrived at nine, and preached on the state of the country at ten. Preached plain, straight-out abolition doctrine; but it seemed to go down well, as far as I could see.

Sunday, September 29. God was very near us to-day. We asked largely for the Spirit, and he was given to us. Text, "Open wide thy mouth." Preached again at four—a missionary sermon.

October 2. Left home for Scioto Conference. Feel empty and much need of help from heaven. Oh, that I were better qualified to do good. What shall I do to get nearer to God. I often tell others what to do. Oh, that I could teach myself.

October 3. Conference tolerably full, but lack of power among the preachers.

Sunday, October 6. Preached conference sermon with some effect. A pointed talk to the preachers on the importance of qualifications for the work in little things.

Bishop Edwards from his own choice attended Sandusky Conference, in Bishop Markwood's district.

October 15. Started at eight for Sandusky Conference. Had hardly time to pray. Ought to have risen sooner, so as to have had time.

October 17. Tried to preach at night. Hampered much. Perhaps tried to say too much. Had I taken a new text and attempted a short discourse, would have had better light. Text, " Open wide thy mouth."

October 18. Self somewhat mortified. Let it die. Feel sad and drawn out in prayer for purity and power.

October 19. Am listening to an old-fashioned preacher. Powerful in prayer, but in preaching covers too much ground to succeed long.

Sunday, October 20. Brother Markwood preached a good conference sermon at ten. One point, that on holiness, especially, melted my heart and the hearts of others. I tried to preach at night on the sacrament. Good meeting. Many hearts melting. Praise God.

November 16. Came to Daleville, Indiana, to a quarterly and dedication meeting. Brother Wright preached at eleven. Good, solemn, and searching. I preached at night from the poverty of Christ. Fear we shall have a hard time to raise the money—nearly three hundred dollars. Some rich ones in the way.

Sunday, November 17. Preached dedication sermon. Good liberty. God made me happy. But oh, what an effort, and what a failure as to the money,—one hundred and twenty dollars back. Can't help it. Did my best.

November 27. Father Lane came to my house to make over some land to the missionary society; also some notes, making his donation, to this time, thirteen thousand dollars.

January 2, 1862. Alleghany Conference opened in usual form. Day passed pleasantly. Something of a revival in progress here. Four forward last night, and twelve to-night. Evidently the mourners depend too much on their physical efforts. Tried to talk to them; but they are not of the talking kind. How strange their views of the method of obtaining religion! But God knows their hearts, and knows when to bless them.

January 4. Preachers of this conference need very much a new consecration to God. Policy too far prevails in all their arrangements. It will ruin them unless they learn a more excellent way.

14

Sunday, January 5. The Lord gave me power to preach at ten o'clock. Five were ordained. One is, I fear, a Mason.

January 17. Pennsylvania Conference begun. Prospects of a pleasant session. To-night Brother K. preached from redeeming the time. A good, very good sermon. What good that man might do if he had good business habits. But his poor financiering spoils all.

January 20. Preached conference sermon at ten. Very plain. Some writhed under it, I think. "I magnify mine office." Conference closed pleasantly. Heard no grumbling. God be praised.

March 6. Upper Wabash Conference. Rose at five o'clock and rode nine miles through a very cold morning. And oh, what a poor prospect for a conference! House cold and dirty. At night Brother D. preached a kind of a sermon. Oh, for a revival spirit.

March 9. Preached the conference sermon. Felt somewhat solemn, and think some good was done. At three a missionary sermon, from "Go ye into all the world."

March 13. Lower Wabash Conference. An exciting session. The conference took steps toward building a school. I preached.

March 15. An unusual melting time at the reading of the appointments. In the evening preached the conference sermon. Good impression.

Sunday, March 16. One of the best morning meetings I ever was in. Preached at ten. A wonderful outpouring of the Spirit. Glory.

October 9. Western Reserve Conference. A stormy commencement. Lord, have mercy upon us. At night preached. A good and profitable time.

October 10. A better spirit prevailed to-day. Peace and love seem coming up.

Sunday, October 12. Preached in the grove. God helped.

October 13. Conference closed in harmony and love.

October 16. Erie Conference. A pretty good conference. Nearly all strangers to me; consequently my blunt manners don't take very well.

Sunday, October 19. God was with us to-day while preaching. At night read the appointments. Some growling. God reigns.

His mother had died during this year. On going to the family home at Delaware, Ohio, he wrote, " One is wanting, who has long been to me a praying mother. Believe she has gone to rest. She died in triumph."

The year 1863 was begun with the invariable prayer for "power, grace, and holiness," to begin his Christian life and work anew. Some occasional entries will now be given upon his trip in 1863 to the East.

January 22. Pennsylvania Conference commenced in a good, moral atmosphere. Yet I feel that I have not the sympathy of the brethren. They seem distant, and suspicious of western men.

Sunday, January 25. God was very near this morning while I preached. Text, "Open wide thy mouth."

On this Sabbath morning Bishop Edwards was in excellent condition, and had a large and appreciative audience. As he spoke of the divine interposition of the past, the whole house seemed lighted up with glory. Many wept, and others

shouted. Among the preachers who occupied a
place in the pulpit with him that day was one
who has since filled the high office of bishop.
After the congregation was dismissed the brother
came round to Brother Jacob Hoke. Weeping
and wiping his eyes he said, "O brother, it seems
to me that I can never after this attempt to
preach."

February 1. In New York, on my way to Massachusetts.
Heard H. W. Beecher this morning. The church ought to
pray for him. Oh, if he had as much unction as talent,
what good he might do!

Bishop Edwards found the mission-work in
Massachusetts not very flourishing or promising.
Stormy weather and small audiences prevented
his doing much while there.

An incident during a visit which he made to
Boston must not be omitted. He, almost from
time immemorial, wore an ample, white, broad-
brimmed beaver hat,—perhaps as a sort of protest
against the folly of Fashion's changes. But he
may tell the story. "The most of the people
seemed to say, Stay off; you don't belong to us.
My white hat may have had something to do
with it. I suffered no little persecution while
walking the streets. Wherever I went I would
hear the boys calling out, 'There goes the man
with a white hat.' 'Who skinned the cat?' called

out one. This was repeated again and again, till my hat really began to seem out of place. One man, riding in a covered wagon, called to me and pulled off a white hat and held it out toward me, as if to say, You have one friend. On my way home, while at East Pennsylvania Conference, some of the brethren, hearing of my tribulations, put a five-dollar bill into my pocket, with the remark, 'This is to get a black hat.' If my friends who have known me for twenty-five years by the same hat object to the change, they can charge it to the ill-mannered Boston boys and the good brethren of East Pennsylvania Conference."

Bishop Edwards preached twice in Delaware, Ohio, the seat of Ohio Wesleyan University, to large and appreciative audiences. After one of the sermons, Dr. Merrick, president of the university, greeted him with tears and exclaimed, "Oh, your sermon has helped me! It has done me so much good." In fact, the educated and illiterate were alike charmed and instructed by his pulpit efforts.

August 12. Left home to begin the fall work. Oh, how much I need help from heaven! Will the Lord help?

August 13. Western Reserve Conference opened in fine spirit. Love and peace seemed to characterize all present.

August 15. Conference continues good,—one of the best. Not a hard time in the Stationing Committee. Left one brother without an appointment. God help him.

Sunday, August 16. At ten preached in the grove to a very attentive audience.

August 17. Conference closed. All is right. No grumbling heard. God, keep and help the preachers to be holy men.

Sunday, August 30. Indiana Conference. Preached conference sermon. Pretty good meeting. Read the appointments. General satisfaction. Praise God.

September 5. Upper Wabash Conference. Some trouble on the Stationing Committee to-day. Oh, what a heap of human nature in men.

Snnday, September 6. Preached at ten, in the grove, upon the itiueracy. God helped. At night on the "Leaven." Not so clear.

September 11. Illinois Conference. Spoke too sharply to Brother J. Dunning, and felt weakened and mortified by it. Felt that he should be reproved; but I did it with too much feeling. God pity me. Oh, for love.

September 12. Took the remark referred to above back to-day, and felt well over it.

September 19. North Michigan. A small mission-conference, but possesses some elements of vitality. Some petty jangling.

September 25. Scioto. Much trouble throughout the conference territory on secession. Fear much loss. But if the purity of the Church can be maintained, all will be well.

October 12. Took the train for home to vote against the traitor Vallandigham.

This concludes the extracts from the journal, except those that belong to the single year that is to follow. The extracts for 1864 will, perhaps, be a little more full.

Late in 1863 Bishop Edwards sold his property in Dayton, and purchased fifteen acres of partially improved land, with a fair dwelling-house upon it, near Sonora, Ohio. He obtained possession of this property and moved to it very soon after the purchase. He had lived a little over ten years in Dayton. His object in making this change was to go where living was not so expensive, and where he could have the benefit of country air, hoping that thereby his health would be improved. To have remained in Dayton would have been better for his work. Besides, the city schools furnished an advantage for his children which he could not afford them elsewhere. Yet his salary and his expenses of living being what they were, he could not remain in Dayton; for he would not ruin himself in his expenses, and he believed it to be his duty to so shift as to go on in his work.

January 1, 1864. Must keep a better memoir this year. God help me to be a good man.

With how many persons the man is forgotten in the incidental prominence of official position, and even our own duties to God forgotten, while the duties and responsibilities of others are urged —function taking the place of character. But no vanity or bewilderment made such self-deception and calamity possible in the case of Bishop Edwards.

January 4. Am led to consider the depravity of man, and the consequent danger to religion and country. Oh, for a trumpet to sound the alarm.

January 5. Home. All well. Thanks to Him who cares for and keeps us and ours. Am waking up somewhat to the importance of help from above. Felt in the cars the spirit of prayer. God help and pour out the spirit of grace and supplication.

January 25. Long will this day be remembered. Old sores healed and old grudges forgiven. God subdued some stubborn hearts. Praise his holy name.

January 31. West Sonora. Preached to-night. Considerable liberty and earnestness in speaking; but the after services proved a little dragging. This day was some tempted. Felt weary of the ministry. May God forgive me, and bear with my infirmities. Oh, when shall I have complete victory.

The above expression of weariness in the work of the ministry is the only one of the kind occurring from the bishop. But he was a man, and not more than a man. It will readily be admitted by all that by acts of faith so renewed that they appeared rather a state, he kept himself much above ordinary experience. Yet sometimes he was robbed to a considerable extent of his triumph, or victory, as he called it, and presented the characteristics of human frailty and wearying conflict. Thus he becomes to us a more encouraging example. At West Sonora he looked oftener upon the same faces and the same scenes. His attention and labor, also, in fitting up a new

home, made the atmosphere about him more secular. Yet he did not succumb to this influence.
He assisted in a glorious revival-meeting at Sonora, and lent a helping hand in various other
meetings.

. *March* 12. Worked hard in planting and transplanting
trees. Think I will divide the time better between books
and work. The tendency with me is to run too much to
physical labor to the neglect of the pen and studying.

Sunday, March 13. Poorly prepared for the Sabbath.
How easy to become secularized, so that the thoughts will
not easily fix themselves on religious things! Tried to
preach on an old familiar theme, but had poor liberty.

March 17. Started east to see "Uncle Abraham," to ask
some modification of the order of Secretary of War concerning southern churches.

Secretary Stanton had issued an order by which
all churches, of the Methodist Episcopal Church
South, not occupied by a loyal minister, appointed by a loyal bishop, were turned over to the dis-
posal of Bishop Ames. The United Brethren
Church had encouraging missions at Vicksburg
and at Davis Bend, and was contemplating quite
general work among the freedmen, and it was
thought that the order of Mr. Stanton would be
prejudicial to the work undertaken. Rev. D. K.
Flickinger and L. Davis were also on the committee. The result of the visit to Washington
was an order from the Secretary of War which, in

substance, was satisfactory.   As this was the first
and only instance of the United Brethren sending a deputation to Washington, we will let
Bishop Edwards tell the story.

Sunday, March 20. Spent a part of this day preparing our
paper to present to the officials. At eleven o'clock went to
hear Dr. Channing. A finely prepared lecture; but it would
take a vast amount of such preaching to save a soul. Worked
till late at night on our paper. Don't know that it was
entirely right; but our time is precious, and this is the
Lord's work.

March 21. Still have difficulties in getting our paper to
suit us, but finally decided upon the form to be used. Went
to the Capitol and made the acquaintance of General Schenck
and Senator Wade. Both promised to go with us to-morrow
to see the Secretary of War. We moved our quarters to the
Woodbine, where we are to get boarding at one dollar and a
half, instead of four dollars per day.

March 22. This morning, according to arrangements, we
went to see the Secretary of War. Obtained some favors
through an order, but could not easily reach the secretary
on ecclesiastical points.

March 23. Visited Secretary Chase. We were kindly
received, and taken by him in person and introduced to the
President, with whom we had an interesting interview. We
also visited Attorney-General Bates, with whom we had an
encouraging and long-to-be-remembered talk. Finished our
work. Feel that it will pay in the end.

March 31. Lower Wabash Conference. Did not arrive at
conference-room until 2:00 P. M. The first time for years
that I have been behind time.

April 1. Flickinger sick. At night preached from the

"precious promises." Fear I do not feel the full force of what I say. Oh, for faith,—practical, experimental.

Sunday, April 3. Preached from the solemn charge of the apostle to Timothy. Preached an old missionary sermon at night and raised two hundred and eighty dollars.

April 7. Missouri Conference commenced well. Reports excellent. What a field for us in Missouri.

April 9. Conference sermon at two o'clock. Pretty good liberty while talking from the charge to Timothy.

April 10. At ten o'clock preached a missionary sermon, from the "blessing of Obed-Edom." Good day. All peace and love. God be praised.

April 15. Kansas Conference. Characters of members not clear. Some must be disposed of before we can have real peace. One expelled and another on the hook.

In May, 1864, Bishop Edwards assumed the pastoral charge, for three months, of the First Church, Dayton. His relation as pastor was agreeable to all concerned; and his labors in visiting and preaching were marked by faithfulness, and were attended with advancement and increased spirituality in the church.

July 18. Came home on the evening train. Sick with fever. This is the third week. This time took the matter to my heavenly Father. I always succeed in going to him, even in the smallest temporal matters.

August 12. Started on my long, long, fall tour of eleven weeks. Oh, that God would go with me and prepare me for a successful campaign. He has promised help, and will give it if my state of heart is such that he can do so without injury to me or others.

August 17. White River and Indiana conferences now in joint session at Hartsville. Preached at night from the faith of Abraham.

Sunday, August 21. Preached to a large congregation. A good time. Six ordained,—three of each conference.

Then followed Miami and Upper Wabash conferences. These sessions were harmonious and interesting.

September 11. Lower Wabash Conference. Preached to a large congregation out-doors. By special request I preached from the subject used at the last conference,—"family religion." At the close a Presbyterian asked me to go four miles and preach the same at the county-seat; but did not go. At night a missionary meeting and a farewell shake-hands with the preachers.

Sunday, September 18. Illinois Conference. At ten o'clock preached from Daniel's character. Ordained four. At night a missionary talk. A good time. Praise God.

Sunday, September 25. North Michigan Conference. At ten o'clock God helped me once more in telling of the transfiguration. Hope it was not in vain. At three o'clock preached the conference sermon. Guess it was profitable.

Sunday, October 2. Scioto Conference. Preached at ten o'clock from the character of Daniel. Had unusual freedom. God helped, and the word seemed to take effect.

October 3. At ten o'clock I talked to the preachers, without a text, about one hour. This was a pleasant conference throughout. Peace and friendship among the brethren.

Bishop Edwards had now attended all the conferences of his own district, except two, for the current quadrennial term. The following resolu-

tions, adopted by Indiana and White River conferences, in joint session, fairly indicate the tone
of resolutions passed in other conferences:

Resolved, 1. That our heart-felt thanks be and are hereby
tendered to Bishop Edwards for the able, efficient, and im-
partial manner in which he has presided in our sessions for
the many years he has been among us as our bishop.

2. As a preacher, as a superintendent, and in his private
walk we esteem him an example in piety, in faithfulness,
and in efficiency.

3. We could have desired no one in preference to him;
and if he should be returned to us again as our president,
we will greet him with words of welcome and with hearts of
love and gladness.

At White River Conference he had now presided for fifteen consecutive sessions, having been
absent the first session through an exchange made
with Bishop Glossbrenner.

Bishop Edwards attended, in October, Muskingum, Western Reserve, and Erie conferences, in
Bishop Glossbrenner's district.

In December he went to Canada, to dedicate
a church, and remained there two weeks,—a time
well occupied and highly enjoyed. When he desired to return across the border he found unexpected difficulties, because of some features of the
passport system. As he had been born on British
soil, the law required the presentation of his
father's naturalization papers, which of course

could not be commanded. Even then the passport would cost seven dollars. But listen to his
own account of the case:

"Here was a trial of faith. I must get over
in a clandestine manner, or remain and send to
Washington for a pass, and thus miss my appointments. I had lately been preaching to others on
trusting Providence, who makes all things to
work together for good. But what good could
come out of this? This I could not see. Yet it
must be true; and I resolved to hold on to my
faith. I concluded to take the day to decide my
course. At noon the kind-hearted consul sent
me word by one of his clerks that if I would be
at his office at 5:00 P. M., he would go with me to
the other side and try to prevail on the custom-
house officers to let me pass without a passport,
and thus save the law, himself, and me too. The
plan succeeded. Faith triumphed, and the promise was again verified."

In March, 1865, he attended his last annual
conferences — Missouri and Kansas — before the
General Conference.

While many of the interests of the Church had
been advanced during the quadrennial term, there
had been an actual loss in members of over four
thousand. The Church was patriotic in the highest degree. In some conferences the feeling for

the Union was such that to be a Democrat was to be regarded with suspicion, or pressed out of the Church; while to be a secessionist was to receive no quarter. Add the losses from these causes to the ordinary loss from the desolating and demoralizing effects of war, and the wonder is that the loss was not greater. In more auspicious times the providential mission of the Church will again be attested by thousands converted and added to its communion.

A few incidents, and this chapter will be brought to a close.

, Several members of one of the conferences had joined some of the minor secret societies. Bishop Edwards had labored with them, but without much apparent success. One Sabbath, in the midst of his sermon, he spoke of the nature and influence of these societies; and after a solemn admonition he said, "Some of you, brethren, will be sure to be like a man who has passed, on a very dark night, through a filthy yard. You will find something very unpleasant sticking to you."

In his illustrations he was not always the most choice; but those who had their minds on the justness and force of his characterizations and the need of something telling, could easily reconcile themselves to his most daring presentations. He never gratuitously offended the taste of the most delicate.

In a certain conference a minister who had made great trouble was on trial. A visiting minister was interposing pretty freely by his frequent speeches to save the man from expulsion. Bishop Edwards, whose feelings were always too surely and strongly enlisted to make it easy for him to keep from manifesting them before his conferences, began to show signs of his displeasure in the drawing of his face and his peculiar whistling through his teeth. The officious brother noticed these evident signs of his displeasure, but did not desist from his offensive course. Finally the bishop wrote a note to the officious visitor in substantially the following terms: "You are always defending mean men, and this half makes me think you are not the right kind of a man yourself. Now, if you don't desist I will expose you." This had the desired effect.

In speaking of the use of tobacco he could but poorly conceal the disgust he felt. More than once in dedicating churches he told those who were addicted to this filthy habit, to take their tobacco out of their mouths before entering God's house, and lay it by the fence or by the side of the house. "But," said he, "it don't matter where you put it, for I can assure you that neither the hogs nor the dogs will carry it off."

Examples of the bishop's faith occur on every

hand. The confidence with which he presents even his least and most secular wants to God, to many would seem like presumption, almost like trifling with God. But child-like faith is not presumption, and can never displease God.

He had been asked to dedicate a church. He got off the train at the place where the dedication was to occur, at midnight, and found no one to conduct him to a stopping-place. It was very cold winter weather. The station-house was closed, and no lights were to be seen in the town. He felt that he must do something. He knew not what to do. But he knew that there was one who did know, and so, lifting his eyes, he asked the Lord to direct him, and started up through the town. He came to a house that looked to him as though a United Brethren might live in it—he afterward remarked that it needed a coat of paint. He walked up to the door and knocked, and in a moment an upper window was lifted, and a voice called out, "Bishop Edwards, just wait and I'll come down and let you in."

One of the sessions of the Illinois Conference was to be held twenty or twenty-five miles away from the railroad, and it was necessary for him to procure a horse and buggy in order to reach the conference. After going about ten miles he came

15

to a place where the road divided. The tracks before him were equally clear, or, rather, equally dim. He was in the midst of a vast prairie, and there was no house at which to inquire. He had no time to lose, and if he should take the wrong road it would throw him late at his conference. "But," thought he, "the Lord is here, and he knows what I do not. I'll trust him." He drove the horse to the place where the roads parted and stopped him. He then dropped the lines and started the horse. He reached the conference without further trouble, and in time.

At one time the bishop had an appointment to dedicate a church the approaching Sabbath, but was unable to get to the station at which he desired to take the train, before Saturday evening. On arriving at the depot he was informed that the evening train did not stop at that place. The agent also said that he was not allowed to stop the train. He knew that if he reached his appointment he would have to take that train, which would be along in less than an hour. God had helped him at other times. So he went away into the dark, and bowed down and asked God that he would move upon the men in charge to stop the train if it was his will that he should reach his appointment. Sure enough; the coming train stopped at the platform without being signaled. The engineer on being questioned said that he did not know why he stopped, but that it seemed to him that he could not pass without stopping.

Bishop Edwards was accustomed to narrate these incidents in his preaching, as a means of stimulating the faith of others. They certainly indicated the nature and strength of his own faith.

CHAPTER X.

THE fourteenth General Conference met at Western, Iowa, May 11, 1865. As the preceding General Conference met at the beginning of the civil war, so the present General Conference met at the close of that great struggle. Rebellion had gone down in a sea of blood, and the way of empire was again open to the great Republic. The results of the war gave the highest satisfaction to the members of the conference and the Church. On the fourth day of the session, a paper containing the official news of the capture of Jefferson Davis was laid on the bishop's table. Bishop Edwards, after glancing over the paper, arose and remarked that the paper in his hand contained important intelligence, which he would be pleased to communicate. He then read the dispatch, amidst the greatest applause. The conference then arose and sung the doxology.

It is worthy of remark that the General Conference elections and sessions in the United Brethren Church synchronize very closely with the quadrennial election and installation of the president of the United States. The feeling of the conference was indicated by a vote as to the obligation of giving to all the inhabitants of the land an equal position before the law, and of giving to colored citizens the elective franchise. All enthusiastically supported the proposition, with the exception of five, who refused to vote. Of course, Bishop Edwards was not one of the five.

This conference fixed the salary of a bishop at seven hundred and fifty dollars.

The subject of ministerial education was here for the first time considered with any favor by a General Conference. The difference between education for the office of the ministry and a collegiate training is not allowed to-day to work any disparagement to the former. Indeed, it seems hardly possible that the idea of raising up and qualifying laborers for the Master's vineyard was not always the first and most prominent purpose of education by the Church. The most that the conference of 1865 was willing to indorse was to favor the formation of classes, in the literary institutions of the Church, for the study of the books prescribed in the reading-course. The slowness of the Church to favor theological education, but nevertheless the fact of a somewhat changed sentiment on this subject, was indicated by the following remarks of Bishop Edwards:

" We are all aiming at the same thing. Perhaps our opposition to theological schools originated from superstition. Our ministers should be educated. We should do something to prevent the evils we fear. We have no theological insti-tution as yet; and now, while we have them not, let us adopt a plan which will give us the thing we want, without the evils which we apprehend. The best plan will be to give the young men who are to become ministers, along with their college-course, the training in theological studies which they need."

At the close of the session Bishop Edwards made the following happy and significant address:

" The history of this General Conference is the history of the triumph of Christian principle. Not less than one hundred persons of different nationalities and different temperaments, and different opinions, in many respects, have been together for twelve days, discussing and deciding upon exciting questions; and not one angry word has been spoken, not one unkind feeling has been exhibited. I do believe that the ministers of this church were never more closely bound together in the bonds of Christian charity than at the present time. But there may be breakers ahead, which may be to us a source of danger. The present is, in some respects, a critical period. It is a period of transition, an age of progress in the political, civil, and social world. And the spirit of the times affects, in no small degree, the Church. We are constantly in danger of agitating to our injury. The counsels of these old men are not to be despised."

He was re-elected bishop. His associates in this high and responsible office were J. J. Glossbrenner, J. Markwood, J. Weaver, and D. Shuck. He was also continued vice-president of the missionary society. The district assigned him, denominated the Ohio District, embraced the following named conferences: Scioto, Auglaize, Michigan, Indiana, Miami, Ohio German, and Muskingum. The new conferences formed during this session were Cascade and Central Illinois. The Indiana German and Massachusetts were discontinued. During the coming quadrennial term Tennessee Mission-conference was organized by Bishop Glossbrenner, and Kentucky by Bishop Edwards. During the term, Bishop Edwards continued to reside at West Sonora.

Besides attending all the conferences of his own district, Bishop Edwards. attended the first two sessions of Kansas and Missouri conferences, Bishop Markwood being sick. He was also given, by Bishop Markwood, in January, 1867, ecclesiastical charge of the West Mississippi District, until the health of the latter would be so far restored as to enable him to attend to his district. This led Bishop Edwards to make some extra visits to the West,—mainly for the purpose of dedicating churches. He also, for a time, in a general way, attended to the wants of the district.

In May, 1865, he assisted in the dedication of a building for Westfield College. The college at that time had been in operation four years. During this term, he was also called to dedicate some churches in Illinois. At that time the bishops in attending dedications received no extra remuneration; and, generally, they had to·pay their own traveling expenses. In his own district Bishop Edwards attended many dedications, and by general oversight and special personal effort promoted the work of the Church.

In September, 1866, a little over one year after the General Conference, four contributing editors were appointed to assist upon the. *Religious Telescope*, of whom Bishop Edwards was one. Rev.

D. Berger was the editor. Under this arrangement Bishop Edwards furnished numerous articles
on current topics of minor importance, as well as
some of more permanent value.

During this term the Church was much agitated on the question of the use of instrumental
music in worship. In the latter part of the preceding quadrennial term, while Bishop Edwards
resided in Dayton, an organ was introduced into
the Sabbath - school of the First Church. The
bishop entered his earnest protest at once. And
during the last part of the same term the congregation at Westerville commenced using an organ
in regular worship. In Otterbein University,
also, in connection with the chapel services, the
organ was used. This gave the bishop, and many
others, no little uneasiness and dissatisfaction.
Emphatic resolutions against this supposed de-
generacy of the university were passed by many
of the co-operating conferences. The General
Conference of 1865 enacted a rule prohibiting
the use of instrumental music in public worship.
True, this was a favorite measure of Bishop Edwards; but it must be remembered that it expressed, very generally, the sentiment of the
Church at large. It was believed that this prohibition could be vindicated as both righteous and
wholesome. Before 1861 the reading of sermons,

the use of choirs, and musical instruments, or, indeed, anything else supposed to hinder the simplicity and spirituality of religious worship, found no place in the Church. The original impulse and conviction of duty leading away from formality and lifelessness in worship, which characterized the founders of the Church, still continued to be so strong that no elements of contention had thus far disturbed from within. Hence no one can wonder that it was difficult for those who were accustomed to this simplicity in worship to turn away to something different. In fact, it could not be done without wounding the feelings of a large number of ministers and laymen of the Church. So these changes and innovations were vigorously resisted by Bishop Edwards. Though he believed in legislative authority in order to prevent the evils feared, he did not depend wholly on this. In reference to the music-question he wrote two quite elaborate articles, which appeared in the *Religious Telescope.* He showed that the fathers and reformers of the Church were with him in opposition to instrumental music in public worship, or at least were opposed to the form in which it existed in their day. His argument was clear and strong. To . these articles Prof. S. B. Allen made a very candid and able reply. Bishop Edwards wrote one

more article, in which the following beautiful expression occurred: "None of us have any interest in being wrong. If our views can not bear
the light of discussion we ought to give them up.
If I can be convinced that God would be glori-
fied and souls saved by the use of instruments in
our worship, I will cease my opposition. But so
long as I see in the organ an instrument of formal-
ism, so long I must vote against it. This is not
a discussion between Brother Allen and myself.
We are good friends, and both want to be guided
by truth; and I think we shall get to heaven by
and by, when we shall understand what the
'harp of God' means better than we do now."
Two additional articles from Prof. Allen closed
the discussion. But it was not long until the dis-
turbing organ was reported as removed from all
United Brethren houses of worship. The disposition to use the organ, however, could not be
kept in check, and gradually the opposition
became less.

January 1, 1868, there appeared an article in
the *Religious Telescope* from the pen of Prof. H.
Garst, in reply to a remark in a previous editorial
contribution by Bishop Edwards, on the subject
of secret societies. Prof. Garst urged objections
to the restrictive rule of the church Discipline
on this question. While not the first to call in

question the soundness of said rule, he was yet
the first to bring modification views prominently
before the Church. Following the article already
referred to, Bishop Edwards and Prof. Garst each
wrote two additional articles. The merits of the
question were little entered into. Prof. Garst
made the declaration that in social and church
circles Bishop Edwards had used expressions indicating that he was himself receding from the
disciplinary rule. To this the bishop made his
reply, in which he denied the charge most em-
phatically, and the discussion did not reach much
beyond this point. But who will question his
fidelity to the principles of the church of his
choice, or suppose it possible for him to offer a
truce with secrecy? In his last article he said:
" So long as we believe the principle of the rule
right, we will neither be alarmed nor intimidated
by the charge of inconsistency. I say the principle of the rule, because I will not be tenacious as
to the form, if it can be shown that we can more
effectually execute the law and keep the Church
free from connection with secret combinations by
a different wording of the rule. But I more than
suspect that the thing objected to is not the form
of the rule, but the test of membership itself."
Bishops Glossbrenner, Edwards, and Weaver had
previously, in an address to the Church, insisted

on the observance of the rule. Bishop Edwards showed his earnest opposition to secrecy, wherever found, by his presence at the National Anti-Secrecy Convention, which met at Pittsburgh, Pa., in May, 1868. He was elected president of this convention. President Fairchild, of Oberlin College, delivered before the convention an able address. Some of the noblest men of the country came a long distance to take part in the convention. A letter from Hon. Henry Wilson, expressive of his sympathy, along with many other similar letters, was read. The influence of the convention, in reference to the evils of secretism, was large and decided.

None of the territory traveled over by Bishop Edwards during the present term was entirely new to him. The establishment for the second time of the Kentucky Conference, however, was almost of the character of a new work. In 1867, when he visited Kentucky, the country was filled with marauders. The morning on which the conference closed, quite a remarkable scene was presented. A large company of people, many of them the bitterest foes of the United Brethren Church, on account of its antislavery sentiments, were present. Bishop Edwards read the report of the stationing committee, and asked all to join with him in prayer. He prayed for the preachers

that would go out, then for the people to whom
they would go, and then for their enemies, so
many of whom were present. The Lord was especially near by the influence of his Spirit. During the prayer an awful solemnity prevailed. The
ministers present cherished the recollection of
that prayer as among their most solemn and hallowed memories. The visit of the next year was
attended with increased danger; but Bishop Edwards rebuked the spirit that would secure his
safety by carnal weapons. A number of young
ministers came into the Kentucky Conference
during the year, and the outlook for the future
became more encouraging.

While attending one of the sessions of the
Missouri Conference he asked a brother to lead in
prayer. The brother kept on telling the Lord
how good and great he was; and at last the
bishop called out, "Brother, ask the Lord for
something." "Lord, bless our bishop," said the
brother. "Amen, amen; that is better; go on,"
shouted the bishop. It was a good lesson to the
brother, as well as to others. He felt that prayer
should be prayer indeed; that every petition
should be prompted by a present sense of want,
and presented and urged by a living faith. He
regarded formality in prayer as the result of a
lifeless state of religion, and as being a proper

subject of criticism. His own prayers were a marvel of suitability to the occasion, of comprehensive and child-like simplicity of faith.

Until 1873 he was opposed to the wearing of beards; and of course he himself shaved clean. But after the date given, his scruples were so far overcome that he himself wore a full-grown and very becoming beard. His opposition to mustaches, however, was the same from first to last. In a sermon at the Kansas Conference he said, "There is one thing that many of you dare not say, but I will say it: It is unbecoming for ministers to wear mustaches; it is bad enough for them to wear a long beard."

A rare instance of resolution and earnestness is furnished in the fact that Bishop Edwards, after he was fifty years old, took up and carried forward successfully the study of the German language. The occasion of this was his relation to the Ohio German Conference. At one session of this conference he told the brethren that he would read some verses in the German Testament every day during the succeeding year. The next session he could read German to the conference, especially using it in the ordination service. This was highly appreciated by the German brethren. By them he was venerated as a father.

At the Scioto Conference sessions of 1865 and

1866 his sermons were examples of great power and acceptability. At the session of 1866, while speaking of a ministry called and owned of God, and accompanied by the Holy Ghost, his own countenance was almost transfigured, and an indescribable awe fell upon his hearers. Always, in his highest state of spiritual emotion, his lips became compressed, his countenance unusually pale, and his voice tremulous and burdened with emotion, in its very nature unutterable. The effect of his preaching at such times no tongue nor pen can describe. All seemed to feel that the message was direct and fresh from heaven.

An example of the bishop's happy faculty of saving himself from going too far, or extricating himself from any difficulty, is afforded in the following: He was speaking in a town, and his subject led him to speak of the virtues of country people. He spoke of the honest farmer and his good wife, etc., etc. The worst feature was the apparent disparagement of the towns-people. His hearers became nervous, glancing around at each other; and all felt that the bishop was blundering. He at once perceived the situation, though he, perhaps, understood his part from the beginning, and concluded that part of his subject with the sentence, "I know that you are towns-people, but all of your parents came from the country." From that moment the people were contented to let him lead.

At one time, after going home from church after evening services, the minister in charge of the work at that place remarked that, as they had all been at meeting, they would omit family worship. Said the bishop, "It wont take long to pray," and asked the minister to lead in prayer.

The point of time at which we have now arrived seems most favorable for the introduction of something more explicit in reference to Bishop Edwards as a preacher. We have already witnessed the way in which the solemn depth and rare loftiness of his spirit were secured and maintained. Thus we see the ground, unvarying except by constant renewal, of his success as a preacher. A marked solitariness with God, a vital communion with Christ, a thorough dependence upon the Holy Spirit, a mind and heart completely yielding to the authority of the Scriptures, were some of the elements of his power. These were either manifest in the materials that were brought forward or were felt as a reserve-force, giving to his words more than an earthly significance.

For his preparation he mainly depended on the stores with which he kept his mind stocked, and the light and quickening which came from

recent experience and immediate surroundings.
His mind, without being especially urged to it,
gathered thoughts and facts wherever and whenever presented, and assimilated and appropriated
them in a convenient way for public use. His
constant study of the Scriptures and diligent
reading of the purest literature, together with
his genius for moral ideas, gave to his preaching great simplicity, variety, appropriateness and
power. Thus equipped, he never had to find
something to say, or to labor in constructing sermons; he found them, or rather grew them. He
believed in truth as something real, having its
own character, branches, and outlines lying like
a continent above the ocean of uncertainty and
doubt. He believed that truth was accessible
and unchanging, and that it should be treasured
for its own sake. Truth was to be the instrument of his ministry; and this love for it made
his life-work more joyous as well as more effective. But he sympathized with men, and felt that
his mission was to employ truth for their sake.
Thus the workings of his mind, the throbbing of
his heart, his daily life, his occupation within and
without the pulpit, were all severally a part of
one great thought and work. With this general,
or rather special, qualification he combined very
careful, almost agonizing, preparation before at-

tempting to preach at any particular time. He wished, under the influence of the occasion, to gather up his subject and secure a present living connection between every part of it and his mind and heart. He thus preserved the conditions of unity, and of an all-permeating life. So if a sermon is the truth of God incarnated, and brought before the people, in a living man, then Bishop Edwards filled the requirements of a great preacher.

His public prayers before entering upon his sermon are worthy of note in this connection; for without them the impression of his sermon could scarcely at any time have been complete. He not unfrequently removed the greatest obstacles out of the way, and even obtained substantial victory for truth, often the conquest and conversion of souls, in an opening prayer. He was at home in prayer. His prayers were as well suited to the occasion as were his sermons. Sometimes in his prayers he seemed to translate his hearers into the awful hush of God's presence and the solemn scenes of fixed eternity. A marked characteristic of his praying was its scriptural tone and expression. This none who heard him could fail to notice. His familiarity with the inspired language of prophets and apostles gave to his diction peculiar warmth and liveliness. The language of Canaan befitted well his lips. Many of his sermons were based upon some Old Testament event or New Testament incident. His strong imagination, guided and controlled by rare tact, and his happy talent for description, usually gave to such sermons indescribable charm and power.

But he was, also, a thoroughly systematic preacher. He was always clear and logical. His positions were taken advantageously, and his propositions rarely came short of the mark or failed of acceptance. He usually closed his sermons with "remarks," or a practical improvement. In his sermon he had not built up an artificial effect which would collapse or vanish while he made applications to the common circumstances of men. He spoke largely from his own experience to the awakened consciousness of his hearers. He asserted, rather than argued. If his hearers did not believe him, so much the worse for them. His sermons and public addresses, however, were never loose or disjointed. They were, in fact, tough and compact. Hence, every one of his sentences was telling, and every one of his sermons was easily remembered. He did not withhold propositions in the beginning from fear that there would be nothing left to state afterward. He was a remarkable example of a practical preacher. He possessed the uncommon power of investing every-day truth with unwonted charm and effectiveness. It was largely owing to his skill in this respect that he so often moved the slumbering susceptibilities of the heart. Thus it was that he used definite truth for definite results. While he would often use principles for inciting action, he was pre-eminently skillful in presenting motives equally strong from facts drawn either from the present or past.

Bishop Edwards had great skill in the use of illustrations drawn from common life. Illustrations, however, were never used by him for their own sake. His own soul had a profound acquaintance with human life; and few men lived day by day nearer the center where all hearts are one. On his lips the simplest story of human woe or conflict often melted down the most stubborn of assemblies. For the purpose of instruction he often used homely illustrations, but never without the effect of increased clearness or emphasis.

But the feature standing next to the direct logical element that has been referred to was the essentially dramatic power of his preaching. He preached to the eyes and imaginations of men. He pursued so natural and so vivid a course that other minds yielded a necessary submission to his leadership. Every step of his course was so

simple that the connection of his mind with the
minds of his hearers was never disturbed, and
the spell which was at first formed remained
unbroken from first to last. On one occasion,
when speaking in a grove, he seized an umbrella
hanging from a tree, and imitating the smiting
of the Jordan by Elijah he exclaimed, "Where
now is the Lord God of Elijah?" Several persons on the stand instantly rose to their feet and
looked over to see the waters part. At another
time he seized a cane from a man in front of him,
and drawing it back and bringing it forward
toward the man, he illustrated, by the dodging of
the man before him, how Peter must have aimed
to take off the head of the servant of the high-
priest, but only took off his right ear.

He had not only a holy veneration, but an im-
passioned soul, for what he called the "higher
truths" of the Christian religion. He was em-
phatically the preacher to lead those who "hunger
and thirst after righteousness" to a higher Christian life. The pulpit never reproved oftener of
sin, nor gave forth higher and nobler ideas of
Christian life, than when it rang and resounded
with his divinely electrified voice.

Along with these characteristics named, the
highly evangelical character of his preaching
ought to be mentioned. Aside from the particu-

lar subject which he preached, there was made
the impression of his sympathetic acquaintance
with men and of his unhesitating faith as to the
fullness and steadfastness of gospel promises.
His faith unlocked the door of hope to many
hearts, and his words conveyed a heavenly balm
to many souls.

It seems proper here to give the reader the
advantage of the sketches of some of his sermons.
Most preachers have a few favorite sermons, while
others can use one text about as well as another.
Bishop Edwards belonged to neither of these
classes. In his earlier ministry he selected his
themes from a wide field, but in later times the
occasions which he met were less varied. Hence
he felt it to be his privilege, and duty as well, to
use those subjects in 'the use of which God's
blessing had been especially bestowed. The
reason why some preachers can not repeat a
sermon frequently with success is, in some cases,
that it is not built up out of a vital or funda-
mental truth, being a mere conceit, which may
collapse at any time. In other cases, the thought
used is good enough, but the preacher has a nature that is not as susceptible to a great truth as
to countless little accidents which can not a second
time be marshaled to the same theme. Bishop
Edwards had the capacity to take a truth right

out of the mine, which frequent use might polish but could never dim. To this he could bring his mind again and again. He never preached a sermon lazily or indifferently. His thoughts never appeared to be dried specimens. He wrote out many sketches of the same sermon, and generally embraced some new thought or made some new application to suit the case in hand. His favorite sermons were topical and historical. He was especially gifted in the latter. Lessons drawn from sacred history and biography were great features in his preaching. It may be said of all his sermons, however, that they had a practical aim. Of those which he preached throughout the length and breadth of the Church, the sketches of not less than one hundred might easily be given. Of this number a few only will be selected, and given as specimens.

THE HATEFULNESS OF SIN.

"Oh, do not this abominable thing that I hate." (Jer. xliv. 4.)

I. Sin defined. 1. Transgression. 2. To know to do good and do it not. 3. All unrighteous. 4. Inward depravity.

II. Does God hate sin? 1. His word says he does. 2. His treatment of Adam and Eve, and his curse upon the earth. 3. Sodom and Gomorrah. 4. The history of the Jews—all history, in fact, proof of God's hatred. 5. Especially the suffering of Jesus as proof.

III. Why does he hate sin? 1. It is hateful in itself,—

loathsome, detestable. Some things so in nature. 2. Dishonors God. 3. Dishonors man and destroys his happiness. 4. Destroys both soul and body in hell.

Application. 1. Divine solicitude for us. Oh, "do it not." God's regard for us benevolent, earnest, perpetual. 2. If God hates sin, so should we. 3. We should be a standing rebuke to sin, and so should seek to save our fellow-men from its power.

DRY BONES.

"Can these bones live?" (Ezekiel xxxvii. 3.)

I. What implied by the bones. 1. Former life. 2. Present death. 3. A helpless state. 4. May refer to the human family in the fall. 5. To backsliders. 6. To the backslidden condition of the church.

II. The means of recovery. 1. The Lord began by leading the prophet among the bones. Direction to him. "A hard question." Referred back to God. That better than to have given a negative answer. 2. The instructions to the prophet — to prophesy on the house, to pray for the breath of life.

III. The result. 1. A noise and a shaking. 2. A coming together of the bones. 3. Sinews and flesh covered with skin. 4. Filled with life and stood up.

Application. 1. The prophet led about, not for himself, but for others. 2. The agency to be employed — prevailing prayer. Go to God, and let theories go to the wind.

THE CHURCH AND THE WORLD.

Introduction. Personal remarks. All men divided into two great classes. Where the line between them. What fellowship allowed, and what forbidden.

I. Negatively. 1. Necessary commercial relations. (I. Cor. v. 9, 10.; I. John v. 19.) 2. Good citizenship. Help to secure the best rulers. Seek the peace and prosperity of the country where we live. 3. Good neighborship. Borrow and lend, visit and converse. 4. Associate for the express purpose of doing. Illustrate. Young lady of the ball. Visiting the afflicted, etc., etc.

II. Affirmatively. What is forbidden? 1. Marriage between Christians and the ungodly. (I. Cor. vii. 29; Deut. vii. 2, 3.) 2. Secret societies. (Eph. v. 11, 12.) Example and precept of Christ. Nothing hid. In secret said nothing. 3. Partnership in business. 4. Intimate social companionship.

III. Reasons assigned. 1. Inconsistent with the *nature* of the parties,—their aims in life, the Master's service, their final end. 2. Incompatibility of sin and holiness, truth and error. 3. The utter want of agreement in their worship. 4. Union between sin and holiness, God and Satan, angels and devils, heaven and hell. Can not hold fellowship together.

HOLINESS OF GOD'S HOUSE.

"Holiness becometh thy house forever." (Psalms xciii. 5.)

I. Explain the terms. 1. *House* is a place of residence; applied to the temple as the residence of God; also to all houses of worship. 2. The human body. 3. The church. 4. Every believer.

II. *Holiness.* 1. Not external conformity to the letter of law. 2. Not great excitement of feeling. Not happiness. 3. A right state of heart and life. The word is from the root to heal; holiness or completeness hence implies unreserved consecration, deliverance from sin, and a corresponding life of purity, temperance, and truth.

III. The doctrine of the text. 1. Holiness a necessity of God's house. 2. Suitable to it—a type and preparation for heaven.

Remarks. 1. Our house of worship should be well built, —not extravagant, beyond our means, nor inconvenient. 2. Kept clean and neat and orderly. 3. So should the church on earth be as pure as possible in this probationary world: Voluntary sinners should be kept out till converted. Difficulty in dealing with that class. Apostles had their difficulties. So all have. Should aim to be ourselves holy. What is a church for if there is no difference between it and the world? 4. Yet there must be charity and patience. We read of the *weak, sickly children*, babes. The church like a hospital, a school. Bury the dead, dismiss the unruly, but *feed* the babes. Care for the sick. And train all for heaven, the glorious temple above.

"OPEN WIDE THY MOUTH."

I. What implied. 1. Not physical. Not loud nor long prayers. 2. A figure of speech implying large asking—blessings great and many.

II. The necessity existing for such asking. 1. We have great guilt to be forgiven. 2. Great moral pollution from which to be cleansed. 3. We need wisdom to direct. 4. Grace to assist in duty. 5. Strength under the burdens and afflictions of life.

III. The encouragement we have for this. 1. The character of the Promiser. 2. The promises themselves—so plain, varied, and full. 3. The history of God's dealings with his people in all ages. The Israelites at the sea, in the wilderness, at Jordan and Jericho. Individual instances—Elisha, Jesse Wilson, and others. God helps. Oh, help for languishing Zion's sake! Oh, that our ignorance of God and consequent unbelief were removed!

THE GRACE OF RELIGIOUS CARELESSNESS.

"Be careful for nothing." (Phil. iv. 6.)

I. Negatively. 1. Not indifference as to right and wrong. We are to contend earnestly; watch in all things. 2. Not slothful in business. Are to have a calling, and be first in it if possible. 3. Not to be unconcerned as to the prosperity of the church and the salvation of souls. "I could wish that myself were accursed."

II. Affirmatively. 1. Freedom from useless regrets about the past,—misfortunes, afflictions, sins even. 2. Freedom from needless anxieties about the future. Do duty in all things; then trust. 3. Submission to the present. God's will revealed in his providence. J. Brown of Haddington would have had none of the circumstances of his life changed. To the believing Christian all things work together for good.

III. The antidote. Prayer. Thanksgiving. Trials will come. Temptations will beset. Disappointments the lot of the best men. Refer all things to God. For a preacher to go where he is not wanted the hardest trial; but this no exception.

IV. Results. Floweth like a river. Passeth all understanding.

CHRIST'S CUP OF SORROW.

"O my Father, if it be possible, let this cup pass from me." (Matthew xxvi. 39.)

I. Why must he drink this cup? 1. The Scriptures declare it necessary. Isaiah liii. 4, 5, 6; Zechariah xiii. 7; Luke xxiv. 25, 26; Acts xvii. 3. 2. The justice of God requires it. If God is strictly just, he can by no means clear the guilty without a sufficient expiation for guilt to maintain his justice. Romans iii. 25, 26. 3. Necessary to harmonize the divine attributes — justice, mercy, love, truth. Psalms lxxxv. 10. 4. To reveal the character and attributes of God. God manifested. 5. To check rebellion and secure obedience in the universe.

II. What were the ingredients of that cup? 1. Not present outward circumstances. 2. Not the crucifixion. 3. No physical suffering, but mental anguish, arising from, 1.) The concentration of human guilt. Isaiah liii. 7. 2.) The sword of divine justice. 3.) The most dreadful assaults of Satan. Hebrews ii. 18. What sorrow was even like this? Behold him in his agony! and learn to hate and shun sin.

III. Why did he pray to be delivered from the cup? 1. The natural shrinkings of his humanity. 2. As an example to us.

Practical improvement. 1. We learn his method of prayer. 2, We learn the Lord's way of answering prayer. Was his prayer answered? How? Not by removing the cup, but by increasing his strength. 3. We are taught resignation in sorrow—the sinner's hope. 4. Also self-sacrificing benevolence. 5. The astonishing guilt of sinners in regard to the Savior!

FAMILY RELIGION.

I. Its importance. 1. The family the foundation of government—civil and ecclesiastic—and of all true reforms. 'Tis the fountain whence good or evil influences flow to the nations. 2. Impressions made and habits formed in childhood and youth generally remain; the Ethiopian and leopard. Thomas Benton; comparatively few are really converted in old age. Look around and ask when were converted those who are now active in the cause of Christ. Look at those who have resisted holy influences for many years, how almost hopeless is their case. 3. The family is ordained of God to be a kind of school, and a church. The father the minister of God to his househeld, and also a king; and the mother a teacher of good things.

II. What is implied in family religion? 1. Government. This is of the first importance; without it there can be no piety. This is the most difficult part of a parent's duty; depravity, selfishness, ungovernable passion, and the snares of an alluring world all combine to baffle them in this duty. Where patience is wanting, how often is the parent's heart almost crushed with care and vexation in trying to control a wayward and selfish child. 2. Training. The children must be instructed in right knowledge. This a positive duty. Train up a child in the way he should go. Bring them up in the nurture and admonition of the Lord. Like a young tree when crooked, must be straightened—branches must be lopped off, etc. 3. Worship—including the reading of the Scriptures, prayer, and thanksgiving. This implies a suitable frame of mind—a converted, or at least a seeking state, so that it may be done with reverence. Must be done at regular times; morning and evening most suitable. Ought to be early in the evening, before the children become sleepy. 4. Should never be crowded out for worldly cares, nor given up through discouragement. The letter from the apprentice—the man whose children grew up without religion, etc. 5. Some of the benefits. It will help govern the children. It will govern the parents themselves. The man that prays will not be likely to fall into scandalous sins. It will keep before the minds of the household the idea of a God, and their obligations to serve him. It will have a good influence even on others.

Application. We will, etc. 1. This resolution made considerately after long trial. 2. Without the surroundings of a revival. 3. Without waiting for others. 4. A fixed determination to serve God in all he dictates—buying, selling, moving, farming, associations—at home, abroad, everywhere and in everything. Salaries. God help.

CHARACTER OF JONAH.

I. Brief sketch of his life; commanded to go to Nineveh; flees to Tarsus; overtaken and miraculously cast upon the land; retraces his steps and faithfully delivers his message. The people repent; he is offended; and God expostulates.

II. His character. 1. A prophet, nearly nine hundred years before Christ—the first whose writings are recorded. 2. He was honest; confessed the truth even when it was against him. 3. Was mighty in prayer when overwhelmed in distress. He had evidently some fear of God before his eyes. 4. But his good qualities were very much neutralized by his defects—natural and moral. He was very self-willed, and hence dissatisfied with his appointment to Nineveh, a hard distant field; and go he would not. Fretful and peevish, faithless and desponding, even unto death.

Practical improvement. 1. God calls and sends his own ministers, even yet, those who hear his voice and understand his will. 2. They must preach according to instruction. 3. How difficult to flee from duty. Our sins will surely find us out. 4. They must preach against the wickedness of the people. This necessary to arouse. A wise minister will know when to present the law, and when the gospel. 5. Learn the need of entire abandonment to the work of saving souls. God help.

ELIJAH THE TISHBITE.

The great prophet who prophesied about nine hundred years before Christ. One of the best and greatest men that ever lived. His traits of character. But first notice the manner of his appearance, sudden, unannounced, and without one word of his previous history. The times in which he lived—of Ahab and Jezebel abominably corrupt and idola-, trous. 1. His life was a life of poverty. No property, no home, no salary, and yet his wants were in some way supplied. He worked for God, and he fed him—once by ravens, once by a poor widow, and once by an angel. 2. His was a persecuted life. The king and his wicked subjects called him the troubler of Israel. Then the queen was sworn to destroy him. 3. A life unreservedly consecrated to God. See his boldness in opposing sin, his faithfulness in delivering God's message, and his singleness of purpose in opposing the prevailing idolatry. A man of one idea; this *one thing.* 4. He was a man of prayer. He shut heaven by prayer, brought rain, raised the dead to life, and brought fire to consume the sacrifice. 5. His firmness in the right though vastly in the minority; a regular old fogy had he lived in our age; he would not have sanctioned any of the new improvements of the modern worship. He was worth a score of our modern time-serving preachers. 6. His was a successful ministry. The prophets of Baal were destroyed. The people were emancipated from their fears, and were ready to acknowledge the true God, and a host of young prophets were raised up. 7. His end was glorious. A sufficient reward for his poverty and perseverance.

ABRAHAM'S FAITH.

"He staggered not at the promise of God through unbelief; but was strong in faith, giving glory to God." (Rom. iv. 20.)

I. Show its strength. 1. Notice the different exercises of his faith. He was first called at the age of seventy-five,—when he was an old man,—and Isaac was promised; then thirty or more years later, when he was commanded to sacrifice him. 2. He firmly believed all that God said to him. 3. He patiently waited through long years of trial for the fulfillment of the promise. 4. He had an unwavering trust, which led him to overlook all natural impossibilities, and even to crucify his noblest affections, in order to obey God. 5. It resulted in complete and unquestioning obedience. 6. He did not stagger under the heaviest duty.

II. Show how strong faith glorifies God. 1. It honors him to implicitly credit his word. 2. It secures our personal salvation, which glorifies him. 3. Our example influences others to give him glory.

Remarks, 1. What more dishonoring to God than unbelief or weak faith? 2. Unbelief one cause of our lukewarmness. 3. The reason we have so few direct and manifest answers to prayer. 4. How can we obtain such faith? By exercising what we have; by self-denial; by implicit obedience in all things; walking in the steps of Abraham's faith.

The above sketches convey but a feeble idea of Bishop Edwards' power in preaching. But any one who will examine carefully these outlines will be convinced that he did not rely on cheap experiences for effect. The wonder is that he could pour his soul into the old-time principles of Christianity so as to give to them the freshness and power of new discourses. Then the amount of solid material which he succeeded in unifying, vitalizing, and compressing into a single discourse would have been baffling to most minds. In an eminent degree he seized truth in its elementary forms, and formed his particular combinations with astonishing power and freshness.

17

CHAPTER XI.

URING the preceding quadrennial term, the Church had prospered in its various interests. The increase of membership was over eighteen thousand, the entire membership being one hundred and eight thousand one hundred and thirty-two. The lingering influences of the civil war and the speculating tendencies of the times were prominent obstacles in the way of the greatest and most satisfactory results. The energies and instrumentalities of the Church, however, were persistently used in enlarging and building up the different departments of church-work. The Church seemed to be in a transition stage, between the wide evangelistic influences prevailing before the war and a more settled condition of home cultivation and careful pastoral methods. In this state of things the fifteenth General Conference met at Lebanon, Pennsylvania, May 20, 1869. Thirty - eight annual conferences were entitled to representation. Bishops Glossbrenner, Edwards, Markwood, Weaver, and Shuck were all present. Bishop Markwood, however, was in extremely poor health. At the hour of 2:00 P. M., immediately on the assembling of the conference, Bishop Edwards preached the quadrennial sermon, from Psalms cxxxiii. 1. The sermon was intended to be preparatory to the sacred and grave duties of the conference, and was listened to with deep interest.

The questions before this conference were more exciting than those of any previous General Conference. Bishop Edwards, by a special motion, was called upon to close the discussion on the secrecy question, after the debate had been running nearly two days and a half.

He said, " It has been clearly proved on the floor that these secret temperance orders are all children of Masonry. They are Mason - born. Masons form the constitutions of Odd-fellows and of Good Templars. I do not know anything about the Rechabites and the Cadets; but I see the foot-prints and the finger-marks of Masonry in all the constitutions of these secret orders. Did you ever carefully look at the Constitution of the Good Templars with this idea in your

minds? Mark the similarity in names. They
have their lodges, grand lodges, charters, degrees,
titles,—such as Grand Worthy Chief,—initiation,
grips, signs, obligations, pass-words, inside and
outside guards, gavel, anteroom, balls — black
and white — for voting. If the fashion of the
Good Templars suits us, hence, also, the fashions
of Masons. Do you see the parallel? And Masons
themselves, understanding these things, laugh in
their sleeves when they see good, true, innocent,
and secrecy-hating United Brethren advocating
the reception of their children, while they turn
the old parents out. Why, my friends, the thing
is preposterous, and they would all laugh at us if
we would undertake it."

This is not the place to characterize this discussion, nor to speak of its results upon the
Church. The above extract, however, shows
very clearly the relation of Bishop Edwards to it.
This much, at least, we all need in order to understand the story of his life. Suffice it to say, that
the large majority of the conference, by the tra-
ditional spirit of the Church and by personal
convictions, were earnestly opposed to any change
in the rule, further than seemed to be required to
make it more easy of execution and more efficient.

The subject of lay delegation received considerable attention; but on the ground that there was no very general demand for it, on the part of the laity, the proposition in its favor was defeated, only thirty-two delegates voting for it. Bishop Edwards was in the chair and of course did not vote.

His position in reference to the use of instrumental music in public worship, and his advocacy of the prohibitory clause adopted in 1865, are already understood. While there was no considerable change throughout the Church as to the merits of the subject, it was nevertheless felt, especially in some congregations, that the prohibitory action referred to was carrying legislation a little too far. Four years had passed; and while the subject was again under consideration Bishop Edwards said, "I think I have been misunderstood. I am not so thorough a convert to instrumental music as these brethren have represented me. I hate it as much as ever, and think with Luther, that so far as worship is concerned, it is still of the devil, in one sense at least. I have not changed from that. But I saw that we could not keep it out by this legislation; I saw the spirit of this General Conference; and I thought it one of those things upon which we could compromise." So he moved an advisory clause against the introduction of choirs and instrumental music, saying as he did so, "We shall thus have a good opportunity to try the effect of advisory law, which has been so applauded here; and I do not know a better subject on which to try it than this." So the amendment of Bishop Edwards providing for an advisory clause prevailed. It was generally conceded, however, that instruments and choir-singing in churches tend to destroy spirituality.

One of the most important acts of this session of General Conference was that which led to the founding of Union Biblical Seminary. The time was past for very much difference of sentiment or opposition in reference to the subject of special education for the ministry.

Another step of much importance was the establishment of a mission in Germany. All these measures received the hearty concurrence and advocacy of Bishop Edwards.

From this time on the General Conference did not attempt to name a uniform salary for ministers. As early as 1857, provision was made for an increase above the salary named in cases in which it was necessary.

The new conferences formed were the Osage and East German. The Michigan was given the name of the North Ohio Conference, and the North Michigan was to be called the Michigan

Conference. The Kentucky was included for the time with the Indiana Conference. During the succeeding quadrennial term the Dakota, Southern Illinois, and Colorado mission - conferences were organized.

Bishops Glossbrenner, Edwards, and Weaver were re-elected, and in the place of Bishop Markwood, who was prostrated by affliction, J. Dickson, of Pennsylvania Conference, was elected. The four bishops were each in turn to visit the Pacific conferences; and they were each to receive, as salary, one thousand dollars.

Bishop Edwards was given the East Mississippi District, embracing the St. Joseph, Upper Wabash, Lower Wabash, Central Illinois, Illinois, Indiana, Michigan; and White River conferences.

After Bishop Glossbrenner had made some remarks in connection with the closing of the session, Bishop Edwards spoke as follows: "I am glad of the fellowship I have enjoyed here, and in previous General Conferences. Whatever I am I owe to this Church. I was converted in this Church, and have been promoted from time to time, often against my protest, notwithstanding my many defects. I am glad to approve the statement of Brother Glossbrenner as to the peace and fellowship that have always existed

among the superintendents. I hope the spirit of
forbearance and brotherly love will be more and
more cultivated among us. Many of us have
much to learn in this respect. We ought to love
one another though we differ in opinion. The
spirit of dissension in conference or in church
will soon prove ruinous."

Bishop Edwards continued to reside at West
Sonora until November following the General
Conference, when he removed to Lexington, Illinois, where he occupied the residence nearly completed for the bishop of the East Mississippi
District. The church and citizens of Lexington
considered themselves fortunate in having the
bishop and his family reside in their midst.

Immediately after the General Conference,
Bishop Edwards went to Chicago to attend the
anniversary of the Antisecrecy Convention, of
which he was president. His opening address
was an excellent production, and received marked
attention. In respect to the antisecrecy conflict
he said, "All who are present to engage in this
struggle are heroes. The time for cowards has
not yet arrived; but when a sentiment sufficiently
strong shall be created against secret societies
there will be enough of that class of men to fall
into line."

These were bold words, yet no one more than

LIFE OF BISHOP EDWARDS. 265

he saw the necessity of genuine prudence. In an interval in the convention he remarked to a minister of the United Brethren Church that great prudence was necessary to the success of the antisecrecy reform, observing that even the precious doctrine of holiness had much to fear from the imprudence of its advocates.

No part of the East Mississippi District was entirely new to Bishop Edwards, and at the different conference sessions nothing very unusual took place. He attended all of the conference sessions of his district during the entire term. His characteristic firmness as an administrator of law was as manifest as it had been during the former terms. In the White River Conference there was a small faction that sought to nullify the secrecy law; and failing to do that, they worked what injury they could, and either withdrew or were expelled. The faintest marks of schism or defection have appeared at different times in several conferences, or perhaps better, in the territory of several conferences; but to the credit of the moderation, piety, and good sense of the United Brethren Church, under the good providence of God, none of the storms and conflicts that have risen in the course of over one hundred years have been permitted to produce schism or permanent alienation. One of the reasons may be that, unlike many. churches, the United Brethren Church was not founded as the result of schism.

Bishop Edwards' report of the conferences of 1869 contains the following: "I am glad to be able to say that though we were threatened with difficulties in some of the conferences we have had general peace and evident tokens of God's presence. In one conference a few were expelled for insubordination, and some others of the same stripe left us, and in one other conference some others breathing a like spirit withdrew. We look for peace and prosperity the coming year. The Discipline will be carried out, we hope, with meekness and love toward such as have been led astray. Our greatest want now is a new baptism from heaven. When the Church is lukewarm all forms of error spring up, and discontent and a spirit of murmuring prevail. While men sleep the enemy sows tares. But it is a consoling reflection that the great Head of the church never sleeps."

In a letter written about four months after his moving to Lexington he said, "The people here are quite clever, and they respect the Church and the ministry more than have the people in any place where I have lived before. The cause of religion is flourishing all around us. Just now we are having a blessed revival here. We have a strong society at this place. I am still going about as heretofore. To-night I am to preach at seven and leave at half past eight to go west to another dedication. Next week I am to be at home one day, and then away for two weeks. God has been very good to me all through life, and my health is of late years better than ever before. In the general way my peace flows like a river. I have the very best compassionate Savior—forgiving, loving, and helping in every time of need. I have some serious complaints against myself, such as mental laziness, and delinquencies arising therefrom. Yet I have some aspirations after better things."

In the spring of 1871 he went to the Pacific coast to attend the California, Oregon, and Cascade conferences, being absent about three months. Going in company with him were Revs. J. H. Watson, J. F. Fields, and E. De Witt—these ministers being under appointment as missionaries to the coast. On reaching Sacramento, the party were unexpectedly met by friends. Like Jacob of old, whose "spirit revived when he saw the wagons," they were made glad when they saw three wagons and seven as earnest and large-hearted brethren and sisters as ever greeted a dusty and weary set of travelers. While on this

trip, Bishop Edwards furnished six very interesting articles to the *Religious Telescope*. In one of
these articles, after describing the advantage of
the country, he said, "Were there not another
side to this picture the country would be a para-
dise. But like every other spot on this mundane
sphere, it has its dark side. It is not the plan of
Providence to give us our heaven here. Everywhere there are evils enough to cause us to look
for a better country. In this world the lights and
shades, the good and the evil, are far more evenly
balanced than people are disposed to believe.
Happy is he who expects no perfect clime here,
but early makes sure his claim in the beautiful
land beyond the river."

During his stay on the Pacific coast he entered earnestly into the investigation of the work
there, sought to remove the causes that impeded
progress, and labored to impart an earnest and
healthful impulse to all the laborers in these distant conferences. Five days were occupied in
reaching Sacramento, and the entire cost, at
clergymen's rates, was less than one hundred dollars. Eighteen years before, when Rev. T. J.
Connor, under appointment as missionary to Oregon, went with teams, he was six months and
eighteen days in reaching the settlements on the
Willamette River, Oregon. It was only in 1869

that the great trans-continental railway was completed.

While in Portland, Oregon, Bishop Edwards called upon Dr. Dillon of the *Pacific Christian Advocate*. Having been invited to share his hospitality, and having had a pleasant interview with him, he was about to leave; but, said he, "I think we should have worship together before we part." A Bible was handed, and opening it he remarked, "I will read that precious portion of God's Holy Word,—the Christian's life-insurance policy,—the ninety-first psalm." After returning he received a copy of Dr. Dillon's paper, in which his visit was noticed and the beautiful title given the psalm referred to. This psalm was a great favorite of the bishop's, and when read by him in the families of those whose hospitality he shared it became very significant.

On his way back he stopped to look into the work a little in Colorado, and then came on in time to meet the missionary Board at Canton, Ohio, August 6.

In August, 1872, he, by the concurrence of the Board of Missions, organized the Southern Illinois Conference. Thus we see him incessantly engaged in the interest of the Church—like his Lord and Master, going about, here and there, doing good. His was indeed a busy life.

In June, 1872, he delivered an address before the students and friends of Union Biblical Seminary, in connection with the closing exercises of this institution of sacred learning. His feelings prior to the delivery of this address are indicated in a private letter written a few weeks beforehand. "I am looked to," said he, "for an address before the school of the prophets, June 5. Well, if the Lord is not with me it will be a failure, I know. But I know that he will be with me if only I am with him. Oh! I hope my heart may be in such a frame that he can bless me without doing me injury. He will help me if he can, I am sure. But how treacherous is this heart of mine; how selfish and how prone to deceive even itself. 'He that trusteth in his own heart is a fool.' Solomon never uttered a more truthful saying. God can save to the uttermost, and is able to make all grace abound toward me through Jesus my Lord."

The address when delivered proved to be most happy. He was favored with a large and appreciative audience. The eulogies upon the sentiments and points of excellence of the address were hearty and general.

Some extracts from letters written by the bishop, and other examples of his familiar and habitual expressions, will be introduced here. Immediately on being introduced to persons he would often inquire as to the state of their souls. Rarely would he close a letter without inquiring as to the spiritual progress of his correspondent. He watched, also, and familiarly disclosed, the actings and progress of his own soul. On meeting at one time with Scioto Conference he said, "Brethren, I have either backslidden or God has revealed a new stratum of my depravity."

The following from a letter written in 1858 is characteristic and very significant:

"I have just enough trial to convince me that my heart is not to be trusted; that it needs just as much the atoning blood now to keep pure as it did in the first place to save from sin. Oh, what a fathomless deep is the human heart! How endless and diversified its forms of depravity! How many lives the old man of Sin seems to possess! He may be nailed to the cross and buried, and yet he revives again in some other form. I have been so often deceived by his manners that I fear to say that he is dead—that I am crucified with Christ. I can with comparative ease profess entire consecration to Christ, because I feel that to be true; but to say that my depraved nature is all destroyed, is quite another thing. Oh, my weakness and infirmities! Lord, help me, and subdue my nature entirely to thyself."

The following is an extract from a letter written in 1859 to a sister in the church, whose way was often overcast with clouds:

"Your letter indicated less faith and less victory than you have before expressed. Perhaps you wrote at a time of peculiar trial. This trial of faith is more precious than gold. My dear sister, do not forget that it is through much tribulation that we must enter into the kingdom. We naturally love ease and prosperity. But these will not crucify the old man; they only prolong his life. In the beginning of this year I was enabled to reconsecrate myself to God's work. Since then I have had more victory and faith, more power in preaching, more fruit of my labor, and better health; can preach every day for a month at a time without weariness."

In a letter written in 1861 he said,—

"I am trying to live an entirely consecrated life. Sometimes I feel a peculiar pleasure in trusting all things, both temporal and spiritual, in the hands of our heavenly Father. The future sometimes looks dark; but when I reflect how God has cared for us for the past two-score years, I find no difficulty in trusting that the same Providence will care for us for all time to come, even in old age, if such a lot should be ours."

From a letter written in 1862, note the following:

"It strikes me that if more time were spent in communion with the ever-present Spirit, more special prayers would be put into our mouths. American Christianity, like everything else American, drives us into society and keeps us there, in a hurry and a bustle all the time. All must go by steam and lightning. Thus we have little time or inclination for silent, closet communication with heaven. Your resolution to gain some important victories during a specific time reminds me of my feelings many years ago, when placed on Circleville Station. The battle was hot, but the victory was gained. I sometimes think that I need to go through anotber such a fight, in order to get a new edge. Even an ax can not be sharpened without being put on the grindstone. I suppose it takes a hotter fire to purify some than others. Guess I am one of the number that need to be often melted over. Oh, that the Master's image could be seen in my life and spirit."

On his trip to the Pacific coast he met a number of old acquaintances, among them Mrs. Olivia Dunning, who had been for a long time widely known in Ohio as a most devoted Christian, and a frequent correspondent for the different church-periodicals. In the following extract from a letter from Oregon the reference is to her:

"Good old Olivia is still clear gold, is doing well everyway, and is exerting a wholesome influence. Her children, too, are doing quite well, and are worthy citizens and Christians. Tell Rev. B. W. I congratulate him on his present position on the secrecy question,—that is, if I understand it, —'no society but the church for Christians.' We must come to that yet to be consistent. Let us lift the church to where it belongs, as containing all the reformatory elements necessary to save the world."

The destructive fire in Chicago, Sunday, October 8, 1871, the largest of modern times, was indeed a notable event. A few days after it occurred Bishop Edwards wrote,—

"It is enough to make one shudder to think of such appalling calamities. It does seem that the vials of wrath are being poured out. I am looking for greater calamities upon the nations. The fire in Chicago and elsewhere in the north-
14

west have not been exaggerated. I was to some extent a witness of them. I am to give a short lecture to-night in our church on the moral lessons to be learned from them. For myself, I have had no losses worth the naming. No serious afflictions of any kind have ever been my lot. God forgive me wherein I may have murmured in the past. I have thought it a wonder of mercy that I have not been cast away long ere this. I shall be at home two weeks; then away three; and so on nearly all winter, at dedication and protracted meetings. I have now nine dedications promised, and more to come."

In a letter to a friend, dated January 5, 1872, he wrote,—

"We have not sold at Sonoro, and possibly may go back there for a home in 1872, should the Lord permit us to live so long. I can not see an inch beyond General Conference. Just the way it always is. I have commenced the Bible again by course. Hope and expect to find new treasures in it."

In another of his letters, dated March 11, 1872, he said,—

"We have one Mason in our church here, and he is giving us no little trouble. He has had a legal notice to leave the lodge within six months; but the majority of the church sympathize with him. Their plan is to get something against the preacher and get rid of him before the six month's period ends. But they will be disappointed, I guess; for the pastor is a good man and a good preacher, and attends to all his duties. This country, after all, don't seem to be like home. We seem to be off somewhere on a visit, or preaching tour. My books are accumulating on my hands. I have not much company to interrupt me, so that my situation for study would be good if I only could be at home more, and had a better heart so that I could improve everything for God. I am somewhat stirred up to the importance of a nearer access to God for my own sake and for others."

A few letters or extracts indicating the deep individual interest he took in others can not, perhaps, be given in any place better than here. Official duties, numerous and pressing as they were, did not wholly absorb him. His personal sympathies were pure and tender. Note the following in a letter, January 14, 1875, to a little boy:

"FREDDIE COWEL: My dear boy. I guess you think that Grandpa Edwards has forgotten his promise; it has been so long since he promised to send the picture of his grandchild, Daisy Bell. Well, she brought it to my room a long time ago, and I put it in my drawer; but I forgot it till now. So here it goes, for if I don't send it now it will be a long time before I can send it, as I shall be away from home most all winter. Tell Eva I had forgotten my promise to send my picture and Mrs. E.'s to her till I looked on my book to-night. But as I have none of mine I will send that of Mrs. E.'s, and send mine some other time.

"Now, Freddie, I suppose you are growing as fast as you can, and when I come out there again I shall not know you. But I shall often think of you as mother's sweet little pet. Daisy is the girl you sent that beautiful trade-dollar to. She is eight years old, goes to school, and is learning fast. Give my love to your pa and ma, Grandpa Hubbard, and Eva. May the Lord bless you and make you a useful man."

The following is a letter written November 9, 1866, to Charlie Jones, at Delaware, Ohio.

"MY DEAR NEPHEW: While writing letters to others, the thought struck me that it would not be amiss to write a few lines to you. I know from experience and long observation that boys of your age need all the encouragement possible to direct them in the right way. Temptations and snares are continually set before the young, by our grand enemy and the world, to lead them astray. But your advantages have been far greater than those of many others. God has blessed you with pious parents, who have watched over you, and prayed for you from your earliest years, You have had school and church privileges to make you one of the best scholars and Christians, if they are properly improved by you. But privileges will not make men of us, unless we are resolved, by God's help, to make men of ourselves. We may not become *great*, but we may become as *good*, as *true*, and as faithful to the trust committed to us as anybody else can be. And true goodness is of far more importance than greatness. Resolve, then, always to be *truthful and honest* in all your dealings; cultivate industrious habits, and be sure and *do*, or learn something useful every day, and you will grow up a comfort to your parents and a blessing to the world. But never forget to trust in the Lord in all things, and he will help you through life, safely and happily. I hope to hear a good account of you in time to come. May the Lord be with you and bless you."

In 1853 he wrote a letter to the members of a literary society in Mt. Pleasant College, on the occasion of their electing him an honorary member of the society, in which he said,—

"Truth is older than the creation, firmer than the universe, and as enduring as eternity. You can afford to stand with the few, or even alone, if called thereto. But alone you will not stand; for God will be with you. Take, then, my young brethren, the advice of an obscure and unseen friend, and cultivate your minds and your hearts for God— and for God only. Consecrate your natural and acquired abilities wholly to him. There is work for each and for all of you. Men who can stand erect in this stooping and crouching world are now needed in all the professions and vocations of life as at no other time. May the richest of Heaven's blessings rest upon you, your college, and your society."

In June, 1872, Bishop Edwards received the honorary degree of Doctor of Divinity from Westfield College. This honor was entirely unexpected on his part. There is no reason to believe that he was unduly elated by it; yet he received it gracefully. If a wide acquaintance with general literature, solid attainments in divinity, and eminent service in morals and religion are a proper basis for the degree of Doctor of Divinity, then was the degree in this place fittingly bestowed.

Another General Conference session was approaching, and with it the work of Bishop Edwards in the West would terminate. He counted himself a western man more than in the mere respect of locality. His spirit, manners, aptitudes, and acquaintances were decidedly western.

It is a matter of surprise when we come to notice what a large part of his time was given to substantially the same field. Through a period of twenty-four years, he was the appointed superintendent of White River Conference twenty years, missing but one session in that time, and that by way of exchanging. For fifteen years together he was present at the annual sessions. He was the regular bishop over Miami Conference for sixteen years, consecutively. The fourth year, however, he was absent through an exchange that had been agreed upon; but this absence was offset by his once having attended this conference previous to his regular appointment over it. He was also regularly in charge, for sixteen years, altogether, of Illinois Conference, missing, however, one session from sickness. He was a member of Scioto Conference more than forty years. He was also bishop of this his own conference, in all, twelve years. One session he missed by exchanging and another from sickness. From the old conferences of the West as a center, through his relation to the missionary Board, and especially through his office as superintendent, the influence of Bishop Edwards extended, with more or less power, to all the West. He felt that great results ought to be accomplished; and to secure these he left nothing untried. He was everywhere present by the inspiration which he exercised, and by his pushing, tireless will. And the power of his · presence thus diffused was everywhere awakening, molding, and always riveting men to their posts and tasks. His attention to details, his requirement of system and order, his exacting expectations and demands, and, withal, the exacting and coercing model which he furnished in himself, made him, in an important sense, the father of the Church in the West.

CHAPTER XII.

S we approach the last General Conference attended by Bishop Edwards, and
his last term of service, we naturally feel
inclined to dwell upon all of his expressions
and actions. The sixteenth General Conference met May 15, 1873, at Dayton, Ohio.
The increase in membership in the Church the
preceding four years was over seventeen thousand, the entire membership at the end of the
term being over one hundred and twenty-five
thousand. The bishop's report referred to differences of opinion among the ministers and members of the Church upon essentially important
principles, but expressed great gratification with
the Christian spirit that in the main had characterized the interchange of thought on vexed
questions.

During the session it was proposed to submit a

proposition to the Church to so change the Constitution as to admit laymen to membership in the General Conference. The measure prevailed, with but twelve dissenting votes. Bishop Edwards voted for it. Some vexing details, however, in reference to the measure arising, and some of the members not caring to make much new law while existing laws were not enforced, it occurred that a majority of those who had voted in the affirmative were very willing, before the session closed, to allow the proposition to fail for the time. It was also feared, on a final review of the question, that if an interpretation of the Constitution of the Church were favored which would admit of the adoption of this proposed change, that other changes not to be desired might follow. It was very evident that some of the opponents, as well as some of the friends, of lay delegation, owed their zeal to their attitude toward another question. Bishop Edwards also announced himself willing to vote for something looking toward pro-rata representation in the General Conference. But that feature was destined to wait for a time.

On the vote to indorse the law of 1869, on secret societies, there were but twenty-two negatives. The struggle of the session, however, turned on an amendment, offered by Bishop Edwards, to the effect that for the expulsion of members against special law—such as the law on secret societies—no vote of the local society should be necessary. The bishop supported his amendment with the following speech:

"There are some great evils that seem not to be easily reached by the ordinary laws of church-government. It has been the custom, not only among nations, but with churches, to have special laws for special evils, just as in regard to slavery—our great organized system of slavery. As a church, we had our general rules; and we had against that great evil special legislation from the time when I came into the Church until slavery was gone. I consider that organized secrecy is another great evil, which has disturbed the churches of America very much as slavery did in its day. It is so insidious, and so powerful and mean, that common legislation will not meet the case. Here we have special legislation against it, and have had ever since I have been in the Church. Another word: I, too, am against one-man power. There is some little power in Masonry and among Odd-fellows. You get one or two of them into a class, and they will rule the whole society. I have seen this during the last four years. I want the one hundred and seven men here present, representing this Church, to say by their authority that men who can not be reclaimed from these wicked associations shall go out to the world where they belong. This question might as well be faced first as last; for the whole issue is brought before us in this amendment. The underlying idea is this: Shall this General Conference open the door for every class to say whether they will tolerate Masonry in its multifarious forms; or shall we be a unit, and bear our testimony against this hydra-headed evil? By your vote on this amendment you will decide whether the United Brethren Church shall tolerate secrecy or not. We must meet the question; and we shall never have peace until secrecy is conquered within our fold, or until it conquers us. The conflict is upon us, and for one I am willing to face it. And while other churches are being divided and torn asunder,—some taking one side and some another,—we, if we live up to our early principles and training, shall be free from all dissensions of that kind. I understand that if the original paper is passed without amendment, it will most surely neutralize and nullify the law that is now in the Discipline. Without desiring to impugn men's motives, it looks as if that were the design. I can easily understand, Mr. President, how men exercising the authority over a congregation, and desiring to set aside the Dis-

cipline, and being unwilling to bear the responsibility of doing so, would throw the responsibility
on the class."

The amendment was sustained by a vote of
seventy against thirty-one. Whatever any one
may think of the policy of the amendment, or of
the merits of the question to which it belonged,
the speech by which it was supported, it must be
confessed, was strong, and prompted by a deep
knowledge of the question. and tendencies involved, and indicative of the highest form of
moral courage and Christian fidelity.

Bishop Edwards had been one of the vice-
presidents of the missionary society from its organization, in 1853, and had been present at every
regular session except the first. The General
Conference now elected him president of the
Board. This was a high compliment, especially
when taken in connection with the fact that
when elected to the office of bishop, at this session, he received a higher number of votes than
any one else. These two facts when taken together clearly indicate how deep was his hold
upon the affections and confidence of the Church.

At this session of General Conference the Nebraska Conference was formed, and the Cascade
was changed to Walla Walla, and the Canada to
the Ontario Conference. The conference pro-

vided also for the union of the Iowa and North Iowa conferences.

The bishops of the preceding term were all re-elected. Bishop Edwards was sent to the East, having for his district the Erie, Muskingum, Tennessee, Alleghany, Virginia, Pennsylvania, East Pennsylvania, East German, and Parkersburg conferences. His feelings in reference to his future work are indicated in the remarks which he made at the close of the General Conference, some of which are as follows: "I was expecting to be sent farther west, and I was ready to go. I am essentially a western man. The second time I was born was in the West. Ohio was then 'west.' I have served the General Conference twenty - eight years—much longer than I could have had reason to expect. I confess that in all this time I have not felt the weight of an appointment as I feel this one. I know that some of the delegates consider me a little rigid; but I tell you I intend to be a right clever, good man. If anything bad comes into my heart I do not intend to keep it there. I intend to live so that I can look up to heaven and say, 'I did the best I could.' In some things, though, I think my crossness has been overestimated, and I think that perhaps I am not as bad as I used to be. But I intend to oppose sin and the devil everywhere;

and I want you to understand that, brethren. I have felt, somehow, during this General Conference, that we are not as humble and prayerful as we ought to be. I pray God that his baptism may come down upon us, and make us what we ought to be."

In August, 1873, he went east to make his home in Baltimore, Maryland. He was to occupy the residence provided for the bishop of the East District. He had spent a little time in visiting and attending to some financial matters, disposing of his home in Sonora, and so forth.

His first work on his district was in the Pennsylvania Conference—the oldest conference in the Church. Ten camp-meetings were appointed for the summer of 1873. Bishop Edwards attended the Orrstown Camp-meeting, August 21. His feelings were greatly moved in approaching his new duties; and on the other side his friends were anxious as to the impression which he would make, while others were simply curious. An appointment was made for him to preach. About ten minutes before the hour arrived he was seen on his knees in the woods in secret prayer. He took for his text "Draw nigh unto God," etc. For forty minutes he swayed the great audience as the forest is swayed by the mighty tempest. A well-known minister who was assisting in the meeting said of the sermon: "The conclusion of this sermon was the most effective I ever witnessed. I had read how men like Whitefield and Finney moved audiences, but here I witnessed it." On the lips of all were the words, "What a man to preach the gospel Bishop Edwards is!" During the meeting he preached four regular sermons. On one occasion, after the dismissal of the congregation, the people lingered in the altar singing and rejoicing. The preachers in the stand were also happy, and shaking hands. The bishop sat looking on with beaming countenance. Suddenly he rose to his feet, exclaiming, "I must get away from here. If I stay any longer I must jump and praise God, and if I do that I am as awkward as a bear." In an account of these meetings furnished by the bishop to the *Telescope* he said: "'The Lord has triumphed gloriously; the horse and his rider has he thrown into the sea.' Every day was a triumph, and the Holy Spirit was present in converting and sanctifying power. We left this consecrated and hallowed spot with our souls filled with praise."

The Erie and Muskingum conferences, holding their sessions in September, particularly the former, were occasions of great spiritual interest and benefit.

In November he held the Tennessee Conference, and preached four times in that mission-field.

In the winter and spring of 1874 he attended, in their order, the Alleghany, Virginia, Pennsylvania, East German, East Pennsylvania, and Parkersburg conferences.

Few knew the struggles of mind with which the bishop set out for these conferences; none, perhaps, the extreme depths of that anguish. If it cost him so much to come up to an ordinary appointment for preaching and other occasions of increased importance, it is not strange that his whole moral nature trembled and cried out under the present burden. He always felt that a fault lay at his door if he did not come up to any duty with the earnest of victory already dilating his own soul. It is very easy to assign ordinary reasons for his mental agitation, but only the superficial would ever think of them. The circumstances were, indeed, peculiar. The bishop knew that one reason why he was sent east was that he might correct, if possible, the very general disregard of the restrictive rule on secret societies that prevailed in some of the conferences. He knew also that his supposed strenuousness had biased many minds against him. His first would be the Alleghany. With, perhaps, a single exception, dissent from the general view of the Church on the secrecy question was understood to be more persistent in this conference than in any other. But Bishop Edwards did not go to the East trembling for his personal success or fearing his ability to maintain the principles of the Church. He did not have the feeling that some may have that the secrecy rule was intended merely to rid the Church of a class of members not in harmony with the Discipline. This was one of its objects, it is true, but with him it meant more. Down deep in his soul, bound up with a love for the worst of sinners, was the conviction that the purity, spirituality, and power of the Church depended on a wide belt between the Church and the world. In his mind the secrecy rule was to save, and not to destroy; and thus he ever represented and employed it. Can he go to the East, not with a mere rule, but with such a conviction back of the rule and such a life and power in his soul as shall enable him with the co-operation of those to whom he went, to create such a fund of motive or delicacy of life in the hearts of others, as shall make the rule a savor of life unto life? If we do not enter into these thoughts, we may yet see that many difficulties were to be overcome, and hence much grace was needed. If his had been an ordinary mind, or if he had put forth an ordinary effort, he would

hardly have been able to lead his audience into
the unmixed marrow and glory of gospel truth,
and an exulting Christian experience. It is most
gratifying to know that Bishop Edwards obtained the inner assurance which he sought, and
that his work in the East may be set down as
a great and increasing good. His reception in the
Alleghany Conference was not simply compli-
mentary, but enthusiastic. True, the conference
did not put their arms around him,— various
reasons might have prevented that,—but they
honored him very respectfully as their bishop,
and as Doctor of Divinity, as indicated by the following in the published minutes: "The doctor is
one of the senior bishops of the Church, and
growing quite venerable in appearance. He is an
excellent presiding officer. Bishop Edwards made
many strong friends, in and out of the pulpit.
We all felt pleased with our new bishop."

The bishop certainly lost nothing in preaching
ability or in appreciative audiences by being
transferred to the East. His administrative ability, likewise, was uniformly commended.

A prominent feature at the different conferences was the attention given to centenary facts
and interests, the year 1874 being celebrated by
the Church as the one hundredth year of its existence. Bishop Edwards enlisted himself very

largely in this feature of the conference sessions. Thus he manifested a diversity of aptitude and a wise appreciation of the many conditions of success in Christian work. His report for 1874 closed with the following sentences: "In the main the ministers are working well, and the prospects for the future are encouraging. We are praying for purity and peace, and an increasing interest on the subject of holiness. A Pentecostal baptism on all our ministers and people would be the best cure for all our present evils. May we not hope and pray for this, believing that we shall receive it during this centennial year?"

In the spring of 1874 he started on a second visit to the conferences on the Pacific coast. His experience did not differ much on this visit from what it had been on the first trip. The work on the coast was prospering somewhat, but not as much as could have been reasonably expected. He also attended, on his return, the Colorado Conference.

But the Walla Walla Conference furnished an episode which must not be passed over.

Some of the ministers of this mission-conference had become strangely infected with a spirit of fanaticism in connection with the subject of sanctification. Some of them had reached the point where they claimed to be the recipients of immediate revelations from God. This was especially so with the younger ministers, some of whom came to conference as applicants for license to preach. Bishop Edwards, who was a kind of authority in most parts of the Church on the subject of sanctification, was boldly told by a young upstart that he was not sanctified. The conference session was held in connection with a camp-meeting. The fanaticism culminated on the Sabbath of the conference. Sabbath afternoon some of the ministers held a meeting at one side of the camp, and arranged for a novel evening service. The question was asked as to who would lead the meeting. The answer was, "The Lord will lead." But one of the wildest of their number was to preach the sermon. This man ranted and stormed about to the disgust of all decent people. During the meeting it was announced that it had been revealed to the brother that the bishop would be converted that night or else the Lord would take him away— cut him off. But the bishop was not converted to either the new views or to the new way of doing things, nor was he cut off. He sat upright, calm, and thoughtful while the zealots were making a mourner's-bench affair over the matter of his sanctification. He was grieved and mortified,

but said little or nothing. Monday morning
he told those who had taken part in the dis-
graceful affair, that he would not sign a license
for such men. He told them, however, that
after a time, if they by their conduct should
be deemed worthy, he would sign and inclose to
them their license. This very clearly indicated to
these fanatical young preachers that the bishop
was master of the situation. At the next meeting of the Board of Missions the Walla Walla
Mission - conference was dissolved. It ought to
be remarked that some of the ministers of the
conference were far from sympathizing with the
prevailing fanatical spirit, and that after a few
years the conference organization was restored
with advantage.

The work of the fall conferences was at hand.
A visiting minister at the Erie Conference wrote
the following: "Bishop Edwards seems to be
earnest in every way in the work of the Church.
His counsels, reproofs, and preaching were able,
appropriate, and pious. His late trip to the Pacific coast seems to have had a tendency to invig-
orate and sharpen him. He is the embodiment
of intelligence and Christian zeal."

The remainder of the fall conferences, and also
the conferences for the first months of 1875, were
duly held. Some of his sermons deserve special
notice.

One of the most impressive sermons he ever preached was at the Virginia Conference, held at Keedysville, in 1875. His subject was the character of Elijah. This was his favorite theme. He had not spoken five minutes until he ascended in an outburst of eloquence and emotion, which melted and charmed the entire audience. Many feared that he had begun in a spirit and scope of thought from which he would have to descend. But it was not so. Every moment seemed to open paths of richer thought and more striking illustration. For almost an hour he preached without any sign of weariness or of losing his magic hold upon the audience. Toward the close of the sermon he described the ascension of Elijah. He pictured the walk of Elijah and Elisha. Stopping as if startled, he pointed out the chariot of fire and the horses of fire. The audience could see the chariot sweeping by as he showed old Elijah stepping within it and being borne heavenward. And then, in an inimitable way, turning the attention upon Elisha, he exclaimed in melting tones, "Oh, if I had been Elisha, I would have tried to get on too!" No one but he could have uttered such a sentiment; but as uttered by him, it was the climax of his wonderful description.

At the East German Conference the bishop

preached a quite peculiar sermon, but a very powerful one, on Jonah, which he introduced substantially as follows: " I shall take for my subject this morning the life of a preacher whose name was Jonah, and the whole book of Jonah shall be my text. A very great while ago there was a conference. The bishop who presided was the Lord Almighty, and the only preacher present was named Jonah. This preacher, by the appointment of the bishop, was sent to Nineveh mission. When the appointment was made known to Jonah he said, 'Nineveh mission! Why! that is a very unpromising field. We have not a single member there, and I shall get no support at all. I can not go there!' When he thus refused to take his appointment, his conscience troubled him so that he concluded that a change of some kind would be necessary to relieve his mind." The bitter experience of Jonah, his repentance, his entry upon his work, and the results, were then narrated with exceedingly fruitful and striking applications.

At the East Pennsylvania Conference the labor of Bishop Edwards was highly appreciated. The published minutes of 1875 contained the following: "At 10 A. M. Bishop Edwards occupied the pulpit and preached a sermon that will not soon be forgotten. It was grand living truth, told in a plain simple way, and accompanied with the unction from on high. The large congregation gave every attention, and many were moved to tears. His subject was the character of Elijah."

At Parkersburg Conference, in 1875, he preached on the Savior's sayings upon the cross, a sermon of rare excellence and power. At this conference he, perhaps, felt less freedom than at the other conferences, as indicated in letters to prominent ministers of that conference, copies of which he kept.

At the Mt. Zion Camp-meeting, in 1874, a number of ministers and a few laymen met under the opening branches of a large tree, and determined upon forming an association for the purpose of promoting the cause of holiness. Bishop Edwards was present, and assisted by his counsels. It is a mistake to suppose that he ever wavered in his devotion to the cause of holiness as held and expressed by him early in his ministry, or that he withdrew his sympathy from those who seemed to be advocating the doctrine in a true or scriptural way. Where he saw fanaticism rising, he felt rather to mourn in silence than to seem to be opposing what he believed to be a scriptural experience. Yet, on occasions when he deemed it proper or necessary, he placed himself strongly against distorted views, spurious experiences, and a mere dogmatic tendency, as occurring too frequently among professors of holiness.

Bishop Edwards' report for 1875 is quite full, and the following extract will be an excellent contribution to our knowledge of the district:

"It is but just to say in behalf of the itinerants of the East District in general, that they are a good class of men and faithful workers. They are men of one work, pure morals, and sound doctrine. They will compare very well with the same number of men anywhere as toiling itinerants. I speak not now on the administration of Discipline on that one 'vexed' and vexing question, which is to trouble us for some time to come. Yet I am glad to say that personally the ministers stand aloof from connection with secret orders, and by moral suasion try to keep their members out of such entanglements, though more might be done in this respect. My hope and prayer is that those who have been led astray by unwise counsels may, by the teachings of God's word and the Holy Spirit, be led into all truth. The nearer we get to Christ and the more of his Spirit we possess, the more will all personal animosity disappear from our discussions and the more completely shall we be united against the world, the flesh, and the devil, and thus be enabled to build up a holy and spiritual church."

Thus Bishop Edwards completed two full rounds upon his district. His work was incessant. Camp-meetings and extra tours of visitation and preaching filled up the interims of the conference sessions. He also delivered addresses on various public occasions, and wrote for the *Religious Telescope* on the sinful and pernicious effects of connection with secret societies, with a view to create a sounder sentiment on this subject and with the hope of leading those who had become entangled out of the snare. In 1874, including a distance traveled of nine thousand two hundred and eighty-six miles on his visit to the Pacific coast, the entire distance traveled by him was twenty-one thousand six hundred and fourteen miles. In 1875 the distance traveled was twelve thousand two hundred and eleven miles. Many incidents might be given of the work of these last years; but whatever is not specially characteristic may be passed by.

We know that Bishop Edwards was kind and gentle; but he could be terrible in reproof when duty seemed to require it. His conferences were blessed in having a suitable method of punishment for the refractory or derelict always at hand, and they often took the convenient course of referring those judged deserving of censure to the "admonition of the bishop."

While the bishop was on the train with a number of ministers, returning from a recent conference session, a young preacher began to tell him how great was the dissatisfaction over the appointments of the preachers by the Stationing Committee. ' Brother A. and Brother B. were not going to their fields, and Brother C. was not likely to go; old Brother S. had just told him that he would not go. The way he represented things, the picture was awful dark. The good bishop was severely tried — so much so, indeed, that he seemed unable to stand it any longer. It happened that the bishop, the young preacher, and another minister got off the cars at the same place. As they started up through the town, the bishop proceeded to administer a terrible rebuke. He told the young man that his besetting sin was exaggeration, using, though, a stronger and more appropriate word. He had himself just talked to Brother S., and knew that he was going to his field. The accompanying minister, who had deemed it best to fall behind, on overtaking the bishop after the young man had reached his stopping-place, said to him, "Bishop, that was rather a severe drubbing which you gave that brother." The response came instantly, "I do not wish to be catechised over this matter. The brother has long needed a plain reproof, and it was hard enough for me to give it." The answer indicated that the reproofs of the bishop were those of a friend, and not, as some may have at times supposed, the mere pastime of a rigid mind.

At a certain camp-meeting, during prayer, and while penitents were at the altar, two or three preachers on the stand were engaged in conversation, speaking so that they could be heard by those about them. The bishop, who was kneeling at one end of the stand, rising from his knees at the close of the prayer, went to the preachers and said, "I am ashamed of you. The idea of United Brethren preachers acting so inconsistently! I am ashamed of you."

At one of the conferences a young man, who had been appointed to preach, preached a sermon exclusively to ministers. When the services were over the bishop shook hands with the young preacher, and holding to his hand said, "See here, brother, what am I going to do on Sabbath?" The preacher asked him what he meant. "Why, you have preached the conference sermon to-night, and it is usually expected that the bishop will do that on Sunday morning," was the reply.

At one of the sessions of Alleghany Conference an applicant for license laid great stress on his "call" to the ministry. Some members made remarks which were taken by the applicant as making light of his "call." This troubled him; so the next morning, before breakfast, he, with many misgivings, went to the bishop's stopping-place and again rehearsed his call. The bishop placed his hands on the young man's head and said, "I only wish that more could say as much of their call to the ministry."

In April, 1875, Bishop Edwards attended the meeting of the Board of Bishops, at Westerville, Ohio. At this meeting it was decided that there is no authority in the Discipline for granting license to preach to women. This was in harmony with a decision long before given by Bishop Edwards. It was also resolved that the clause of the Constitution specifying that changes could not be made except by a two-thirds vote of the whole society, which clause had been referred to the bishops for specific interpretation, should be referred back to the General Conference, the bishops not being able to agree. At this meeting the bishops issued an address in which the different interests of the Church at large were specifically remembered. The address closed as follows:

" We would most earnestly urge upon you the importance of harmony among yourselves. 'A house divided against itself can not stand.' To this end we should pray often for one another. We should put the most charitable construction on one another's motives and actions. We should avoid evil surmisings, and forgive from our hearts the trespasses of others as we hope God in mercy to forgive us. Let us feel that in Christ we are one."

In May, Bishop Edwards, by special arrangement, attended the Ontario Conference in Bishop Weaver's stead, and then proceeded to the meeting of the Board of Missions, at Dayton, Ohio.

He was also present at the commencement exercises of Union Biblical Seminary, and gave the charge to the graduating class. In his address to the class he told them that they should have the courage to tell the truth, whether palatable or not to their hearers. He said: "You must not be like a certain colored preacher, in the days of slavery. When he was questioned by his ecclesiastical superior as to whether he had preached against this, that, and the other sin, he got along admirably until he was asked if he had preached against stealing chickens, the prevalent offense among the slaves. The colored preacher answered, 'No. Whenever I attempt to preach against that sin it brings a coldness over my audience.'"

While speaking at the funeral of Rev. J. Hoffman, who died during commencement week, the bishop spoke of himself as follows: "My health has been so good during these late years that I began to think, contrary to all my earlier expectations, that I might be good for twenty years' service yet. But the death of Brother Raber, of the Pennsylvania Conference, which occurred during the last session of his conference, has affected me so that I have been caused to think that my time, after all, may not be very long. Just a short time before his death some one had said to Brother Raber, 'It may not be very long until our work will be done.' 'Not so,' said Brother Raber, ' You and I belong to long-lived families. We shall not go yet.' But how soon and suddenly he was taken away! This incident was what impressed me."

Bishop Edwards' health continued apparently good until about the time when he commenced his fall conferences. Even then his devotion to his work and his fixed and determined method of labor carried him forward with no diminution in his efforts, or of the work accomplished. He attended the Erie, Muskingum, and Tennessee conferences, and presided and preached with his accustomed ability.

In November he wrote an article for the *Religious Telescope* on the "Fullness of Christ." In the article he quoted, among other expressions, the following: " Of his fullness have all we received, and grace for grace." " That we all come unto a perfect man, unto the measure of the stature of the fullness of Christ." " My God shall supply all your need according to his riches in glory by Jesus Christ." He concluded as follows: " Christian brethren, here is a theme for you—one on which you may profitably dwell. It is vast enough to engage your best faculties and greatest learning, and is worthy of your highest ambition. Study the character of your blessed Master, and

304 LIFE OF BISHOP EDWARDS.

remember that you are bound as a Christian to
walk as he walked. This you may and can do,
not by resolutions, or merely trying to conform
your external life to this standard, but by seeking
Christ himself as an indwelling presence. This
presence he has promised to his faithful followers. When you have received of his fullness,
when he comes and brings the Father with him,
and makes his abode with you, you will begin to
understand something of the meaning of the
great promises of the Bible, and of the exhaust-
less fullness there is in Christ."

In December he published an article on sinful
anger. He drew the lines very close against much
that many are accustomed to treat with indulgence.

He was enabled to attend all his winter and
spring conferences, and thus complete his third
round. At the Alleghany Conference he preached what was pronounced an " excellent sermon,"
and delighted the people with one of his " hap-
piest efforts." His subject was Elijah. It seems
that the Lord directed his mind to this theme
very frequently in the later years of his life. The
character and career of this grand old prophet of
ancient times seemed to give ample scope to the
mind and heart of the bishop. It was a perfect
treat to hear him while dwelling upon the moral

grandeur of the character of Elijah; his lofty zeal; his intimacy with God; his superiority to ease, suffering, and persecution; his power to work miracles; and, above all, " how he stood up as a fire, and whose word burned as a lamp." And then while he drew the pictures, so vivid and life-like, of Elijah's translation into heaven, the effect produced upon his audience beggared all description. All intervening time seemed to be lost while he portrayed this sublime scene. No one could hear him on such occasions without intense emotion. How could it be otherwise, when the veritable Elijah seemed to ascend into heaven, and that, too, in order to assure good men of their future existence in a state of glory and felicity. But the time comes apace when the good bishop himself will realize all the glories he so frequently and eloquently portrayed.

At the Virginia Conference he was quite indisposed; but he was favored with the assistance of Bishop Glossbrenner. Rev. W. J. Shuey, who was also present, wrote a communication for the *Religious Telescope* in which the following occurred:

" It was the lot of Bishop Edwards to be seriously afflicted during a part of the session. Age and hard work are making marked inroads upon the strength of Bishop Edwards, and a faithful and indomitable servant of God and the

20

Church will before long lay down his armor and rest from his labors."

He next went to the Pennsylvania and East German conferences. At the East Pennsylvania Conference he presided, but was unable to preach on Sabbath. Rev. J. B. Resler preached the conference sermon.

The last conference attended by Bishop Edwards was the Parkersburg, which met at Parkersburg, West Virginia, March 15, 1876. He labored under great affliction, but presided during the session, and on Sabbath preached, though in an abbreviated form, on Elijah, his favorite theme. At this session he ruled against sending before the committee an applicant for license to preach, who was understood to be connected with the Odd-fellows. His ruling in the case was appealed from, and the appeal sustained by the conference. Manifestly the bishop should have received the support of the conference—not for his sake alone, but more especially for the honor and integrity of the Church he so nobly represented,—in his decision. Without saying more, the action of the conference, it must be confessed, was very unfortunate. At any rate, it was so viewed throughout the Church as soon as the facts in the case were made public. It must be remembered, however, that there was no personal disrespect intended by this action against the authority of the bishop. He was, in fact, very highly esteemed by all the members of the conference. The resistance offered was not personal, but official. The bishop understood it to be a deliberate attempt to set at naught the rule of the Church on secret societies. It was this view of the case which so deeply affected him. Nor is it too much to say that this action of Parkersburg Conference was the occasion of a sorrow which he carried to his grave. He bravely bore the burden, however, using his oft-repeated expression, "The Lord reigns." On his leaving the conference, broken in health, a brother said, "Bishop, when you go home take a good rest." The reply was characteristic—"I must work now." His prayer was, "Let me cease to live and cease to work at the same time." But the "beginning of the end" had already come.

In returning to Baltimore it was necessary for him to pass a night on the cars. The weather was cold, and he cast himself down on a seat near the stove and fell asleep. His brain was fevered, and his mind seemed to wander, during this long night's travel, and at times was unable to direct itself. In the night he found himself standing in the midst of the excited passengers, repeating his conference sermon. His own voice finally awakened him, and after facing the people for a moment, he turned away without saying a word, and left his fellow-passengers to their reflections upon this strange scene.

He reached his home in a broken-down condition, but was very slow in giving up to be retired from the post of duty. It might be said of him that he closed his days, not with his eyes fixed upon the glorious hope before him, but turned backward upon the field of action. He had no fears as to the future; but his constant inquiry was, What more can I do for the Master's cause? "It will be time enough to think of going to heaven when my work is done," said he. When urged to be quiet and take rest the reply was, "I must work now."

Just about the time when he was closing up his round of the conferences he wrote his last article for the *Religious Telescope*. His caption was, "*Too Slow.*" Always seeking some practical good, his remarks in this article were directed by the same spirit. Consider the following:

"Some preachers are often, if not always, behind time. What will become of such men? They will get so far behind that some passing event will knock their heads off. Such men must wake up and put on more steam, or they will founder at sea, or stall on the grade of life. They can not be useful anywhere, and hence must be put on the shelf. Some of these times they will be asleep at roll-call, and their names will be struck from the list. Brother, move on

a little faster; jog up a little—yes, a good deal. Make yourself useful, and you will always have a place."

It has been supposed by some that a change
took place in the mind of Bishop Edwards during the last few years of his life in respect to the
restrictive rule of the Church on the subject of
secret societies. For this there is no ground; but
on the contrary, there is abundant evidence of his
adherence to the principle of a prohibitory rule.
This is seen in addresses delivered and letters
written on the subject, after he went east, and
but a short time before his death. We have,
moreover, the unqualified testimony of Mrs. Edwards, who is still alive, to the same effect.

By the time the bishop reached home he was
almost completely exhausted, and under the power
of his disease. From the first it was feared that
his malady, a mysterious affection of the head,
malignantly fixing itself upon the brain, would
terminate fatally. He suffered much, but was
never heard to complain. His devotion to his
great life-work and the welfare of the Church
was never more conspicuous than during his sickness.

Said the bishop one day to Rev. J. H. Young,
who had called to see him, "Brother Young, can
you pray the prayer of faith? If you can, I want
you to kneel right down here and ask the Lord

to make me well." Said Brother Young, "I can ask the Lord to restore you if it is his will." "Oh," said the bishop, "I can get hundreds in Baltimore to do that; but that is not what I mean." What he did mean might be understood, perhaps, from the case of his own prayer offered at a camp-meeting, in the previous August, in behalf of Brother J. Hoke, who was suffering under a severe and alarming prostration. Said the bishop at that time, "There, Brother Hoke, under that tree, I was praying this morning for you; and there the Lord assured me that you will get well. I never am mistaken when receiving such assurances." The prayer was signally answered in Brother Hoke's slow but steady recovery.

As the hope of getting well and of a longer term of service became less, the spirit of Bishop Edwards expressed itself in the following utterance, which more than anything else may be received as his last testimony and message to the Church: "If it might be the Lord's will, I would like to live to preach awhile yet. I would preach, as never before, salvation by faith alone. Oh, the church has so much machinery, and there is such a disposition to interpose so many things between inquiring souls and Christ! Oh, I would tell them salvation is by faith in Christ alone. I see this now as never before, and I would like to live and preach it."

But his work was done. This sad fact became more and more apparent as the days and weeks passed by. His suffering was intense and protracted; but he bore it all as a Christian. The very best medical service in the gift of the profession, in the city of Baltimore, was employed to give relief and save his life, but without effect. Surrounded by his family and a number of his loved and trusted friends of the Church, he breathed his last, June 6, 1876. Great anxiety had been felt in respect to his recovery, and everywhere in the Church the news of his death was received with feelings of deep personal grief and a profound sense of the loss that had been sustained. Accompanied by the stricken family, Rev. S. A. Mowers and J. Hoke, who had been much with the bishop during his sickness, and a number of sympathizing friends, the remains were brought to Dayton, Ohio, and taken to the First United Brethren Church, where the funeral took place. The officiating minister, a life-long friend of the deceased, could do little more than give expression to the sense of loss and personal grief which filled his own heart. Bishop Weaver and Rev. S. A. Mowers followed with interesting remarks. The attendance was large and the services were deeply impressive. The interment took place in Woodland Cemetery, the beautiful burying ground near the city of Dayton. Not long afterward a subscription for a monument was opened, and through the grateful and generous contributions coming from all parts of the Church, a handsome and becoming monument of Scotch granite was erected at the head of the grave where repose the mortal remains of Bishop Edwards, awaiting the resurrection of the just.

The annual conferences of the East District, and many in other parts of the Church, in their next ensuing sessions, devoted a liberal amount of time to appreciative and impressive memorial exercises. Bishop Glossbrenner, on the first Sabbath morning during the next General Conference session, by request, delivered a fitting memorial sermon on the life and character of his departed friend and colleague, using as his text the following appropriate words: "For he was a good man, and full of the Holy Ghost and of faith." Every one who heard the sermon felt that it was fit that such a man as the departed bishop should be held up in such a simple, scriptural portrait as the sermon presented.

The plan throughout this biography has been, for the most part, to present facts, and let them make their own impression, and in as many cases as possible to allow the noble subject of the biography, through his own sayings and through personal incidents, to present the many sides of his mind and the recesses of his heart. If at any time the author has erred in his judgment, he has certainly placed means in the hands of the reader for forming a proper opinion.

But little in the way of summing up or reviewing needs to be done. Yet we must linger a little under the sacred influence of the presence that has gone out from among us, and turn our eyes once more down into the valley, torn by the plucking up of this mighty oak of the Lord, under whose spreading boughs, in the years past, so many have found goodly shelter.

Bishop Edwards, at the time of his death, was one month and one day over sixty years old. He had spent just two weeks more than forty-one years in the ministry, twenty-seven of these years being spent in the bishop's office. During these years, as traveling preacher, editor, bishop, and member of the various general boards, in labor, official duty, or administering any trust, he was never charged with delinquency or intentional fault. Those who knew him best were always the most ready to testify how pure he was in personal character. In this respect he was ever regarded as among the foremost. Christians may well congratulate themselves that so pure a character has existed to adorn the walks of life. No one ever questioned the purity of his motives or designs.

He was favored, physically, with a strong constitution. His large, stoutly-built form, penetrating eye, frank and honest face, could not fail to make an impression at first sight. He kept his person and attire clean and neat. It may be said that he was careful and exact in this respect, but not over-nice. He sought to appear neat and comely not alone for his own sake, but in part to set an example to young ministers.

After what has been given in the preceding pages it is unnecessary to speak at much length of the power of his mind or of his capacity for work. This much may be said, however, that no one could be in his presence any considerable length of time without feeling the superior vigor of his mind, and, especially, the keenness of his moral perceptions. And in taking even a cursory view of his life and labors, we can not but feel amazed at his power of endurance. Tireless and persistent, he worked for the Master's cause to the last. Nothing but death itself could quench his zeal or cut short his struggles to save souls and preserve the purity of the Church.

While rigid, and, it may be admitted, sometimes harsh in his bearing toward men, his heart had the tenderness of a child. A little more than a year before he died, at a time when the four bishops were together, he said to his associates that he had an incident which occurred on a railway train that he would like to read if he could. "I have never," said he, "been able to read it through without breaking down." He produced the incident in the form of a scrap, and read it through, but during the reading broke down a number of times. The touching incident was written by Rev. J. M. Dosh, of the West Des Moines Conference, and was first published in the *Religious Telescope*, and afterward published and re-published under various auspices. In his last years the finer elements of his social nature manifested themselves more and more, and his personal attachments, which were always ardent, became more tender. He, of course, was not in harmony with any movement or tendency of things which seemed to antagonize those principles which were dear to him all through life. Nor did he cease to assert and maintain his long-cherished convictions, as some have incorrectly affirmed. He, nevertheless, became increasingly kind and conciliatory toward those who held views different from his own. This was very observable during the last few years and months of his life.

Through all his life he practiced a tender-hearted and sympathetic benevolence. At least for twenty-five years of his active work in the ministry this was his method of giving. The 5th of May, 1851, he recorded in his diary a solemn promise to thenceforth give one tenth of all his income for benevolent purposes. He observed this promise, tithing even what he received as marriage fees and what Mrs. Edwards received for sewing. He kept this rule till the time of his death, the yearly tithes of the last three years being a little over one hundred and fifty dollars. His sympathy for the distressed and destitute was large and unvarying. He did not stifle benevolence with the inquiry as to the cause of the wretchedness, or the blame, real or supposed, of those appealing to him for aid, or as to whether the duty of yielding relief might not belong to another. He assisted church-enterprises uniformly out of his "dedicated funds," but his benevolence was not confined by denominational wants. He freely gave of his scanty means outside these limits.

Composure and serenity of mind were marked features in his life and character. With his ever-recurring maxim, "The Lord reigns," he put the most troublesome fears aside, and, on many occasions, re-assured his doubting brethren. "Truth,"

he would say, " is imperishable and it must prevail." Many despondent and doubting souls he
led into light and joy by urging the faithfulness
of the promises of God. His own faith was
strong and steady. He knew how to live and
walk by faith. In this respect he had few if any
equals. Indeed, he seemed to have been specially
appointed by divine Providence to adorn and instruct the Church respecting a life of faith. He
held that the many " exceeding great and precious promises " of God were not only to be accepted as true, but especially to be trusted in all
the affairs of life.

His relation to the ministry was helpful almost
beyond comparison. He would urge his young
brethren not only to try to do more and better
work for the Master, but he would show them, by
precept and example, how it could be done. He
had the courage and frankness to say, many
times, to the careless or inexperienced, " You fail
here; by doing thus and so you can better your
sermons, pastoral work, or management." Nothing affecting ministers and their work seemed to
escape his notice. He even undertook to tell
them how they could preserve their health, how
they could protect themselves in their long and
hard winter travels, and how they could best
economize their time and strength so as to do the

most work. He always urged studiousness and diligence. While giving attention to these details, and such as these, on the human side of a minister's life and experience, he never failed to urge the necessity of being divinely called and qualified for the work.

Next after the strength and positiveness of the bishop's character, nothing surprises us so much as the degree to which his most marked characteristics were complemented and guarded by other qualities. Said one intimately acquainted with him, and himself a bishop, "I have looked upon Bishop Edwards on every side. He is the best man this Church ever had. It has never seen his like; it will not in the time to come." This language may be a little too sweeping. Doubtless many will so regard it. But after making all due allowance for the esteem and enthusiasm of a warm-hearted colleague, there remains in this noble eulogy the just recognition of a strong, symmetrical character, and a well-guarded life. What is the secret of this surprising blending of various and seemingly irreconcilable elements of character? The answer can not be given in a word, nor in a few brief sentences. The story of his life and labors, taken as a whole, can alone answer the question. In the light of all the facts connected with this story, it may be easily seen that Bishop Edwards never fixed his mind and heart upon a few theoretical centers from which he blindly pushed out to the different points of the moral compass. True, he was not without well - defined theories which he could state and logically defend when necessary; but these were formed and modified by the manifold teachings of the Scriptures and the facts of human life. He did not seek so much to reconcile thought with thought as thought with facts. In this he was right. Science, philosophy, and divinity, alike demand this practical method. It was this that made him so mighty in the Scriptures.

The difficulty of harmonizing a large spiritual insight into the nature and universality of God's kingdom on one side, with the tangible demands of actual life, and the divinely established claims of the visible church on the other side, was beautifully solved in his life and character. Without his affluent spiritual nature he never could have been the " great Christian " that he was; without his appreciation of the relation of things as seen in the common affairs of life, he never could have become eminent as a Christian bishop. In a word, his extraordinary piety, strong common sense, and liberal culture made him one of the brightest ornaments of the Christian church.

These elements of strength and beauty rarely meet in human character; but in Him they were happily combined, and, by consequence, placed him among the foremost of Christian workers.

He will live in the memory of the Church as a wise and efficient administrator. His knowledge of men, wisdom and ability in influencing the action of others, thorough understanding of the genius of the Church, sympathy with its spirit, and full belief in it as an agency providentially called forth and divinely acknowledged, were each and all elements of strength which entered into his qualification for the work required at his hands. How nobly and grandly he wrought for the Master, in the use of these gifts and graces, we have already seen.

But it is especially as a preacher that he will be remembered by the multitudes of the Church. It was in this character that they met and heard him and received their impressions of his power and worth. His strong imagination, vivid power of description, skill in drawing from the Script-ures, fruitful mind, thorough system, direct state-ment of truth, and great earnestness were the characteristics, on the human side, on which his fame rested. But on the divine side, his reputa-tion appears as the pure and free gift of God. He was inflexibly devoted to the will of Heaven; and

God made him honored by giving him the Holy Spirit without measure.

The sermons which he loved most to preach during his last years were those on the sayings of Christ on the cross and the character of Elijah— the former adapted especially to sacramental occasions, and the latter convenient for conferences, or any desired use. In the character and career of Elijah he saw realized his best conceptions of a heroic and successful life. Hence to this sublime theme his mind naturally turned, especially in its more lofty moments. In using the sayings of Christ on the cross he was especially happy and effective. Here he found that which awakens the purest and tenderest emotions of the soul. In the use of these sayings the Lord signally blessed him, in showing that man's only hope of salvation is found in the cross of Christ. But he had other themes upon which he dwelt with eloquence, pathos, and power, seldom equaled. Indeed, it may be said that he never entered the pulpit without the "beaten oil," or without the "blood in the basin." The gospel which he preached was a gospel of life, but a life purchased by the death of Christ, and accompanied by a death unto sin.

But Bishop Edwards has passed from life to life; and now nothing remains but to breathe a prayer that these pages may be owned and blessed of Him who has said, "The righteous shall be in everlasting remembrance," and that, besides helping to commemorate an honored name, they may be of some use in perpetuating and enlarging the influence of the noble life which it has been the author's aim faithfully and affectionately to trace.

www.ingramcontent.com/pod-product-compliance
Lightning Source LLC
Chambersburg PA
CBHW060533030726
47498CB00004B/1173